JESUS IN SPACE

A Christian Space Opera

Part One of the Jesus in Space Trilogy

I0673442

Mike Phoenix

New Testament verses from the Oxford Annotated Bible, 1973
Revised Standard Version.

ISBN   978-0-9851191-5-7

Then Jesus was led up by the Spirit into the wilderness to be tempted by the devil. And he fasted forty days and forty nights, and afterward he was hungry. Mathew 4.1-2 RSV

The Spirit immediately drove him out into the wilderness. And he was in the wilderness forty days, tempted by Satan; and he was with the wild beasts; and the angels ministered to him. Mark 1.12-13 RSV

And Jesus, full of the Holy Spirit, returned from the Jordan, and was led by the Spirit for forty days in the wilderness, tempted by the devil. And he ate nothing in those days; and when they ended, he was hungry. Luke 4.1-2 RSV

TABLE OF CONTENTS

1. Baptism by Fire

We'd been on the road two days when we hiked into Bethany. Passing ox carts, street vendors and a detachment of soldiers, we heard commotion up ahead. My buddy spent his last shekel on a couple of corn dogs and a big elephant ear. "Do you want to share some of that?" I asked as he stuffed a wad of hot sugary dough in his mouth and continued walking. "It's not like it's your last meal or anything!" I yelled after him and he started laughing, tore off a piece and tossed it back to me. "Nothing cures your ills like deep fried food," I thought to myself as I followed him along the path to the river.

It was like a concert down there. There were hundreds of people: cute girls and little kids and married men and women, and big families and some folks out on blankets with lawn chairs and picnic baskets. Most of them didn't know us from Adam, but when we got maybe fifty feet from shore, my friend kind of "disengaged" from me and the crowd started moving aside so we had a clear shot all the way down to where a man with long, ratty hair looked up from the water. The guy was waist deep and he pulled out some lady he'd been holding

1

under the surface and she was sputtering and splashing and shouting "Praise the Lord" or some such nonsense, but the guy soon forgot about her and she was floating away. Maybe some teenagers dove in and rescued her.

The man in the water didn't break his gaze; he stared up through the crowd on the riverbank at my friend. For a minute it was like everything went into slow motion and the sound of the crowd switched off and there was an open path for us as we headed directly down to the water.

"Hey, watch it, you SOB!" I shouted at some little dude who accidentally elbowed me in the side as he tried to squeeze past. He gave me a dumb look and I almost popped him in his big ugly nose, but he crowded in ahead of me without a second glance and now the whole mass of people sprang to life and I was getting pushed back. Everyone was chanting, "John, John, John." He was the nut job out in the river who started a long speech about making the path straight, and I don't know what all, but I had seen enough, so I stopped in my tracks and the crowd flowed around in front of me and I figured I'd hang back while Jesus did whatever.

I walked up the embankment and sat on the grass next to a metal cooler. A middle aged guy slammed the lid shut and gave me a dirty look and he and his middle aged wife, holding hands like little kids, headed down the hillside. So what? I kicked back, pulled out a pack of smokes and lit up. At least I had a good view. I leaned over and opened the cooler for a cold one. Wait a minute. On second thought, I guess I wasn't smoking back then. I sure could have used a smoke, though. No, I must have picked up the habit another time. I do remember for a fact that I was messing with fire, out of boredom I suppose. I never really stopped to think what I was doing. Maybe somebody had a little camp fire going or a hibachi or something and I was writing my name in the air with a burning stick. S T E V E – hanging there in letters of smoke and the darn stick got loose in some dry weeds behind me.

Meanwhile, my pal stripped to his loin cloth and stepped off the embankment into the river with the crazy man, whom, I later learned, was his cousin. When the two men were chest deep in the water, the crowd dialed back the volume to where you heard the cousin's voice boom over the surface. The sun was at an angle that made each ripple look like strings of wavering silver coins, and these millions of tiny flashing flecks of light were shimmering around the men, while way up on the river bank a flash of orange was dancing in the bushes where I'd started an accidental fire. It sent plumes of black smoke into the sky.

If Jesus thought I was attempting to signal him, he didn't let on. I had nearly finished tramping out the fire when I looked back to the water where Jesus had disappeared. "One one thousand, two one thousand, three one thousand..." I counted to myself as a murmur of voices came up from the shoreline.

"Man, he's been under a long time," I thought to myself, "I've never seen one of these before, but do they always take so long?"

I started to panic a little, like maybe I needed to get down there and stop the proceedings in a HURRY, when all of a sudden, across the river there was an explosion of water and Jesus bounded back to the surface. A cheer went up from the crowd. A trained pigeon sailed out of the sky and landed on Jesus' shoulder like they were partners from the carnival side-show up the river. I could see a Ferris Wheel and a Tilt-A-Whirl up there above the tree line. Maybe it was a dove? Thinking back, I'm not sure there was a carnival up there, but the crazy cousin went into hysterics when he saw the bird and the crowd sure dug it.

* * *

Pretty soon Jesus walked up to where I was waiting on the shore. He was drying his head with a towel.

"Is that it?" I asked.

"Yep," he said.

"You're kidding?"

"Nope."

"Two days on the road and that was it?"

That was it all right.

2. On the Road

We made it back to Joseph's carpentry shop at dusk the next day. Joe was working at his bench and I didn't know whether Jesus had said anything about the purpose of our four-day sojourn in the middle of the work-week, so I figured it best to say nothing. It was all work with Joe, or "Mr. Joe" as the help called him. It was past eleven when we finally knocked off for the night. The old man gave Jesus a hug and thanked the three apprentices who departed for their homes or the local watering hole on the edge of town where I was headed. Mr. Joe looked at me as he climbed the stairs at the back of his shop.

"Goodnight, Stephen."

"Goodnight," I said and we looked across the workroom where Jesus was returning wood clamps to their hangers on the wall.

"He's a good boy. You are wise to follow him," Mr. Joe said to me in a whisper.

He reached over the banister and squeezed my shoulder. It felt like he was trudging up those familiar stairs for the last time and I would never see the old guy again who had taken me in off the street and pretty much raised me. When Jesus turned around, Mr. Joe was gone. For a minute, I felt out of place, as though I was supposed to say something.

"Let's get the rest of the chairs out to the storehouse," said Jesus with a smile.

"Sure," I said. If this was helping, it was the least I could do. After all, I was getting paid. I'd made a lot of money over the years working for Joseph the Carpenter and Son. Carrying one of the big chairs, I stepped out into the quiet alley behind the workroom. There was a lot of dough riding on this project. The daughter of some rich guy over in Capernaum was getting married and this was all from a set of twelve killer chairs and a big, ornate, dining room table ordered as part of the bride's dowry.

The air had cooled down since the sunset. I walked to the storehouse, went in and set the chair beside its companions. Over the next hour I made a dozen trips back and forth. The storehouse wasn't all that big and rather than take the time to do it right, I just started stacking the chairs onto the table, one on top of the other like a house of cards, really large, heavy cards covered with gold.

As I worked, I thought about maybe one day sailing to one of the big cities like Ephesus, or Athens or even Rome. Maybe when I was older, I might start a fishing business on the coast. Tucked in the corner of my mind were hopes of someday finding a girl and starting a family. I had no definite plans.

It was during my last trip to the workroom for the last chair that I heard a rumbling sound in the distance. It sounded like thunder. I looked west over the roof tops for the thunderhead, but it was a cloudless night and a million stars illuminated the sky and I saw nothing like rain. Back in the quiet workroom, I lifted the last chair and noticed Jesus at the table where I had left him marking in the ledger.

"Don't forget to put out the lamp," he said.

"Got it," I replied, stepping once more into the night, and I crossed the alley into the storehouse. They'd kill me if they ever learned how I'd stacked those chairs.

This time the rumbling sound was very close, so that its source seemed to be just beyond the alley. The floor boards rumbled. I held my breath and pulled the door shut. I hadn't done a very good job stacking those chairs. Actually, I had done a really lousy job. I guess I had been in a hurry to get some smokes at the inn and taste that first cold beer. Was I smoking in those days? I should have stayed put, but for some reason I got scared by the noise and forgot where I was standing. I jumped back from the door. My arm bashed into something and the last thing I remember was the clatter of falling wood and a terrific blow on the top of my head.

I thought it had been dark. It got really dark. It's a wonder the place didn't burn down, but a blast of air had extinguished the lamp. In the next instant, the cracks and spaces between the slats of the storehouse wall were shot through with light. The rumbling rose to a violet shudder. The storeroom door flew open and blinding white light flooded the room. There was a metallic clicking sound from outside and then, nothing.

I never looked back into the storeroom at the tangle of broken chairs. I had forgotten about the blow to my head; something enormous was outside in the alley, something foreign. Gleams of electric fire described the outline of a gigantic wagon of gleaming metal. It was borne by many wheels, but where were the oxen? I had stumbled into the open, only an arm's length from the monstrosity when I smelled oil, thick and smoky and I coughed. The sound of my voice startled me and I nearly ran back to the storehouse when I heard Jesus.

"Come here," he said, "We haven't much time."

As it turned out, the big thing in the alley was a motor home with a diesel engine, refrigerator, propane stove, toilet, shower, two DVD players, a big aluminum canoe lashed up top to the cargo rack and a trailer hitch with two dirt bikes in tow. There were some other things too. The outfit apparently belonged to the driver, a lean faced young man about my age in jeans and cowboy boots. Jesus and I stood in the light of the open passenger door looking into the eerie glow of a face illuminated by the console lights.

"You ready?" said the driver.

"Always ready," said Jesus.

"What about him? You leave him here, I'm going to have to kill him."

"No, that wouldn't be a good idea."

"Have it your way then."

The driver flicked a switch on the console and an interior light cast its glow from the cabin into Jesus' face. The driver adjusted a pair of dark sunglasses on the bridge of his narrow, perfectly formed nose.

"The trip'll probably kill him anyway."

Without turning, Jesus motioned me to follow and in an instant we were on board. He guided me into the passenger seat and passed behind me out of the cabin down a short hall to the rear of the vehicle.

"Grab yourself a bite," called the driver, with a friendly smile. I was about to thank him, when I realized he hadn't been talking to me. He looked at me with a broad grin revealing a set of bone white, perfectly formed teeth.

"No, thank you," came a reply from somewhere in back.

"Suit yourself," the cowboy called over his shoulder.

He twisted a key in the ignition and the motor home roared to life. We headed up the main thoroughfare leading out of town. After ten or fifteen minutes, I cleared my throat and tried to make small talk.

"Where we headed?"

The driver only nodded in the direction of the windshield and drove into the night.

* * *

When I awoke, there seemed no end to the flat barren desert that stretched before us. The cabin was filled with glaring sunlight which reflected off miles of sand and sun-baked mud. I held a hand to shade my eyes, and squinted through a windshield spattered with a smear of bug entrails and the skittering wings of smashed locusts.

Already shimmering in the morning heat the road ahead dwindled to a point on the horizon that seemed a thousand miles distant, slipping to the very end of the earth. The driver was bouncing almost imperceptibly to the sound of something plugged into his ears, what I later learned was a song about alcoholism, infidelity, and faith in someone from the future named Christ. I looked out my passenger

9

window and tried to recall the scene outside. Never in my life had I been this far to the east.

We drove for hours. I must have dozed off, because when I awoke I felt the parched roof of my mouth and could barely swallow. I looked at the driver, self-absorbed behind the wheel. I guess he didn't notice me, and for the first time I saw him without his cowboy hat. On his armrest it perched, grey and worn, with a narrow brim angled to a point. A long, coal-black raven's feather knifed back from a snake skin hat band. Steering with one hand, the driver pulled a red bandana off his head and wiped his brow. He was entirely bald. He massaged his scalp with one hand and I noticed the dome of his head was covered with a black tattoo, an intricate web pattern that shot blue highlights like the raven's feather.

"I prefer a shaven head in the warmer climes," he chuckled, fitted the bandana atop his skull and returned the hat to his head. Flexing sinewy hands on the wheel, the driver leaned back as we drove on.

3. In the Wilderness

It was dusk and the sun collapsed in a murderous blaze behind us. I slept restlessly in the vinyl seat and was plagued by dark, disturbing dreams, the memory of which vanished like mist when I awoke with a sudden start in the passenger seat. No one was around and I went back to the living quarters and helped myself to the last of the milk and cheese from the small refrigerator and the last few eggs which I heated on a gas range. With my plate and picking food with my fingers I sat on a sofa and watched out the picture window. It was still cool outside and the driver stood way off the road with a bag of metal poles. At the time, of course, I had no idea what he was doing. He placed small, white balls on the ground, stood over them with his legs spread evenly apart, and waved the pole slowly back and forth over a ball. Then, in a continuous motion he brought the pole back over his shoulder and swung down, striking the ball. A percussive "whack" echoed across the desert and the white object sailed through the morning air.

He repeated this sequence with a series of balls for nearly half an hour. With a glass of water from the faucet I returned to my window and saw the driver leading Jesus to the bag of poles. Jesus shook his head and started toward the road, but the driver insisted he remain. In the end, Jesus had a go. Whereas the cowboy's ball would go left or right, or the cowboy's stroke would miss the ball entirely, Jesus hit the ball straight just about every time. I finished my meal and walked out the side door and took a deep breath of fresh air. Whatever we were doing here was kind of fun, a nice break from the routine in Nazareth, but when I looked back into the desert I heard the driver shouting. I couldn't tell what was being said, but he had thrown his hat to the ground and was beating it with the metal poles and kicking the bag and bending the poles into impossible shapes while Jesus returned to the road.

"What's going on?" I asked Jesus.

"Golf," he said and disappeared into the motor home.

* * *

We drove all day in silence. Late in the afternoon, the driver yelled at a light on the control panel. He stopped the motor home, climbed out of the cab, and unlashed a large canister from the back of the vehicle. He opened a little door over the rear wheels, inserted a funnel, raised the canister, and poured something inside the motor home. The spent canister he left on the roadside, climbed into the cab, slammed the door and we drove the remainder of the day.

* * *

Cramped, exhausted, and drenched with sweat I awoke the next morning. On the horizon, like an evil eye searing the dusty road ahead, the sun had risen. We drove for three hours, until, in the middle of who-knows-where, the massive vehicle coughed, sputtered and stopped. The driver cursed, banged the steering wheel with his fists, climbed out of the cab and kicked the side of the motor home. Jesus appeared from the rear cabin and looked at me. I rolled my eyes and nodded toward the driver's empty seat. Jesus went out the side door and talked to the driver out front while I put a sandaled foot up on the molded ledge beneath the windshield and began to bake. I had failed to appreciate the cool air once streaming through floor vents. I supposed the air flow had something to do with the key in the side of the steering column. I looked at the floor between the seats at what I imagined was the driver' stuff: an old shoe box and a dusty back-pack. The half open flap bore the embroidered initials L.S. I turned aside the open flap and saw a leather wallet lying in the mouth of the pack. Looking out the windshield, I learned over and pulled out the wallet. Inside were tucked embossed cards bearing the name Lawrence Strathmore. Of course, at the time, I had no idea this junk had any value. It was that way with a lot of things.

I was getting hot in the cab as the sun came up and I looked out the windshield. The driver stood down the road maybe fifty feet away yelling at Jesus about something or other. Actually, it really wasn't much of a road anymore, maybe more of path or a trail in the desert that just sort of faded away out there to nothingness in the level landscape. It was getting mighty hot, and I glanced at the keys in the ignition and the lighted instrument panel. I'd seen the driver use the power windows on his side of the cab and so I pressed the button in my door and the glass slid open. A faint breath of air moved across me and out the opposite door. I looked at Lawrence Strathmore's wallet and pulled out a tattered stack of pictures of the driver. He looked pretty much the same but somehow more of a boy than this creep and I wondered whether the pictures were very old. Maybe something had happened to him since the pictures had been taken? In all the pictures he appeared with a young woman. She was beautiful, tall and slender, with a brave, open face. She wore a backpack of powder blue, embroidered with the initials S.B., but the photograph that most impressed me was one of them standing together with their backpacks looking up at an enormous green colossus. It was the statue of a gigantic woman who stood in the background holding something up into the sky out of view. The driver had not always worn a shaven head, for in the pictures his hair was sandy blond like the girl's. I was wondering why he'd gotten that ugly tattoo on his head when I felt a searing pain on the back of my right hand. I looked beside me where it rested on the open sill and, to my horror, stared into the face of a horse fly, its mouthparts buried in my skin. I smacked the back of my hand and the pictures flew up in the air and the fly was loose in the cabin, buzzing, darting, and skittering up against the windshield. I shouted and tried to smash it again, but it flew out the driver's doorway and Jesus and the driver turned from their conversation and were looking at me pressed up against the inside of the windshield.

At the crescendo of his tirade, the cowboy had taken a handful of stones he'd gathered from the desert floor and thrown them down in front of Jesus' feet. To punctuate his displeasure he'd taken off his cowboy hat and thrown it down and stomped on it. He picked it up again along with one of the flat, smooth stones. He dusted his hat against the leg of his jeans, readjusted the raven's feather in its snake skin hatband and marched back toward the motor home.

I fumbled with the wallet, scooping up pictures from my seat, the dashboard, the floor. Had there been that many pictures? It seemed impossible that I could cram them back into the billfold. With less than a second to spare, I had just returned the wallet and replaced the flap of the backpack when the driver reappeared beside the open door, adjusting the hat on his head. With one hand he grabbed the wheel and pulled himself into the vehicle and slammed a palm sized stone on the dashboard. Next, he leaned toward me in a move that made me jump, but he reached up and adjusted the rearview mirror. He was examining his lean face, and looking at various views in the mirror as he spoke off-handedly.

"You find anything to eat in the backpack there, or are you just being nosy?"

I stammered, "What?"

He turned his head and looked at me sideways.

"Oh, that?" I said, "That's a backpack?"

"Come on now," he smiled, "You're can't lie to a liar."

It didn't make any sense. One could lie to a liar, but I was afraid to say anything in answer. He never mentioned the backpack again.

* * *

We were there all day. There was water in the living quarters from the basin faucets, but that was it. Whoever had planned this trip hadn't bothered to get much in the way of provisions. Perhaps they had left unexpectedly? Around noon I awoke beneath the picture window on the sofa in a pool of sweat. I scrambled out the side door and the hot air about knocked me back into cabin. I scanned the horizon and walked to the rear of the vehicle where I saw the driver standing on the trailer hitch unfastening two wheeled machines.

"Where's Jesus?"

"Hell if I know," he said without looking up, "Out there somewhere."

The driver unlatched a metal ramp and kicked it with his booted toe. The ramp swung up and clattered to the ground behind the trailer. Having freed the machines of their lashings, he rolled them one after the other down the ramp and set them side by side on their kickstands in the sand.

"What are those?" I asked, making small talk.

"What are what?"

"Those things with the wheels?"

Without answering he walked over and inspected one of the machines. He grabbed the handle bars, kicked a leg over the seat and sat down as though he'd ridden such machines his entire life.

"I knew a German officer in World War I. Swore he would not be caught dead on the battlefield without one of these."

I had no idea, at that point, what the driver was talking about. He looked like a raving lunatic. I left him there rocking back and forth on his "bike" in the shadow of the motor home and went out into the desert to search for Jesus. Once I started looking, it didn't take too long to find him. He was sitting on a flat rock a hundred yards away in the desert. I stood beside him and was about to speak when he looked up at me with a bright smile.

"Good morning," he said.

"Two things," I replied. "Where are we? When are we getting out of here? And you have to do something about that nut case back there!"

I was waiting for my answer when the roar of a motorcycle erupted on the desert air. The driver had pulled off-road into the wastes and raced the motorcycle in vicious circles. The engine bleated and the rear wheel sent up terrific clouds of dust. Now, the infernal machine bounded across the landscape toward us. I jumped behind Jesus as the driver, yelling and laughing, barreled directly into our path. The machine bounced to a halt one foot from where Jesus stood.

"Whooee…" laughed the driver, "I bet they don't make fun like this in Nazareth," he barked and settled back in his seat and twisted one of the handles which made the engine roar.

"What do you say, Jesus?" cried the driver and he spit, "Take a spin?"

* * *

I don't know how it happened, but twenty minutes later I found myself a mile down the road, staring into the sunset with the driver's red bandana raised over my head and looking back up the road at the two of them on motorcycles.

"On your marks! Get set!" I took a deep breath as they had instructed me and screamed the last word, "Go!" I pulled the bandana down through the cool evening air like my death sentence.

The buzzing of the bikes grew louder, deeper, and the ground quaked as they sped toward me on the road. I held my breath, shut my eyes and clamped my hands over my ears. ZOOM to the left of me.

17

ZOOM to the right. I opened my eyes and spun around. To my right now, but still clearly in front, Jesus throttled down, made a sharp turn and stopped as the losing driver sped past. The driver braked and jumped off the still moving bike. He ran a few steps, slowing down, and spun on his heels as the abandoned vehicle proceeded twenty yards, slammed into a boulder, bounced and fell in a ruin on the desert floor.

"You cheated!" the driver screamed at Jesus as he marched back up the road. He walked past Jesus, right up to my face.

"You had your eyes, closed. I saw you. Your boss is disqualified," he said and he snatched his red bandana from my limp hand.

He shoved past me and continued toward the motor home. He wasn't more than ten feet away when he threw up his arms in a sign of victory, to the sunset, apparently. He was still hooting and hollering as Jesus came alongside me. Jesus and I walked his bike up to trailer where he rolled it up the ramp and lowered it down into a grillwork of metal tubes. I watched as he carefully lashed the bike down with the elastic cords. We could hear the driver inside the motor home kicking things and cursing. We heard the sound of falling objects. Meanwhile, Jesus bent down and raised the ramp, returning it to its travel position and secured the latch. We looked up at the sound of a dish breaking. This was followed by the sound of a metal salad bowl. It must have struck the floor at such an angle as to send it spinning face down on its rim about its center of gravity. I imagined it going around and around, the cadence intensifying with each revolution. It was spinning rapidly now. The pitch grew higher and higher followed by a loud pop. Then silence. Jesus and I stood there in the dusk listening for another outburst.

I asked whether Jesus wanted me to go back down the road for what was left of the other machine. I felt guilty about having closed my eyes during the race.

"Don't worry about the bike," he said. "One should be enough."

We looked at the gleaming blue machine on the trailer. "Enough for what?" I wondered as the driver bounded out of the motor home with a lantern and a chessboard.

"Either of you guys ever catch the <u>Seventh Seal</u>?" he called out.

He set the lantern on the ground and disappeared back into the vehicle. Two lawn chairs flew out the doorway and tumbled to the ground. The driver reappeared with a card table. He set up the table, chairs, lantern, chessboard, and dumped a set of wooden chessmen onto the checker board. Gleefully he went about setting up the pieces in rows and ranks and then took a horseman from each side, put the two pieces behind his back and walked to where we stood at the rear of the motor home.

"What'll it be?" he smiled, "Left or right?"

He stood there like a mischievous little boy, smiling, with his hands behind his back.

"Listen," began Jesus, "You're supposed to present both hands holding the concealed pieces within your opponents view."

"Don't you trust me?"

"What about me?" I said, "Don't I get to play?"

"You'll face the winner," said the driver without turning his gaze from Jesus and he presented Jesus with his closed fists.

"All right," said Jesus shaking his head, "I choose the piece from your right hand!"

The driver smiled, but instead of turning over his right hand and opening his fingers, he put his hands behind his back again and looked up at some point in the sky. We could hear the clack of the wooden pieces.

I turned aside to Jesus. "I think he's making a switch."

The driver stepped forward and presented us with both hands extended. He slowly rotated his right arm and opened the fingers.

"Black," shouted the driver, triumphantly, "You're black!"

"Is that bad thing?" I asked Jesus.

"I don't know," he replied, "I've never played."

* * *

Although the game had yet to be invented that night as the two contestants climbed into their aluminum lawn chairs in the glow of the lantern to begin their opening moves, I was pretty excited by what promised to be a really awesome contest. After the first hour, when nobody had scored, I walked out of sight to relieve myself, which took a little while, but when I returned, the pieces were in exactly the same positions they had been when I left.

"What kind of game is this?" I said and when no one answered I looked up beyond the circle of light and realized the stars had come out in the sky. It was then that I first noticed the eyes in the dark. They were big green eyes with long narrow irises. Jesus had his back to where they burned in the dark no more than twenty feet away, a distance a beast might have closed in a heartbeat. It was all I could do to inch over to the driver and whisper, "Excuse me but, over there, by those rocks…"

"I seen him," the driver said softly without looking up from the board.

"Seen what?" said Jesus, as though coming out of his trance, some sub-atomic connection he'd established with the printed paper of the checkerboard, the grain of wood in the individual chess pieces, not to mention the inspiration, from who knows where, for what his next move might be in a game no one, besides the driver, evidently, had ever played.

"It's my move," warned the driver as he slid from his chair and went into the motor home.

"My move," he mouthed from the doorway.

I watched the green eyes glowing just over Jesus' right shoulder, but held a finger to my lips and Jesus understood my signal to say nothing and remain motionless. In the next instant, the driver emerged from the motor home, walked up beside the card table and fired a double-barreled shot-gun across the road. There was a flash of light and a terrific explosion.

"Don't give me the evil eye, you mangy son of a bitch!" he shouted into the dark.

The driver pulled the gun stock to his shoulder and fired the second barrel. Thunder rolled across the desert. Had he turned 45 degrees to his right, the driver might just as easily blown off Jesus' head, at 70 degrees, mine too, come to think of it, but he walked back, nonchalantly cracked open the weapon, dumped smoking shells on the ground, reloaded, and set the shotgun against the motor home.

He returned to his lawn chair and slapped four fresh shot gun shells on the table.

With amazement on our faces we looked at the driver.

"Don't worry, he's plenty wounded. Dogs will get him one way or another."

"Are we going to finish this game?" asked Jesus.

Out of sheer boredom a couple times I'd say something like, "If you guys don't mind, I think I'll go for a little walk," and Jesus might nod or the driver grunt and I'd leave the table. It was getting mighty cool out there on that desert road. I'd start thinking about the lion and whatever the driver was saying about wild dogs being out there and I'd head back. This went on all night until I had just about had it.

When I came back the third time and it was close to three in the morning, they had a bottle of bourbon and two glasses between them on the table. That's when I noticed the driver's pack of cigarettes. He lit up and I smelled tobacco. I don't know when I picked up that habit. Maybe it was Oakland? I can't remember, but it sure smelled good that night. Anyway, I'm sitting on a camp stool which I had pulled out of the motor home, and all of a sudden the driver cheers and snatches Jesus' queen off the board, and I see Jesus slump down in his chair.

"Good move," said Jesus.

"I'll say, buddy," laughed the drive, "I got your Queen!"

"Are you winning?" I asked the driver. I'd counted up the number of pieces they each had lost or captured and it sure looked like Jesus was on the ropes.

"You might say that," said the driver and he cracked the seal on the bottle and poured three ounces into a glass.

"Jesus?" he said, offering the bottle.

"Normally I would, if only just a taste, but I'm trying to keep my head particularly clear tonight. I appreciate the offer. Thank you."

"Oh, you do? You appreciate it? Well, you are very welcome, sir."

"Not a problem."

"I'm glad it's not a problem. I am mighty freaking glad. I am mighty freaking glad you don't have a problem with my offer of a little celebratory libation, something that has been used throughout all freaking history in virtually all cultures and societies, with rare exception, as a symbol of good will and fellowship. But who am I? I'm just a chauffeur! Run you all over the freaking outback while you get your head together, like I got nothing better to do with my time. Well the clock is ticking, pal. The meter is running on this trip!"

The driver was the sort of guy who always wanted to have the last word. Jesus was fine with that and wasn't out to prove anything as far as I could see, and for the moment he seemed pretty absorbed in how he was going get out of his situation on the board without his queen. The driver turned to me with the bottle.

"Bob?"

"Steve." I corrected.

"How about I just call you Bob?" he said with a grin, "That'll just be my little nickname for you."

"Sure."

"All right then, Bob," he said and he handed me a lit menthol cigarette and poured an ounce or two of bourbon into the empty glass and handed it to me. Jesus gave me a warning glance. I shook my head for him not to worry. I couldn't handle anything if not my spirits.

* * *

I never did manage to see who won the chess match. Come to think of it, when the <u>Seventh Seal</u> was on cable in our hotel in Oakland at the turn of the second millennium, I never finished the movie to find out who won that match either. This time, at least I had a good excuse. I drank myself sick. The card table started spinning and I stumbled away out behind the bike trailer and threw up. I had the dry heaves for what must have been twenty minutes. After that I wandered out into the desert. Hell! I wasn't worried about dogs or lions then! I remember falling onto my back and seeing the stars spinning around in the sky and that was that. Sometime before daybreak I remember my telling Jesus what a great chess player he was and him carrying me somewhere on his back.

Bunnies and kittens on a bright yellow field. Bunnies and kittens: that's what I saw. My head was pounding when I awoke on a big rectangular shag carpet on the floor. I must have rolled off the sofa onto the carpet with the pattern of little, big-eyed animals earlier that morning. My mouth felt like someone had stuffed it with sand. I stumbled over to the basin and got some water from the tap. For some reason it was warm, but I didn't care. I wheeled around and through the driver's compartment I saw the sun burning in the windshield. I rubbed my eyes and staggered over to the sliding door. The sound of the ball bearings rolling along inside the recessed tracks hurt my head. I hadn't even really noticed the sound before that morning. I looked at the ruin of our make shift porch and managed a smile. The card table was cracked in two halves. One of the lawn chairs had its webbing torn out and the other had its frame bent up into a ball. The chess board was in tatters and the pieces were strewn about and some of them crunched underfoot as I stepped from the cabin.

I kicked the empty bourbon bottle and walked to the front of the vehicle and winced at the sun coming up in the sky and I could see the silhouettes of Jesus and the driver. About a quarter mile up the road the driver had taken a stick and drawn a circle in the dirt fifteen feet in diameter. They were both stripped naked and squared off for the next competition. It was Greco-Roman wrestling, old school.

When the driver walked up to Jesus and sucker punched him in the face, I guess rules went out the window. When Jesus picked up the driver and threw him out of the ring, the driver said it didn't count and lunged back in. The contest lasted fifteen minutes. I felt sorry for the driver. Jesus was faster and stronger and just never seemed to take any of it personally. He kept his cool no matter how many hits he took or what the driver swore about his parents or anything. In the end Jesus had thrown the driver out of the ring twice and a third time pinned him on the ground.

"You want to say, uncle?" asked Jesus.

Oh, but the driver was fuming mad, all tied up in a knot, his butt crack up in the air and his face all scrunched over and pressed down into the dirt and sand.

"Never!" snarled the driver and then in a voice so low I thought it almost a whisper or that he might have lost his mind he added, "This body is strong, filled with desire. I should have beaten you easily! You were supposed to be man of flesh and blood!"

"I am."

"You are superhuman!"

"Good enough," replied Jesus, releasing his hold. He stood and walked to the side of the road where his loin-cloth, robe and sandals lay on the ground.

"I never said Uncle!" shouted the driver and he spit.

"No, you never said Uncle when it might have made a difference," said Jesus as he slipped his feet into his sandals and cinched up his loin cloth.

"Then I win," the driver cried.

I stood off to the side, afraid to move as Jesus pulled on his robe and walked down the road toward the motor home.

"I know things about you Jesus," shouted the driver, stumbling to his feet.

Jesus stopped, his back still to us.

"You ever think about the future?" continued the driver. "Huh? Ever wonder? You don't even exist where I come from! You hear that? You're dead! You hear me? Deader than that lion up over that hill in the dust! All of you, and everyone who ever lived to meet you or hear your name! Dead! You hear that? You hear your old driver, now?"

Jesus took a step and then continued on his way and he disappeared into the side of the motor home.

The driver stood naked in the middle of the road. His fists were clenched and his shoulders heaved and it almost sounded as though he was growling, a long, low growl. Finally, he hung his head and walked to the opposite side of the road and dropped down in the dust beside Lawrence Strathmore's clothes. He wiped the back of his neck with the red bandana, and fitted it over the black tattoo on his glistening white skull. He looked over at me as he pulled on his jeans.

"What are you doing here anyway? That's what I can't figure." He laughed and pulled on his shirt. Then, out of the blue, "You like the ladies?" he asked.

"What?"

"Ladies? Women? You know," he smiled and made an obscene gesture.

"Sure. I know about that."

"Sure you do. I know what you been doing back on that sofa when you think nobody's around."

I stared at him without blinking. I didn't know where else to look.

The cowboy slowly pulled on his boots. "So, then, how would it be if I was to set you up with a fine looking lady?"

"I don't know, Mister. I don't think it's a good idea for me to be talking to you."

The driver put on his vest and stood. "That's why I asked what you were doing here." He smiled and picked up his hat and preened the raven's feather between his thumb and forefinger.

"Why don't you run along Bobby," he said at last and looked back over his shoulder at the rising sun, "We'll be moving on soon."

I realized I'd been holding my breath just about the entire time and that I'd been standing there with my knees locked, frozen like a rabbit in my tracks. I got dizzy as I finally took a step. I moved slowly away back toward the vehicle as the driver placed his hat on his head and picked up a smooth, flat stone. I was walking really fast now, and I don't know why, but I looked back just in time. He side-armed the stone with terrific force. It skipped three times in the dirt sending up plumes of dust and struck me in the back of my right hand.

"Ouch," I yelled, grabbing my hand, "What did you do that for?"

"That ain't nothin," laughed the driver. "You're running with the big dogs now!"

* * *

Audio cassettes, even those with digitized metallic tape, represented an antiquated technology in many of the places we would one day visit in the far future. Even in the driver's day, the media was being replaced by a new standard. Still, for all his vulgarity, the driver had a profound appreciation for some of civilization's crowning achievements in military science, medical research, high finance and on-line gaming. At the same time, being a student of history, he had nostalgia for some of the old ways of doing things too: hence the stack of books on tape he listened to through a machine in the control console up front. At mid-morning I heard him yell at Jesus that he had to go down the road to check on something and that he would be back "after-a-while" and that we should be ready to leave that afternoon.

I climbed off the sofa in the main cabin where I must have dozed off. I peaked out the side door. Way out there on the desert floor I could see Jesus on his rock meditating. It was getting mighty hot in the van, but seeing that the driver was nowhere in sight I went up front to take a look at those tapes. I climbed into his seat and opened a plastic compartment in the armrest. There they were. Apparently there were some great authors of world literature represented in these audio cassettes. True it was "miraculous," that only semi-literate in my native tongue, I read some titles: The Prince, Rise and Fall of the Third Reich, Helter Skelter, The Qur'an, The New Testament.

There was something about the last one that sounded vaguely familiar, and I decided to give it a listen. Then I realized everything in the van was turned off. I saw the key was still in the side of the steering column and I turned it to the same midway position I'd seen the driver use. Lights instantly glowed on the instrument panel. That's funny, I thought. They're dimmer than I'd seen them before. Wait a minute, on this stick over here. Lights. High. That sounded good. I turned the dial to "high" and a little blue light added its glow to all the other lights on the control panel. Not much of an improvement, I thought, but I picked up the New Testament and stuck it in the slot. Power: on. What next? Wait a minute. What's this? "Select." I was about to push "cassette" when I saw another button called "radio." I don't know why, but I pushed that button instead. I heard a faint sound come over speakers, like running water. I needed volume so I spun the volume to the half-way mark.

The passenger door flew open and I about had a heart attack. Fortunately, it was Jesus.

"What are you doing, Steve?" he asked.

"Oh, I was just going to listen to the New Testament. It's a book on tape. Ever hear of it?" Jesus thought for a moment and shook his head. "What's it about?"

We were interrupted by a warning chime that sounded from somewhere in the console.

"What's that?" Jesus asked.

"Come in and close your door."

In a moment the chiming had ceased and we were both in the driver's cab listening to static on the radio. The expression that overcame Jesus' face reminded me of the one from the previous night when he'd examined the chessboard.

"Try the FM button," he said. "Frequency…" he said slowly. He repeated the word and turned his head to the side and looked at the control. "Try the tuner," he said.

I slowly turned the dial marked "tuner" and watched the numbers on the LCD display change in response. A smile was slowly forming on Jesus' lips.

"What is it?" I asked.

"Stop there," he said, "Turn up the volume a bit. Good."

A rushing sound like wind poured from the loud speakers.

"It's static," said Jesus, "White noise is what they call it."

"And they listen to this for entertainment?"

"No…" he said, "Perhaps they should."

"What?"

"It's deeper than that."

We sat there in that hot cab for a full minute.

"I'm sorry, Jesus. I don't hear anything."

"No," said Jesus, softly, "It's something inside the noise. It's coming from a very long time ago."

"What?"

"Listen."

"You're creeping me out, dude."

"I don't have a word for it yet, but it's from the very beginning of this world. I've been listening and waiting for it my entire life."

That did it. I moved uncomfortably in my seat. Maybe this had been a bad idea. Jesus looked out the passenger window to the spot where he had spent the majority of the past three days.

"Do you want to listen to this tape or not?" I said.

"Sounds like a great idea," he replied looking into the passenger's rear view mirror, "But it looks as though our friend is coming up the road." He paused and looked back at me, "What's wrong? Didn't you ask his permission? Steve, you did ask his permission to get into his things, didn't you?"

I rubbed my hands together nervously, leaned forward and popped out the tape.

"What are you doing?" he asked, "I thought we were going to listen to this one? The New Testament? Steve?"

I snatched the tape out of his hands, gathered the cassettes, stuffed them back in the driver's compartment, climbed out of the seat and started toward the back of the motor home when I stopped and ran back up front.

"I almost forgot," I leaned forward and turned off the "power" button on the audio console. Jesus gave me a bewildered looked.

"Just try to act normal," I said and climbed onto the sofa in back. I grimaced as the driver's shadow passed by the picture window above me. He went up front to the passenger's side where I heard him address Jesus.

"Where the hell's that shotgun?"

"Out there," said Jesus.

"Oh, that's just great!" replied the driver.

"Is that where you've been?"

"Don't think I couldn't find it if I really wanted to. I've been through these parts before and I have plenty of friends."

"Well?" asked Jesus.

"I had some business to attend to; let's just leave it at that."

"Fine." said Jesus.

"About the shotgun?" asked the driver again.

"You don't really need a shotgun do you?"

"I happen to like guns. It's a free country, isn't it?"

"We're under Roman occupation," said Jesus.

I heard the cowboy's fist bang against the metal panel beside the passenger window. I'd crept out from my place on the sofa and leaned against the partition separating the living quarters from the drivers' cabin. Just then, Jesus lowered his voice to a whisper. It was everything I could do to make-out what he was saying to the driver.

"Have we been on this road trip before?"

"What kind of a question is that?" asked the driver.

"You're good with questions."

"What of it?"

"It's just that a lot of this feels familiar to me, like in a dream I've been having."

"Like you're in a gap?" asked the driver.

"A 'gap?' Yes. Something like that -- as though we're in an empty space."

"Like a bump in the road between all that was straight and true on one side and all that's bright and sunny on the other? Legion…"

"What's that?" Jesus asked.

"Nothing," smiled the driver. "I had a dream once."

"Did you?

"Oh yes. But it wasn't bright and sunny on the other side."

There was a long pause.

"Am I in it?" asked Jesus.

"In my dream? Oh yeah, you're in it all right," said the driver.

They seemed to mull this over for some minutes, when the driver spoke excitedly.

"So, what about me?"

"What?" asked Jesus.

"Am I in your dream?"

"I don't know. Perhaps. You certainly remind me of someone."

"Well, it was all a terrible misunderstanding: some words were spoken, a few oaths taken, that business with the First Sphere and the experiments…"

"Excuse me?"

"Hardly what I'd call an insurrection!"

"Insurrection? What on earth are you talking about?" asked Jesus.

"Oh, just stop with the charade will you?"

"What?" said Jesus.

"Snap out of it, man. You've seen the program! Wake up! You're almost as dense as that idiot you pulled out of the fire back there."

"Steve?"

"Granted, I may be a 'man of mystery.' That's my style. But you! Don't you realize who you are? I mean who you really are?"

"I like to think that I'm a man of God." said Jesus.

The driver paused, exasperated. "Man of God?" he said and I heard him spit, "That's all you got?"

They must have been lost in thought. After a while the driver spoke. "So, what do you say? A few laughs? See how things turn out this time?"

"This time?"

"You were wondering whether you'd done any of this before."

"If only I could get back out there on the desert for a while longer. That's what I really need. That's what I expected." said Jesus.

"Vacations are like that aren't they."

"Vacations? This is a vacation?"

"Why don't you just sit back and we'll be on our way shortly. Okay?"

I heard movement in the compartment up front. It was Jesus.

"Steve? Steve, are you there? The driver says we're about ready to head out!"

I jumped from my spot by the partition and rolled onto the sofa below the picture window. I pretended I was asleep as Jesus tapped me on the shoulder, "Hey buddy, wake up. Someone's coming down the road."

I followed Jesus outside as we both exited the motor home through the sliding door and stood on the road by the trailer hitch as the driver walked down the path to meet a traveler. The hooded figure dressed all in black robes sat on a wagon drawn by a pale horse. Our driver hailed the stranger, and in a few moments the horse and wagon were at a halt behind motor home.

As the driver talked to the fellow at the reigns, Jesus turned to me, "Did you ever manage to listen to any of that audio tape on the New Testament?"

"The what?" I had no idea what Jesus was talking about and I moved to one side to get a better look at the wagon master. Our driver walked alongside the motor home and flipped open the small door above the rear wheels. He reached in and twisted something inside and when he removed his hand, a small black disk was left tethered on a wire beside a small round hole in the open compartment. The driver motioned the wagon master to move ahead with his cargo.

"Who is that?" I asked the driver.

"Who?"

"On the wagon?"

"I wouldn't stand too close," our driver said in a whisper and then, with a knowing look to Jesus, added, "Leprosy…"

I backed away after that as the wagon pulled up and stopped alongside the motor home. Our driver climbed up and unlashed lengths of rope from the mouth of a large clay cistern on the back of the wagon and peeled back a large piece of oil soaked leather.

"What's he doing?" I asked Jesus.

From the wagon floor, the driver produced a black coil of hose. He stuck one end inside the cistern, and holding the opposite end, jumped off, crouched beside the motor home's rear wheel and stuck the hose in his mouth. His jaw worked on the hose and then he pulled it from his mouth and spit and jammed the end of the hose into the hole in the side of our vehicle. He spit again, climbed back atop the wagon and held the hose down into the cistern. After what seemed ten or fifteen minutes we heard a sucking sound reverberate from the mouth of the cistern.

"He's siphoning fuel," said Jesus.

The driver spit again, slapped the silent wagon master on its humped shoulder and jumped off the wagon. Without a word, the wagon master cracked a whip, snapped the reigns and guided the horse and wagon off the road in a short slow turn and back onto the road in the direction it had come.

Our driver disappeared to the front of the motor home and climbed aboard. I rubbed the back of my hand. I felt weird and unsettled.

"What's wrong?" said Jesus, "You should be happy!" he said. "We're finally getting out of here."

Suddenly, a blood curdling scream erupted from the driver's side doorway. "The lamps! Who left the head lamps burning?"

Jesus turned and went up front. I swallowed hard and stood there with a sinking feeling as I watched the wagon recede in the distance. It had stopped about a mile down the road when something horrible happened. The wagon master stood and threw off his black robes. The exposed back flashed weird rainbow iridescence in the hot afternoon air. Then, and I shall not forget the sound for the rest of my life, I heard a distant buzzing, like the cicada in summer, and the creature darted into the air and disappeared in the shimmering heat on the western horizon.

Next, I felt the pull of a hand on my shoulder. I spun like a top in time to see the driver's fist slam into my face. There were bright flashes of light and I fell on the ground beside the black tires of the motor home with the driver standing over me yelling and Jesus trying to pull him back.

"You know what a battery is?" he shouted. "You left the headlights on and drained the battery! You damned fool! Have you got any idea what sort of monkey wrench this throws into things? Some of us are on a schedule! Some of us have goals! Some of us have a reason to exist!"

Jesus succeeded in pulling him away, but not before the driver landed blows to my legs and side with his cowboy boots and I would have ugly black bruises for weeks. The driver pushed away from Jesus and marched to the front of the vehicle.

"Get that little monster together and ready to take off," he barked.

"You said the engine won't start," called Jesus.

"It'll start," replied the driver reaching into his side door and then circling angrily around to disappear at the front of the vehicle.

"Just get that good for nothing side-kick of yours into the van."

"I'm sorry," I said, looking up at Jesus.

Jesus helped me to my feet and back inside through the sliding door.

"Hurry up now," sounded the drivers' voice, "I'm going to need you up in the driver's seat. Hey, Jesus, you there?" shouted the driver and he spit.

"I'm here," called Jesus coming up from the living quarters and he climbed into the driver's seat and called through the open door, "What do I need to do?"

The driver unlatched something on the front of the vehicle. A metal panel flew up and obscured our view as he went to work. Nursing my jaw, I peered down through the windshield in the narrow gap between the raised hood and the dashboard. We could see arms working inside the engine.

"You in the driver's seat?" he called.

"Yes," replied Jesus.

"All right," said the driver. "See the big pedal on the floor on the right? That's the gas pedal. Put your right foot on it, and when I say, 'give it some gas,' ease down and pump it, slow and steady. You got that?"

"Yes."

"Now, see that key in the ignition on the steering column? Turn it all the way forward on my count. One... two..."

Outside, like a picador at a bullfight, the driver stood over the metal poles of the car battery. He licked the fingers of his left and right hands. "Turn on the ignition," he shouted.

There was a low tortured lugging sound from the engine compartment. The driver seized the battery terminals in his bare hands. Blue sparks shot up along his arms. With an otherworldly voice he barked, "Give it the gas."

Jesus obeyed the driver and pressed his sandaled foot to the accelerator. Instantly, the engine coughed, and as Jesus pumped with his foot, the motor home roared to life. The driver slammed shut the hood and came around to Jesus' side, "Move over," he said. Jesus climbed into the passenger seat and I took a step back to see what would happen next.

"Oh, no," said the driver, "Bob, you get up here. I'm not going to let your boss ride shot-gun with this bad boy!"

Jesus acquiesced and passed me in the narrow passage.

"Things will be just fine," Jesus reassured me.

Slowly, carefully, I returned to my seat beside the driver. We got underway as the sun was going down in the desert behind us. It wasn't long into the ride on the rock strewn way that I smelled burned flesh and hair coming from the driver's seat. It was much later, as night fell and the driver turned on the vehicle's head lamps, that I finally stole a look at him. He had an uncanny ability to anticipate my every move and he turned and looked me full in the face with a smile. The flesh surrounding both eye sockets was blackened as though he'd received a fatal blow to the head.

"You think old Larry Strathmore would recognize himself in that mirror?" he said and looked back down the road.

4. Truck Stop

"Do you suppose we could get something to drink?"

No answer.

"Hey! I'm dying of thirst over here!"

No answer.

It was morning and the sun had come up, more cruelly than it had the morning before. We'd driven all night and I could hardly speak, I was so thirsty.

Still, there was no response from the driver. He wasn't listening to his audio tapes with the ear pieces so I knew that he could hear me. I tried again.

"I wondered whether we could get something besides water? Do you have anything else back there I could drink?" No answer again. It was as though I didn't exist.

It was just then that I noticed the glove box. I had never considered opening it, certainly not in the presence of the driver. Out of sheer boredom, and maybe to get his attention, I pushed the latch mechanism and the compartment door fell open.

Without even bothering to look at me the driver drawled, "You might want to be careful with that crap in there."

I snorted, leaned forward and pulled out a maintenance manual. I thumbed through, glancing at some color photographs of the motor home and many curious diagrams. Meanwhile, Jesus was back in the van's water closet with a face full of shaving cream and a disposable razor. He looked at his reflection in the vanity mirror and carefully, deliberately shaved his face.

I was tired of looking at the manual. When I looked up, expecting to see the same, endlessly repetitive landscape, I gave a startled shout and grabbed the door and the edge of my seat. Everything had vanished behind an onrushing cloud of yellow dust and sand.

"What is it?" I cried.

"Dust storm," said the driver.

"Dust storm?"

"Yep."

"Shouldn't we pull over?"

"We're okay."

"Okay? We can't see the road."

"What road?" said the driver.

And now something curious, that lasted only a few seconds, but the color and consistency of the particles coursing over and around the windshield changed to a fine, white mist. Suddenly, there was a terrific BUMP as though we'd hit a pot hole. I cried out and bounced up and down and nearly grabbed hold of the wheel, but the mist suddenly streamed away and we could see the road ahead as though nothing had happened.

"What was that?" I shouted with a laugh and settled back in my seat.

"Bump."

"A bump?"

The driver grinned and looked to his rearview mirror for a moment. Satisfied, he looked back at the road. It was then that I noticed the landscape seemed somehow different than it had only seconds before. I hadn't really been paying all that much attention to anything, but now on the horizon, for the first time I could see a faint blue-grey band of what must have been distant mountains. I noticed too the road had changed.

The Romans had done a mighty nice job to the edge of the city. Out into the desert it had been hard-packed clay, and then for that long stretch, nothing, but now we were on a kind of road I had never seen before. It was coal black, and shimmering and marked with a pattern of white and yellow lines. The motion of the craft had changed; it felt as though we were traveling over a road of silk.

I looked out the passenger window. Off the shoulder at some distance was a curious structure. It resembled the head of bird on a long pole. The pole was attached midway on a tower and the triangular head was dipping down to the ground, as though retrieving something from the desert floor. Up and down, mechanically it moved. And now I saw another, perhaps a hundred yards from the first. As we drove over the smooth black road, I marveled at the field of these strange bobbing machines. I could not help but wonder what they were doing and who had built them. I shoved the booklet back into the compartment. I leaned forward. There was something else in there, tucked away in back, and I reached further in and pulled it out. Printed on the front panel were the words: Road Map.

I smiled and started unfolding the paper.

* * *

Jesus was finishing the last strokes with the razor. He taped his blade on the sink and drew his hand across his lean, square jaw. He looked intently at himself in the mirror and noticed a faint, half inch cut on the side of his chin where the razor had nicked him when we'd hit the bump in the road. A thin red line appeared on Jesus' skin. He drew his index finger across the mark and looked at the blood on his finger tip as though he had never seen his own blood before. He rinsed his fingers and reached for the neatly folded set of clothes prepared for him on a narrow shelf by the basin. He pulled on a pair of khaki shorts and a bright yellow Hawaiian shirt covered with a brilliant pattern of tropical flowers. He was lacing black, high top tennis shoes when he heard a scream from the driver's cabin.

"Help," I cried, writhing in the passenger seat as light blazed in my face and electricity arced over my head from the unfurled road map in my lap.

"How do I fold this thing up?" I cried.

"Thought you wanted to know where we were going?" laughed the driver.

I had modest success folding the map, and like a trap door over a basement of burning lava, only partially closed, light leaked out the sides and sparks of electric current still snapped at my fingers.

"Here," a powerful arm reached over my seat and snatched up the map. Despite the blaze of energy in his face, Jesus' deftly returned the map to its original, folded configuration.

Like holding a snake I took it from him with my thumb and forefinger, tossed it back in the compartment and slammed shut the door.

"What the hell was that?" I wailed.

"Looks like you're both sporting new looks," said the driver and he leaned toward me and flipped down the sun visor. I stared at my reflection in the vanity mirror. My beard had streaks of grey. My face was sunburned, my cheeks blistered. In horror, I looked up at Jesus; whose face too was sunburned. I hardly noticed that his beard and mustache were gone, but his long hair was streaked with grey. I did not for an instant notice his loud Hawaiian shirt.

"Maybe you fellas seen more than men were meant to see?" said the driver.

In horror I recoiled at the sight of the glove box and looked back at Jesus, "But I didn't SEE anything!"

Jesus shook his head, a sad downcast expression on his tanned face.

"Not that you'd understand today, anyway," laughed the driver, "Maybe you need some of these?" the driver grinned, tapping a nearly opaque lens of his shades with the long sharp nail of his little finger.

"Where are we?" I demanded, of either one of them, really, but the driver only laughed his dry, self-satisfied laugh.

"Where are we?" I shouted back at Jesus and lunged out of my seat, but my legs had gone asleep and I stumbled and knocked into the driver. Off guard, he fell against the wheel. The enormous motor home fishtailed wildly across the highway. The motorbike on its trailer shifted violently behind the motor home. For a precarious moment we were riding along only on the motor home's passenger side wheels. I slammed into the passenger door. The driver snarled and wrestled with the wheel. Jesus fell forward and his head slammed into the dash. The motor home crashed back to the highway.

"Where are we?" Jesus demanded of the driver.

"We're at our first stop on the other side of the valley. You fella's may want to stretch your legs and grab a bite. I need to gas up."

Jesus and I looked through the windshield. To our astonishment, not more than two miles up ahead was a truck stop with a filling station, restaurant, and convenience store.

"I might get me some more of these books on tape. You fella's like audio books on tape?"

* * *

We pulled into a crowded truck stop. There were vehicles similar to ours lined up in a lot outside a long, two story building covered with signs and numbers. There were even larger vehicles lined up in a lot beside the outpost, where they waited, murmuring like a huge heard of gigantic, grazing cattle. The driver brought our motor home to a stop beneath a bright red, white and blue awning nearest the highway. He reached down to the floorboard to a shoebox. He flipped open the lid and scooped out a huge fist full of silver coins.

"Here," he said, holding his fist toward me. His clenched fingers opened palm up so that some of the coins slipped out and fell to the floor mat.

"Don't bother about them. We got plenty more."

I picked up every one of the coins and placed them into the leather money purse strung to my belt.

"Them is what they call silver dollars," said the driver. It's what they use for money around here. You can get anything you want."

He poured even more of the coins into my open palms. He slipped on a leather jacket, adorned with tassels of leather fringe and loaded a pocket with audio books on tape. He smiled at Jesus as he opened the driver door and stepped out.

"Anything you want, Jesus." The driver spit, "Well, come on then, we ain't got all day."

I climbed out of the cab and scurried after him across the lot beneath rows of awnings toward the convenience store. I was reminded of the pungent smell of fuel from the sinister wagon master's cistern. Everywhere beneath the awnings people had lined their vehicles and were sticking black hoses into their sides, watching numbers display on the facades of rectangular metal monuments.

Through a doorway that opened automatically I walked into an enormous indoor market and my senses were overwhelmed by the sounds and colors and the beautiful things for sale. Soon enough, I felt that people were staring at me; apparently I was the only man dressed in a robe and headdress. Indeed, most of the men and women dressed in a fashion similar to Jesus and the driver. Still, I found my way to a room in back where the men were assembling to relieve themselves. I urinated against a porcelain fixture on the wall as was the custom and went to an elaborate basin before a mirrored wall to carefully wash my hands.

"A little early for Christmas," I heard one of the men snort to a companion. I had no idea what the man was talking about.

"Hey, Abdul, you got a bomb up under your dress there?" laughed another man.

I took the opportunity to fill my palms with water to drink and did so in this manner for a full minute. The men in line behind me seemed displeased and made other comments about Christmas and a character named Muhammad. I returned to the main room. Down an aisle I saw the driver, loading a basket. I also selected a hand basket from a stack by the entrance. I was enjoying myself as we walked along the aisles filling our baskets. We arrived at a metallic counter where people were filling containers with drink.

The driver poured himself a huge container of bubbling green liquid. I did likewise and followed him to another counter where we waited in a long line. He pulled a long, slender, tube of meat from a clear cylinder and waved it at me. "This here is all beef and spices. Mighty good eating, and it don't never go bad." I took his example and was soon munching a meat stick when Jesus walked into the convenience store.

Suddenly, everyone in the place froze in his or her tracks and looked over, slack-jawed at the man in the door way. A bunch of women coming out of their own special room in the back stopped and gasped. Now, the only sound in the place was the voice of the driver, trying to get the clerk's attention.

"I'd like to exchange these here audio tapes for these." From the confines of his leather jacket the driver withdrew a handful of audio tapes, and a pink receipt. Evidently, the driver had been to such an oasis before.

"Okay…" said the clerk, a corpulent man, perspiring heavily despite the artificially cool climate in his market. He glanced at the slip of paper, "I'll need to see some plastic and a driver's license," he said.

Like a magician, the driver produced the two items and presented them to the clerk who was still half watching my friend in the doorway. Now the man was evidently satisfied with the driver's identification.

"Massachusetts, huh?" grunted the clerk.

Greedily, the driver snatched up his new tapes and slid his basket of items in front of the attendant. Having placed the precious tapes in his pocket, he nonchalantly dumped handfuls of silver dollars onto the counter.

"This ought to take care of this here meat stick and the drink. Plus, I want me three big buckets of that chicken over there and one each of all them sides and a box of biscuits. Make that two boxes of biscuits. This fellow has some stuff too. He's got plenty to cover it. Throw a cartoon of them menthol smokes in there, and I'll just take me one of these."

He pulled a disposable lighter wrapped in imitation snake skin from a POP cardboard standee at the register. He tested the flame, and, satisfied, slipped the object into his vest pocket.

"If you'd all just take your eyes off that big fake in the doorway long enough to let a fellow do his damn business. I'm going out to gas-up my rig at pump 13."

Aware the clerks and patrons had shifted their collective focus back to him, the driver smiled rakishly in the direction of the ladies by the cold beer storage units and tipped his hat.

"Ladies..." he said with a smile.

He strode past Jesus in the door, and he regarded him, not as a traveling companion, but as a total stranger, "Well, aloha to you, too!" He walked outside and spit on his way across the lot.

Even with the assistance of several apprentices, it took the clerk a long while to fill our order. I had to send Jesus to the motor home with a load of beer, wine and snacks and to retrieve more coins from the driver's silver shoebox to complete the transaction. By the time we were done, I even had to sacrifice the coins from my money pouch to pay our debt.

Through the large plate glass windows of the building I could just barely see our motor home. Our driver had taken off his jacket and climbed up the silver ladder to the rooftop luggage rack and sat astride the metallic canoe. The canoe and the canvas covered luggage had shifted drastically during the moments of our close call back on the highway. The driver had inserted a black hose from one of the monuments into the port side of the motor home and sat astride the behemoth with elastic cables, lashing everything down in place.

The driver's large chicken order was taxing the servants behind the counter, but I didn't mind the wait in the least. I was enjoying my bubbling green drink and sugary maple long john when I suggested Jesus load up on some food for himself. I was busying looking at some dark eyewear, similar to that sported by our driver when a beautiful young woman appeared from the back of the shop. She must have been in the ladies' room the entire time. She stood in line at the counter and asked Jesus whether he would like a drink of her orange soda. I don't think I ever saw him look so grateful, before or since, than when the lady raised her big 32 ounce cup and Jesus took it from her hand. His hand was trembling. I even took off my dark blue shades to get a good look at his face. Sure enough, a tear was coming down his cheek. The blond offered for him to go on and keep the thing, but he wouldn't have anymore, just that one, long grateful sip.

We paid for everything, but had to step back out of line to let other folks through as the clerks finished with our biscuits. Evidently they had to thaw some out in a thing called a microwave oven. There would be hell to pay for those biscuits, is the way the driver put it later. The blond haired girl with the orange soda had settled up and was just kind of hanging around at the door. That's when I noticed her sandals and how dirty her feet were and that she had a dirty powder blue back pack slung over her back. I think she was probably more my type than his, closer in age to me, around twenty-five. I pictured her lying out beside me on the beach, looking at our little fleet of fishing boats setting out from the harbor with our seven sons each the captain of his own boat. There was something familiar about her.

I heard a bell sound which indicated our biscuits were thawed and heated. Jesus was in the doorway with buckets of chicken and several drooping bags of the driver's sides, when I noticed that the girl was gone. In the same instant, several uniformed men came through the doorway. These were not Roman soldiers, but they had a manner about them that suggested an unseen authority. As I left the counter with boxes of biscuits and bags of snacks I felt the chill of trouble as I passed these men in blue.

I quickened my pace behind Jesus as we threaded our way between arriving and departing vehicles. Those amazing self propelled machines, long since explained to me and infinitely more primitive than those I would encounter later in my travels, were built the world over in a staggering variety of sizes and shapes, but each with one important caveat. Only those reserved for authorities permitted the flashing lights on their roofs. The wail of sirens split the late afternoon air; suddenly the lot had become a hornet's nest with blue garbed men in cars with flashing lights all drawn to the front of the convenience store.

"Where's the driver?" I cried, as Jesus opened the side door of the motor home and stepped inside hauling my bags and boxes onboard. I thought our captain had lashed himself to the rooftop, but he had vanished. The side door slammed shut as I rushed to the front door, tripped up in my robes, and stumbled. That's when I noticed the driver, leaning up against the side of the motor home. One hand on the nozzle of the gasoline pump, he looked like a chameleon, frozen, and silently counting off numbers on a display screen.

"Hey," I shouted, "Let's get out of here."

I threw open the passenger door and climbed up into my seat. Far across the lot, I saw the big convenience store clerk in the middle of what seemed an army of police officers. He was stabbing a finger in our direction. I flung myself across the cab to the driver's seat. Through the window I saw the reflection of the driver in the side view mirror. Workmanlike he was spinning shut the gas cap on the motor home. He closed the gas cap security door and walked to the end of the motor home as far as the black pump hose would reach. There he tipped back his head, raised the nozzle to his lips, and jammed it into his mouth.

"Jesus… Jesus, I think you better have a look at this," I said.

Jesus had come forward into the cabin beside me.

I looked back to where the driver stood with the pump nozzle in his mouth. The driver's head jolted to the side as he squeezed the pump handle.

"He's siphoning fuel, right?" I asked.

"I don't know think so," said Jesus.

"Can people do that?" I asked without turning my eyes from the mirror, but now a new concern had drawn our attention to a view through the windshield at the convenience store as a loud, electronic voice sounded.

"Attention! Attention, pump 13. This is the police! Step out of the vehicle with your hands in the air!"

Before I could speak, I heard the passenger door open and watched Jesus obediently climb out of the motor home. I shook my head, momentarily forgetting about the driver and our hope of escape and climbed over to the passenger seat and joined my friend on the pavement.

"Now what?" I said, slowly raising my hands over my head.

"Render unto Caesar that which is Caesar," replied Jesus.

"Well sure, but these guys look like they're planning to kill us!"

"Don't make any sudden moves." He suggested without looking at me. "Those are weapons they are pointing at us."

"Yeah," I whispered, "Isn't that like the one the driver had back in the desert?"

A bristling array of service revolvers and shotguns were aligned in our direction.

"These are ten gauge," said Jesus.

I had no idea what he was talking about, but from the tone in his voice I held still, even as my eyes moved in their sockets to the right and observed an obscene and impossible sight. The driver, or what was left of him, appeared slowly from behind the rear of the van. His boots dragged along the blacktop. He no longer held the pump nozzle. He had no need.

"Oh, my God..." I murmured.

"Pray for them," I heard Jesus say as I watched the creature to my right. The driver's vest and shirt had burst open and his torso flowed out. His stomach was distended impossibly down to his knees. Black veins bulged across exposed gray flesh as the legs lurched forward two steps in the direction of the police line.

The apparition stopped them in their tracks. The blaring voice from speakers in the eaves of the metallic awning squawked.

"Raise your hands over your -- what in the name of God...?"

The bloated creature slowly raised its arms. Numb fingers pulled something down from the skull. The hat with the raven feather fell away and the red bandana fluttered to the blacktop. The hand settled on top of the skull with the black tattoo and slowly massaged the scalp. The other hand lowered in the direction of the gasoline pumps across the breezeway.

"Hey, you by the motorcycle, keep your hands RAISED," warned the electronic voice.

The fingers on the driver's extended hand made a series of gestures and instantly the LCD display screens across the rows of pump islands pulsed a simultaneous message: "You may remove the nozzle and select your grade."

Obeying unseen force, the nozzles popped from their cradles or dislodged from the gas tanks they had been servicing or wrenched themselves frighteningly from the hands of customers beneath the awnings, and in a horrific ballet, swaying and snaking, finally pointed at the wavering police line. The fuel swollen maestro in cowboy boots motioned with his arm, as though throwing an invisible missile at the offices. Instantly, thirteen nozzles sprayed petrol at the astonished men. A few patrons, still in their cars, bailed out. A woman shrieked in terror. The voice squawking over the P.A. system had become unintelligible. Someone dropped the microphone inside the convenience store.

Brandishing a pistol, the leader of the troopers walked slowly toward the driver. One of the nozzles veered from the others on its black tether and sprayed gasoline on the man. He wiped his face and shouted.

"I don't know what the hell you are, but I'm warning you for the last time!"

The driver pulled the cigarette lighter from a pocket of his vest. His thumb spun the striker wheel. Holding a tiny flame a foot from his distorted, grinning face, the driver took a deep breath and disgorged. Thirty gallons on high octane gasoline streamed from between the

54

driver's teeth with the force of a water cannon. The stream knocked the state trooper back fifteen feet like a toy doll before it ignited.

Like an ancient dragon, the driver turned his head slowly side to side belching a steady stream of fire as the cobra-headed gas hoses burst into flames. Metal awnings over the islands beside the convenience store exploded with a boom and agony of rending metal. Patrol cars caught fire. People screamed and ran for their lives.

The driver returned to his original shape. He snatched up his hat and his bandana and shouted at us.

"You can put your hands down, you damn fools! Let's go."

I watched the misery and horror of the conflagration, and I have no idea how I got back on board the motor home. I believe, in the end, it was Jesus, crouching from the open side door, who reached under my arms and pulled me, like a dead man, on board. A steel paneled door slid between me and the sight of the truck stop consumed in flames.

5. Evening News

I lay on my side on the sofa beneath the picture window as the motor home barreled down the open road. The afternoon slid into evening. The driver and my friend were sitting up front.

"That was a pretty bad thing you did back there," said Jesus.

"Bad?" said the driver with a chicken barrel between his knees. He spoke between enormous mouthfuls of fried flesh and occasionally tossed a stripped bone on the floor between them.

"You'll see them on the other side one day," he chuckled.

The driver took a sip from his long-necked bottle, "This stuff sure beats hell out of gasoline," he belched and dropped the empty bottle on the floor.

Nonchalantly, the driver opened a box and stuffed a biscuit in his mouth.

"Biscuit?" he offered.

Jesus looked into the box and took a deep breath. He sighed, picked one up, raised it to his lips, and then looked over at the driver who was staring at him intently from the corner of one eye.

Suddenly a thought struck the driver and he stabbed a button on the control console. In response, two glass fitted panels came to life with sound and light. One extended from the ceiling on the passenger side beside the sun visor. Another and much large screen was attached to the cabin wall partition and faced back into the main living quarters where I lay on the sofa. The electronic voices startled me, and I stared at the pictures flashing across the wall.

A family was seated at a dinner table and someone had said something that had made a hidden audience burst into laughter. In the next instant, the picture was replaced by a blue field and banner which read: "Special Report: Tragedy in the Desert."

A bearded man at a desk was speaking earnestly, "Events today on a stretch of highway in the desert southwest have taken a terrible turn. Early this morning a young man identified as Lawrence Strathmore of Cambridge, Massachusetts allegedly stole a motor home parked at a truck stop on Highway 5 outside Bellport, Texas. He returned late this afternoon with a team of terrorists and unleashed a devastating attack against the nation's heartland. We go now to our correspondent in the field, Beth Williamson."

The scene was frighteningly familiar. Behind the woman, in the distance, black smoke rolled into the evening sky. Vehicles with flashing lights rolled past as the woman spoke,

"Hello, Terrance… I am speaking to you from a highway outside Bradford Brothers' Truck Stop where the scene of devastation is indescribable. The death toll here is placed now at fifteen. That's fifteen confirmed deaths. This man…" Now a picture of our driver, but looking as he did in the billfold photographs, appeared in a corner of the screen.

"Lawrence Strathmore allegedly stole a motor home belonging to Warren and Beverly Johnson of Palo Alto, California. He outfitted the stolen vehicle with incendiary devices and returned here at about four o'clock Mountain Time with an elite terrorist team. This truck stop which has served the surrounding community and travelers along Highway 5 for the past sixty-five years has been completely destroyed. We have the Stephenson County Sherriff, Captain Leonard…"

A man in a brown and tan uniform appeared on screen with the woman and was about to speak when the voice of the first man interrupted…

"Beth… Beth, excuse me. This is Terrance, but we're about to go live to a press conference with the head of Homeland Security at the White House."

The image returned to a picture of the man at the desk. He seemed confused for a moment and then looked ahead. I did not know this man, but he seemed to be addressing me directly.

"All right, as we're standing by for that press conference, Beth, we have some footage from the Bradford convenience store security cameras. We have obtained a copy of the video provided to us by Western Security Contractors, a local security firm which has released a copy to the Stephenson County Sheriff's Department. We understand the Sheriff's office has released this footage to the FBI and…"

Now, as though in a hall of mirrors, another window opened behind the desk and I watched a scene replay from the convenience store.

"Jesus!" I called out, my eyes riveted to the screen above where a ghostly image of Jesus appeared in the convenience store doorway. The picture was taken from an odd angle as though from above and it was blurry, but I watched in horror as I saw myself step into the picture.

"The FBI is particularly concerned with this man…" The picture zoomed in on my bearded face. I must have put on the sunglasses. "…This man, whose identity has yet to be determined, appears to have masterminded the attack…"

The image lingered and now was replaced by another sequence with me standing beside Jesus and the girl in the checkout line. I was eating my meat stick and drinking my green bubble water. Again the man at the desk interrupted,

"We are going live to the press conference at the White House."

I hung on every sound and flickering image as the scene now transported me to a room where a grim-faced, middle age woman, stepped to a lectern and spoke.

"Ladies and gentlemen, the tragic events of this afternoon appear to be the work of a domestic terrorist organization. I stress that at this hour it has yet to be determined whether this represents a single, isolated incident or part of a series of attacks. The FBI and CIA are working to see whether any links exist between the assailants and any overseas terrorist organizations. However, I must mention the report of an incident which has been circulating through the various social media this afternoon of grave concern to the President and the Chiefs of Staff regarding a possible break-in at one of our military installations."

Instantly bright lights began flashing in the woman's face and voices from people I couldn't see on the screen started calling her name. It became so confused that a young man got up and was about to say something to shut them up when the woman continued.

"Hey, Bobby!" shouted the driver from the cab up front. "You catching this? We're on TV! Hear that? National news, Bobby! I'll wager that folks are watching this all over the freaking planet!"

The driver was really not all that interested in the report, using it only as a distraction while he waited breathlessly as Jesus turned the uneaten biscuit over and over in his palm. Evidently the distraction had failed.

"Hey, Jesus! Are you going to eat that thing!" snapped the driver.

"Man shall not live by bread alone..." recited Jesus.

"Oh, brother, you can't be serious!"

"...but by every word..."

"Hey Jesus!" I cried from the back room "Are you watching this!"

"...that proceeds from the word of God," continued Jesus.

"Damn you!" cursed the driver and he did not see the wrecked automobile directly in the beams of the motor home headlights. A young woman with a powder blue backpack, lay stricken, hanging out the door of an over turned car in the middle of the lane.

"Look out!" Jesus cried and he sprang to the wheel. The driver shouted and the two grabbed the wheel, turning the vehicle and narrowly avoiding the accident. The motor home barreled down the road.

"Pull over," said Jesus immediately.

"Gonna eat that biscuit?"

"Pull over!"

"Eat it!"

"Pull over!"

"Just a bite."

"I said, pull over!"

"Hell! By the time anyone gets around to writing this down, do you think it will matter whether you ate that damn thing or not!"

"Pull over!"

"In ten thousand years you think anyone is going to actually care! Do you think anyone will even remember?"

I was listening to several conversations at once. For the moment the one that most concerned me was the story of a guy in a motor home breaking onto a military base and stealing something called a thermo-nuclear device. I wasn't sure what that was, but it didn't sound good, and somehow I suspected it had something to do with what our driver was saying up front.

"What they will care about," continued the driver, "What they will remember, is that bad boy I got stashed up underneath the floorboards back there. Hey Bob!" the driver shouted and I could see his black eye sockets in the rear view mirror, "Kick that carpet out of the way. That's right! The one with them bunnies and kittens there. Just roll it back."

I did as I was instructed and found beneath the carpet, embedded in the floor, a rectangular panel three by eight feet long.

"Good job," continued the driver, "Now unlatch those fasteners and fold back the compartment door. It's on hinges. That's right. Careful. That door's heavy."

I completed the task and looked down at the object concealed in the cargo well beneath the floor. It seemed unremarkable, a large metallic cylinder about seven feet long and perhaps two feet in diameter. The enormous tube was covered with stickers. Each sticker bore the same three black triangles, arranged against a circular yellow field.

* * *

As I look back on the events that transpired in and around the motor home that evening, it's a wonder that anyone survived. It was unsettling to look down at that thing buried in the floor of our motor home and then see Terrance on the television monitor share a photograph of the very thing I was sitting on. From what Terrance and some of his guests were saying, Jesus, the driver and I weren't the only ones involved in the apparent theft. Jesus was catching bits and pieces of the very same report on the tiny screen up front.

"You've involved others?" Jesus asked the driver.

The driver grinned proudly, "A colonel, three enlisted men, two civilians and a couple of..." The driver searched for a word, then shrugged, "Let's just say a couple of old friends of mine."

Defeated, Jesus held his head in his hands, "All I wanted to do," said Jesus, "Was go out in the desert and meditate for a few weeks!"

"Life will throw you some curve balls," said the driver, "But listen, you stick with the driver, and I'll make you the MVP."

"MVP?"

"King of the World!"

"King?"

"What do you say?" laughed the driver. He craned his neck in the direction of our unexpected cargo. "There's plenty more where that one came from. Come on, now. What's it gonna be?"

"I have to leave for a few minutes," said Jesus, "But I'll be right back. You won't be getting away with any of this, I promise you."

"Excuse me?"

I had heard most of their conversation and had crawled to my feet and made my way into the cabin, "Will someone tell me what's going on?"

Jesus handed me something, "Have a biscuit!" he said, and with that he opened the passenger door.

The driver punched the gas pedal to the floor. The motor home lurched ahead, speeding down the highway as Jesus reached up outside the cab, grabbed a bar of the roof top luggage rack and hoisted himself up and out of the cab into the night.

"Get back in here!" the driver demanded, "Gonna be hell to pay for that biscuit, you wait and see!"

I guess the driver abandoned hope of getting Jesus safely back inside the cab, and just as suddenly decided to kill him. He tried several maneuvers, swerving in the road, slamming on the brakes, running along the rough shoulder and finally pressing the motor home's engine to its limit and somehow hoping, through sheer velocity, to throw Jesus from the rooftop

I stumbled into the living quarters, tripped and fell backward into the open cargo bay atop our nuclear bomb. Stunned on my back, I saw straight up through the moon roof as Jesus crawled overhead to the rear of the motor home. He scrambled over canvas bundles of luggage like a crab, edged along the inverted canoe, scrambled down the rear ladder and jumped across the hitch onto the bike trailer.

"What's he doing back there?" yelled the driver.

Through the rear windshield I watched Jesus tear loose the restraining bands from the remaining bike. He kicked the ramp release on the trailer. The metal incline banged on the pavement sending up a shower of orange sparks. Mounting the blue bike, Jesus threw his weight against the pedal, and the machine roared to life. Up front, the driver was laughing manically at the speedometer; it climbed past eighty five miles an hour. In the twilight desert wind Jesus was scooting the idling machine backwards down the gang plank off the trailer. He looked at me and nodded as he pushed back and twisted the throttle.

Free of the motor home and the trailer, the motorcycle shimmed violently in the road. Jesus hunched down, fighting for control. He soon came to a stop on the shoulder of the highway, and I let out a triumphant shout as he looked up and waved again, his figure receding in the distance. I turned and looked back the length of the motor home toward the driver's cab. The big screen showed a picture of my face taken at the convenience store against a backdrop of the blazing parking lot with people running and screaming. With the determination of a zealot, and screaming at the top of my lungs, I stormed forward, burst into the cabin and leapt onto the driver.

"What are you doing?" he cried.

I grabbed his head, tore off the hat, the stinking kerchief and began bashing his skull with my fists.

The motor home swerved violently. Somehow in the battle, the cabin lights switched on, and I could see myself on top of him, absurdly pounding away, the entire scene reflected in the mirrored light of the windshield. He got one hand off the wheel up between us and with incredible force threw me across the cabin into the passenger door. The unlatched door banged open and I tumbled headlong out of the vehicle above the rushing pavement, but snared the shoulder harness on my way out and using it as a lifeline, pulled myself back in. I collapsed on the passenger side floor. Wounded from the force of the driver's blow, I struggled to catch my wind. He seemed to have forgotten me, stuffing his face, filling an insatiable appetite for fried chicken. Bones rained on the floor mat where I'd fallen.

Without even looking down at me he crowed, "That was quite a stunt your buddy pulled back there." He consumed another long neck and tossed the empty to the floor. "Guess I'd better turn this rig around and go back and kick his ass."

We were still doing at least sixty when I reached out and with both hands, grabbed the floor mounted transmission stick and jammed it in reverse. An ear-splitting scream of metal sounded from beneath the floor boards. Shocked, the driver looked down at me as I grabbed the steering wheel with both hands and pulled it down toward my shattered chest. Instantly, the driver side of the enormous motor home jumped up from the pavement.

In the last half second before the driver's tattooed head slammed into the cabin ceiling, I looked again into the face of the boy I had seen in the photographs. I had no idea how this had happened, but in that instant I wanted to undo everything, to take him back home to his parents, to go back to Joe's storeroom in Nazareth and stack those chairs properly. I remember getting the words, "I'm sorry," out of my mouth as the craft wheeled into the gravel shoulder and rolled down, and over and over into absolute and total blackness. Soon, the only light was from the cold, distant stars above the desert. A single inverted tire turned and stopped. Far overhead, a meteor hit the earth's atmosphere, arced quickly across the heavens, and then, everything was still.

* * *

If any of this was ever to make it into the Bible, my friend's heroic ride back up the highway on a motorcycle to rescue the girl from the convenience store would have been on the top of the list. As it turned out, the cardinal assigned to that particular passage of text at the Council of Trent in 1546 AD thought it the ravings of a madman. I suppose God just preferred to leave that part out. With all the technical references from the future, it might have made the New Testament even more confusing. Of course, since I wasn't there myself, I can only rely on what Jesus told me of the events long afterwards.

He arrived at that stretch of highway where he had seen the car accident in about ten minutes from the time he bailed from the trailer. He and the "Holy Spirit" weren't that familiar, having only met, publically, at any rate, the week before, but it really went to show the level of trust, under the circumstance, in a small still voice, to manage a piece of machinery as complex as a motorcycle. You might argue he'd learned how to handle the bike back in the desert. Still, to drop a off a ramp traveling eighty-five miles an hour gets mighty technical even for an accomplished cyclist. I prefer to think it was with the Spirit's help that Jesus managed it. Back where we came from, a wheel was still pretty complex technology.

Jesus drove like a man possessed all the way back to the crash site, dumped the bike and rushed to the girl. He knelt down on the asphalt still hot from the afternoon sun and prayed for her. Why he went back for her, I'll never know. He may have been impressed by her frailty, or her courage, or the kindness she had shown him back at the convenience store checkout line. Although she had a twenty-thousand dollar line of credit on her mom's card and five hundred in traveler's checks in her backpack, the girl had spent her last remaining cash, two dollars and thirty-nine cents, for that orange soda she shared with Jesus.

And what did she get for thanks? She walked up the highway, stuck out her thumb and the first ride she got was from some pervert who put the moves on her with a knife at a hundred miles an hour. For all I know it was probably another friend of the driver's. When she resisted, things got crazy and the next thing you know the car spun out of control and there was a dead guy smashed in the driver seat, and an innocent girl, crawling from the wreckage when she passed out in the middle of the highway.

A lot of heavy armored vehicles were converging on that twenty mile stretch of highway as Jesus knelt down and brought the girl to her feet and placed her carefully behind him on the blue motorcycle. At a top speed of one hundred miles an hour, the motorcycle flew back up the highway. Jesus overshot the place where we'd gone off the road. Clinging to his back, the girl looked to the side and in a one in a thousand chance saw an empty fried chicken bucket lying on the shoulder.

"Stop!"

"What?"

"Back there!"

"What?" shouted Jesus.

"Fried chicken from the truck stop!"

Jesus got the idea, pulled another 180 degree maneuver on the motorbike and headed back. Soon, Jesus, the girl and the bike were airborne. They hit the slope below the skid marks where the motor home had left the road and it was all Jesus could do to slow the machine down and turn into the hill. It was almost impossibly steep but he brought the bike to a stop. He and the girl scanned the ravine where a fast moving river threaded through its canyon below.

"There," shouted the girl, stabbing a finger into the darkness at the outline of an over-turned vehicle. In the same instant they heard the wail of sirens from above. Jesus killed the motorcycle headlamp as a convoy of law enforcement vehicles rocketed past on the highway above them. Jesus silently pushed off with the bike in neutral and he and the girl traversed a series of treacherous switchbacks down slope to the bottom of the ravine.

Like a broken giant, the motor home lay on its back beside the fast moving water. I felt disembodied, as though I was floating hundreds of feet in the air, looking down past the highway and its stream of flying blue lights, down the rocky canyon walls to that narrow strip of stony beach where I lay, crumpled on my side outside the driver's cabin. Strewn outside the door on the rocks and glinting like ghost eyes in the dimness among the chicken bones and beer bottles were the silver dollars from the driver's empty shoebox. I scrambled back inside to the driver. He was strung upside down in his seatbelt. His skull had come to rest against a jagged rock protruding from the shattered driver's side skylight. I pulled loose the inverted cowboy hat. Pieces of skull and brain spilled over the brim and a blood-soaked bandana. I expected to see the shaven head, but saw only a shock of blond, blood-matted hair. I reached out and touched it to see whether it was real.

I was startled by the appearance of Jesus on the motorcycle as it rolled to a halt only yards from the motor home. My voice shook as I gripped my bruised ribs and staggered toward Jesus.

"I tried to stop him." I said and held up the driver's hat with its snakeskin band and black raven's feather.

Jesus' eyes were brimful of tears and he looked at me and took the hat. For the first time I noticed the girl who brushed past us and disappeared into the wrecked motor home. I noticed she was without the backpack, evidently left behind in the wreck on the highway. Jesus shook his head and crumpled the raven's feather in his fist and dropped feather and hat to the ground.

"I forced him off the road," I said, "That's not our driver is it?"

Jesus shook his head.

"Did I do the right thing?"

"Lawrence!" a woman's voice cried from inside the overturned motor home. Jesus grabbed me by the shoulders and looked me straight in the face, "Leave her for minute," he warned.

I pushed his arm aside and crawled inside the motor home through its ruined side door and over the slumbering atomic bomb. It had fallen out of its cargo well onto the inverted roof along with its yellow stickers. I made my way up along the cool metal cylinder to the driver's cabin. The girl was on her knees, looking into the face of the driver.

Something unexplainable had happened to her friend. It might have ended differently had Lawrence and Sarah simply flown from Cambridge to Los Angeles three days earlier. But no, they had determined to "rough it," hitch-hiking cross country. They had gotten off the interstate at a truck stop in the desert. Something had happened to Lawrence. He left his friend in the ladies room in the convenience store, crawled into the open cab of Walter and Beverly Johnson's motor home while the couple ate sausage and pancakes at Bradford's Diner, and he drove off.

Jesus has a way of comforting people when they are sad, and by the time the girl looked up from the face of her fallen companion, Jesus was at her side. She wasn't buying his consolation, however, and she stood up and slapped him hard across the face.

"That went well," I thought to myself as I crawled up out of the van, but before I could say anything she had spun on me with a haymaker to the jaw that knocked me to the ground.

"Let Jesus help her," I mumbled to myself rubbing my jaw and my bruised ribs and a new thought struck me and I scrambled into the inverted cab and reached up to the glove box. I pulled the latch and the little door fell open and brochures and travel guides and the owner's manual tumbled into my lap. I tore through the items and found the road map. I squinted, turning my head to one side, bracing myself for the otherworldly blast. I unfolded the map as though defusing a nuclear bomb, but this time, nothing happened. No blinding light, but only a torn and tattered highway road map. I looked down at my map, rolled it tightly in my hands and stuffed it into the empty leather pouch on my belt as Jesus bent down and crawled into the cab and went over to the stricken young man. He said a silent prayer and with a gentle hand, drew closed the bewildered eyes.

We heard something in the distance and looked up, listening. I tumbled out of the motor home, followed by Jesus to where the girl stood at the bottom of the ravine, looking up at the thin ribbon of starlit sky above the canyon rim. The rotor beats of attack helicopters resounded along the canyon walls. Jesus scrambled to the side of the motor home where the roof had buckled over a large boulder, leaving a dark void between the inverted roof and the canyon floor.

I looked in through the crumbled side door and saw the silver cylinder dreaming its atomic dreams on its inverted shag blanket of bunnies and kittens.

"Are we going to hide the bomb?" I asked.

I admit this was a fairly ridiculous idea, but somehow at the time I thought having a concealed bomb would be useful leverage in our upcoming negotiation with the authorities. Instead, Jesus had hold of an object from underneath the ruined luggage rack. He was dragging something big and metallic.

"Come on," he shouted, "Quickly!"

"What about that thing in the there? The bomb? Everyone's looking for it."

"They'll find it soon enough. Now, come here and help."

With renewed vigor I joined Jesus beside the motor home. Together we unlashed the remaining rope stays and pulled a gleaming aluminum canoe out onto the beach.

"I'll bring the girl!" he said.

I looked dumbly from the canoe to Jesus.

"Don't just stand there!" he cried, "Into the water with it."

From every direction, police cars and military vehicles were converging on the highway at the point where the motor home had left the shoulder. As I dragged the canoe over the rocks into the cold, surging water, I saw thin, v-shaped shafts of light flickering at the canyon rim where lawmen were making their way cautiously down slope in the darkness.

I was in the canoe. But where were with the others? The girl was scrambling up the hill toward the lawmen. Jesus followed behind, shouting, "Come back, Come back! Come with me!"

"You're crazy!" replied the girl, shouting, "I haven't done anything wrong!"

"Please," cried Jesus, stumbling up the hill.

They might have argued there on the side of the ravine for the rest of the night. In the end, it was the sound of semi-automatic gunfire whizzing past her head that convinced the girl to turn from her path and follow the man in the Hawaiian shirt.

Without a word, Jesus grabbed the gunnels of the canoe in both hands and with the sound of metal grating against granite, shoved the craft free of the land and jumped aboard the stern. He quickly settled in behind us, pulled an oar from its stays and the swift current pulled

72

us down into the river and away from the site of the ruined vacation home.

6. White Water

Light was breaking in the ribbon of sky above as we slipped along the ancient canyon. By noon, the sun was high overhead and shone down along the narrow walls to the bottom where our canoe drifted into a broadening section of the river. The girl and I lay on our sides, stiff and half-asleep, watching Jesus gently guide our progress with an aluminum paddle. He paused for a moment, reached into the river and with a cupped hand withdrew a mouthful of water. He drank, wiped his mouth with his forearm and noticed we were staring at him.

"Good morning," he said with the smile. There was no reply from either the girl or me and Jesus knitted his brow, "You're hungry," he said.

The girl glanced at me and then back at a Jesus, "Yes," she replied.

Jesus nodded.

"What's that?" asked the girl.

"What?" said Jesus. I shook my head.

"That sound?" said the girl suddenly.

The current had picked up speed and was swiftly threading toward a narrow passageway ahead.

"Maybe we should pull over," I suggested.

No sooner were the words out of my mouth than Jesus was paddling for our lives toward a thin strip of shoreline. The girl and I reached over the sides and paddled with our arms, trying to help steer the craft to that one last stretch of beach along the sheer canyon wall. Up ahead the river piled into its narrow channel. Water rolled up into a wall of foam and spray on the brink of a towering waterfall.

We shouted encouragement, paddling, splashing, and trying for all we were worth to reach that sliver of beach, but the current was inexorable and now we were caught up. The paddle was torn from Jesus' hands. The canoe spun wildly into the center of the channel and for an instant all I could see was a band of brilliant blue sky over head. We uttered a prolonged, collective scream as we slammed into the whitewater and then, the three of us were flying head over heels outside the canoe in a wide open space of air. I saw the canoe, glinting sunlight turning end over end beside us.

I hit the water hard, and the air was slammed from my lungs. I found myself in a silent, dark space, for an instant wondering where I was and then, swimming like mad until I popped up on the surface of the waves. The roar of the waters returned and through the dazzling spray I fought the weight of my heavy robe and kicked and tried to catch my bearings as again the current seized me. We were in an amphitheatre of rock. The shinning hull of the canoe reappeared. I saw the girl clinging to its side. I reached out and felt her hand in mine.

"Jesus," I cried.

"What?" choked the girl.

"Where's Jesus?"

"What?"

I gripped the canoe alongside the girl, dog paddling for our lives, clinging to the hull as it pin-wheeled through the water.

"Where is he?" she shouted, "Your friend...! Where is..."

We both trailed off, looking back toward the falls, and beyond the spot where it pounded down from the cliffs. Jesus had reached a shallows, dragged himself through smooth stones and looked down river. We saw him climb to his feet.

"Hey! Hey! Over here," we cried.

But we were drifting further and further away.

Jesus scanned the waters and spotted the canoe. He stumbled over the stones, trudged forward, threw his arms overhead and dove back into the river.

"There he is," shouted the girl. For an instant, I thought I saw the flash of a smile on her face.

Jesus was in the water, his long, strong arms cutting the waves. Soon, he had closed the distance and the three of us clung to the canoe as it drifted down the canyon, leaving the waterfall and the amphitheater in the distance. Our chance to reach the shore had been swallowed up and we were again in the middle of the channel. Although it was wider and sandbars were visible along its banks, this section was filled with white water. Gigantic boulders and debris threatened our way. We clung to the canoe.

"We must get to shore," shouted Jesus.

"What?" shouted the girl.

"We've got to reach the shore!"

She shook her head, unable to hear. We heard nothing but the incessant roar of water. The canoe was banging against submerged rocks. Now, we were headed toward a huge pile of debris where a sandbar jutted out into our path. The girl reached out and grabbed a branch of driftwood. I saw the black, web like branches of a submerged tree as the canoe wheeled around. I grabbed hold and smiled in her direction. We had halted our forward progress. Then, suddenly, the canoe was torn from our hands. It slipped forward, five or six feet and lodged itself against a rock. A huge wall of water leapt over the inverted hull, sweeping Jesus forward. The girl and I exchanged a look of horror, as Jesus disappeared below the waves.

"He's under the canoe!" I shouted.

The girl looked at me in terror, then closed her eyes and dove into the white water. She wrestled her way down to my friend, down in the darkness to the point where his shoe had wedged between the boulder and the submerged trunk. She pulled on his leg, but the foot held firm. She was running out of breath and swam upward along his body. A small pocket of air was trapped inside the canoe and here Jesus was gasping for air in the darkness.

Into this space the voice of the girl erupted, "Your foot's stuck," she cried.

"Save yourself," he gasped.

"We aren't going to leave you," she said and would have said more, but the canoe shifted violently and the bubble of trapped air slipped away, displaced by cold water. She dove back down, and tugged and tugged on his leg, but soon Jesus' body crumpled and sank down in a heap. She looked at his stricken face and redoubled her efforts, tearing at the laces of the high top tennis shoe. She had gotten through a knot and pulled the laces from their eyelets: one, two, three, four. His ankle was exposed.

I stared down into the roaring rapids at my feet. Suddenly, the canoe lurched to one side and bounded over the line of debris. From below the waves, the body of my friend appeared with the girl. Around his upper torso, her arm held his chin above the water. In the next instant they vanished beneath a crashing series of waves and then reappeared twenty feet downstream. I picked my way along the debris damn, jumped to the gravel bank, and ran alongside, shouting

The woman was a strong swimmer and had succeeded in catching up with the canoe and now, dragging Jesus in one arm and holding the canoe, with her powerful legs she propelled them into a pool at the head of the sandbar. I arrived ahead of her and helped drag the canoe into the gravel shoal and pull Jesus ashore.

Immediately she was kneeling at his side, listening for a breath.

"Is he all right?" I cried.

She put her mouth against his and blew into his lungs. She pushed him to his side and river water erupted from his mouth, followed by a gasp for air. His body shuddered and then settled back.

"Now, we're even," she said.

I doubt he heard her, but she was evidently satisfied, and got up and walked to the pool and dragged the canoe further ashore, past where I was crouched beside Jesus. She stopped at the intersection of the narrow river bank and the vertical rock wall of the canyon. She flipped the canoe right side up and unfastened a box attached inside the canoe. She brought it over to us and dropped the box in the gravel. The front panel read: "Survival."

"What's that for?" I asked.

She opened three latches on the water tight box and removed a clear plastic bag of what I learned later that night were water-proofed matches. She took another bag marked fishing tackle and set it beside the matches. Next she opened a pouch and removed a fist sized pack of silvery material.

"Here," she said, "Put this on him and gather some driftwood for a fire."

Dumbly I took the silvery packet, "What is this?" I asked.

"Haven't you ever seen a space blanket?"

She took the bag of fishing tackle and walked down to the water's edge.

* * *

By dusk we had established a camp below the canyon wall. She had six large trout laid out on a slab of rock below us. We had pulled Jesus up to the canoe and wrapped him in the silvery film that she insisted would keep him warm. Soon, his shivering subsided and he slept deeply. In the dimness, she took her matches, crouched, and drew one across a rock. The match flared up and she applied it to the kindling she had prepared.

"Do you think that's a good idea?" I asked.

"Do you like sushi?"

"What?"

"Raw fish. Unless you like raw fish we're going to need a fire. Aren't you starving?"

"Well, yes but with a fire down here, won't they be likely to find us?"

"I hope."

"What?"

"It's a signal fire, idiot!"

"Hey, now…"

"I haven't done anything wrong. There's been a misunderstanding. They're sure to have figured it out by now."

The fire burned in the dimness illuminating our faces as the flame caught hold of the kindling.

"Have you?"

"Have I what?"

"Have you done something wrong?" she asked.

"No, of course not." I looked over at the form of Jesus, wrapped in silver foil like an Egyptian mummy.

"What about him? Your partner, over there? He's the boss, isn't he?"

"Jesus?"

She burst out laughing. Her laughter was so deep and so earnest that I began to feel uncomfortable. Finally, her laughter subsided so that she was able to speak.

"All this time, I've been hearing you shout, 'Jesus!' 'Jesus!' Back up there in the river this afternoon. I thought you were cursing!"

"Cursing?"

"You know like 'Jesus freaking blankity blank' or 'Jeeezus!'"

I didn't know what she was talking about. She poked the base of the fire with a stick and eyed me through the flickering flame.

"You've got to be kidding. That's his real name? Jesus? Like Jesus Christ?"

"No, just Jesus."

"Jesus?"

"Yep."

She seemed satisfied by this and poked the fire with her stick.

"From Nazareth," I added.

A laugh burst from her mouth. She dropped her stick and sparks flew up into the sky as she held her side, laughing in a fit that seemed almost to hurt. I was smiling too, at first. I didn't know what else to do.

She looked up from the fire and smiled as she took a fish on a spit and waved it over the flame. She was still laughing to herself, in little fits and starts as she cooked the fish.

We ate in silence. About ten minutes passed.

"You guys are nuts." She shouted and she stood in the darkness. "My friend gets kidnapped and murdered – I nearly get raped on the side of the highway. Oh, I've had a great 48 hours. Jesus! That's right! I feel like I've been down on this stupid river forever! Come on! Is there anybody up there! Come on, then. Get me out of here!"

She fell down in the stones. I made a move to comfort her,

"Stay where you are, you little creep!"

"Hey!"

"You're a nut case. You know that? Look at yourself! For all I know you're the ones who kidnapped Larry and put him behind that wheel."

"Now, hold on a second."

"You're the ones who probably sent that pervert after me on the highway. Part of a team? Are you kidnappers? Is that it? "

"No. Please!" I said, "I don't know what you're talking about!"

"Were you planning to hold us for ransom? Is this all a scheme to get money out of our relatives? Well, I've got news for you 'Ahkmed,' or whatever the hell your name is," and she picked up a heavy, club sized piece of driftwood that I had collected for the fire.

"Somewhere along the line you screwed up!" She kicked at my feet and I scooted backwards on the gravel as she brandished the club overhead.

"You don't understand!" I shouted.

"Maybe I ought to bash in your head like you bashed Larry's?"

She held the club above me to strike. Our eyes were locked in the firelight. She was trying to read the truth, I suppose, but it was probably too fantastic to be believed. The club wavered in the air over my head.

"Put it down, Sarah Bennett." A voice rolled over the canyon walls.

The club was still in the air as Sarah stopped in her tracks above me. From behind her, my friend had leaned forward, propped up on two elbows and spoke from his silvery cocoon.

"My friend and I had no hand in the evil done to you or your friend."

"What?"

"We have done no wrong."

"Go back to sleep!" she said.

"What I tell you is the truth."

"Go to sleep," she yelled.

"Why don't you start by putting down that stick?" I said.

That was probably an ill advised comment on my part. Looking back, Jesus had things pretty well in hand. Maybe Sarah, for all her education and modern ideas, still had some pretty crazy notions ruling her and the sight of me in my headdress and robes, must have tipped the balance somewhere inside her and with a guttural cry she wheeled and brought that club crashing down. I had just enough time to shield my head from the first blow, but it nearly broke my arm. I was getting a real beating and Jesus was trying to wriggle out of his foil pouch when someone turned on the lights.

High intensity halogen lamps from the canyon rim instantly illuminated the stretch of beach like the infield during a night game at Fenway Park. Our shouts were obliterated by the rotor beats of army attack helicopters. Pebbles and shards of gravel vibrated across the shoal as helicopters descended with black armored pilots leaning over their controls and gunners aiming at us in their sights.

Despite the whirlwind of sand and noise, Sarah continued to smash me with the stick. Jesus finally had hold of her waist and they wrestled. His shouts were lost on the waves of air stirred by the black helicopters. Sarah broke free and throwing up her arms ran down the beach shouting upward.

"Here! Here! I'm down here." She waved her arms and smiled jubilantly.

Jesus grabbed me by the collar and hoisted me to my feet.

"Get the canoe!" he shouted.

"What!"

"Get the canoe into the water!"

The helicopter furthest upstream had dropped within fifty feet of the river in the narrow canyon. Sarah looked directly across at the hovering machine. A flash of flame and a rocket shot from a starboard tube and traced a black line in the air twenty feet from where she stood. There was a deafening explosion. Jesus and I looked up from the canoe in time to see her thrown down onto the beach. Jesus and I were dragging the canoe to the water when a second helicopter opened up its fifty caliber machine guns. Enormous exploding bullets ripped trenches in the beach gravel and chased us to the river's edge.

"They're firing at us."

"Into the canoe."

"There's no paddle."

"Into the canoe!"

He herded me into the canoe with the very club that had beaten me, shoved it into my arms and pushed the canoe into the waves.

"Meet us at the end of the beach."

Machine gun fire whipped through the sandbar and out into the water as Jesus dashed away. He was running across the stones with only one shoe on his foot. Another spray of machine gun fire dogged his steps and he threw himself down over Sarah. I looked at the club in my hands, stuck it over the side and did my best to pull the canoe along the beach. That's when I noticed the raindrops.

* * *

High above the desert floor, enormous black clouds had assembled in the sky above the helicopters swarming at the canyon rim. Lighting flashes suddenly illuminated the scene as sheets of rain began to pour over the helicopters and down into the canyon. Jesus had Sarah to her feet. This time there was no resistance as he guided her to the water. We were in the sights of a third helicopter. The gunner was about to fire a rocket when his cabin was struck by the brilliance of a hundred suns.

"Lightning!" cried the pilot over his headset.

The craft careened toward the canyon wall. Veering rotor blades ripped through the waves alongside the canoe.

"Pull up," crackled voices over the headsets.

I helped Sarah into the canoe as torrential sheets of rain swept between us and the helicopters. The aircraft wobbled, their engines whining against a sudden down draft of air. Panic was in the voices on the radios as the pilots fought their way up and out of the canyon.

* * *

The three of us stared upward with amazement. In the next instant our craft was surrounded by the downpour, so intense, we could no longer see the canyon walls. The canoe swayed only slightly and it was impossible to say whether we were making forward progress or had simply come to a complete stop in the middle of the river. The rain turned to a fine, white mist, that streamed past us, and I was about to complain about the flying machines when we experienced an uncomfortable BUMP that threw each of us half a foot up and back down into our seats. We were left staring, wide-eyed at one another. No one dared speak. Each of us patted our garments and felt our heads. We were dry. I extended my hand over the edge of the canoe and felt hard stinging rain.

"Ouch!" I said and pulled back my hand rubbed it.

I pulled back the sleeve of my robe and looked at my bruised and swollen arm. It was then that I noticed the girl was looking at me. I shifted in my seat and looked out at the wall of rain.

"We're dry," she said.

It was pretty incredible, but after all the things I'd seen that week, I didn't know what to say.

"It's raining and we're not getting wet," she continued.

Another moment went by as her eyes darted back and forth between us. Then she bolted. The canoe dipped to the side and Jesus grabbed her by the waist and pulled her down. She was kicking and her foot struck me in the jaw as I grabbed her legs. She was screaming for us to let go of her, which gradually, we did as her struggles subsided. I guess she was satisfied we weren't trying to rape her or anything, and she just dropped back into her seat. Again, we sat in silence for what must have been half an hour, until finally, she spoke.

"I'm sorry." Sarah's voice startled me. "About hitting you back there with the stick."

There was another long pause as we three sat in the canoe and watched the rain stream down.

"Look you guys," said Sarah at last, "Just tell me who you are. What do you want with me?"

There was another long silence. Sarah and I stared at Jesus intently.

"You tell her," said Jesus.

"Me? She won't listen to me."

"I will. I'll listen to you," said Sarah. "Go ahead."

"Well…"

"Go on," said Jesus patiently.

"Well, this here is my friend Jesus of Nazareth. We're from Judea. Judea is a province of Israel. Have you ever heard of Israel?"

"Of course I've heard of Israel, but…"

"Call me Steve. That's short for Stephen. My friends call me Steve. Well, they would call me Steve if I had any friends, but I don't, except my buddy over here." I smiled at Jesus and he nodded. I continued, pausing to look back and forth between them. Evidently they were listening. Oh, well! I'd take this strange girl into my confidence. What did I have to lose?

"Stephen's not my real name," I said in a whisper. "We don't know my real name. My real parents were killed when I was a little kid, or maybe they abandoned me, but Jesus' mom and dad took me in."

"Go on," said Jesus.

"Is there a point to this story?" asked Sarah.

"My real mom and dad were merchants from Ethiopia. Maybe they were just passing through, but I might have been born there, which could make me an Arab, and so it's been this big dark secret we've had to carry around all these years back in Nazareth. The folks in town would probably have stoned me to death ten times over if they were to find out, so don't go shooting off your mouth, Sarah."

Sarah shook her head in disbelief. Jesus scowled.

"So, I've worked at Joseph's carpentry shop all these years, went to temple, learned my lessons, more or less, grew up, and that's pretty much it until a week ago when I went down to the river with Jesus and his cousin John."

"You're insane," said Sarah. She looked at Jesus again. "You honestly expect me to believe that you're from the Bible?"

Jesus and I looked at one another.

"You're here from two thousand years ago?" she said, "Is that what you expect me to believe?"

"No," I replied, frustrated by her inability to understand a simple fact. Both Sarah and Jesus looked at me, expectantly, "We aren't, are we? Jesus? I mean, from two thousand years ago?"

"It doesn't feel that way," he admitted.

I nodded.

"But we might be from the past, Sarah's past. I don't know," said Jesus.

"What?"

"I said, I don't know, Steve!" said Jesus sharply.

"Well, that's just great. We're in the future? Is such a thing even possible?" I asked.

Sarah grabbed Jesus by the elbow, "And you expect me to believe that you're Jesus? Jesus from the Bible?"

"I don't know. You keep saying 'Bible.' What exactly is a Bible?"

"The New Testament!"

"I honestly don't know, Sarah. Now that you mention it, that name does sound familiar," said Jesus and he turned excitedly to me, "That's it. The audio tapes! That was one of the tapes in the motor home."

"Audio tapes?" said Sarah, suspiciously.

"What's important is that we complete our journey together," said Jesus.

"Our journey? What journey?"

"Into the wilderness."

"Well, you guys can just let me off at the next stop, okay? I was going to spend two weeks at my friends' parents' condominium in Los Angeles. This isn't what I had in mind," she said and she held onto the sides of the canoe, like she was looking for the next stop and would climb off the bus and take a cab to the airport.

Jesus wore a pained expression on his face as he half watched the girl looking desperately around the confined space for a break in the weather. She started again, more slowly,

"I have to be back in Cambridge in three weeks to begin my third year of grad school at Harvard. Tell me that you've heard of that. Have you ever heard of Harvard?"

She searched our faces for some sign of recognition.

I shook my head sadly and looked at Jesus.

"I'm sorry, Sarah, but had I left you on that roadside back up there, I don't know what would have happened," he said.

"Thanks, but aren't you supposed to be a God or something?"

Jesus started laughing.

"What? Isn't that what you want to hear?"

He dropped down in the canoe, just trembling with laughter and I can't recollect having ever seen him laugh so hard in the nearly twenty years I'd known him.

Finally, he wiped his eyes and spoke, "Do I look like a God to you?"

We looked at him there in the bow of the boat in his Hawaiian shirt and khaki's, wearing one black tennis shoe, and the first blush of stubble showing on his shaven face.

"No." Sarah said, "As a matter of fact, you don't. You don't look like God at all."

"What's she talking about, Jesus?" I asked.

Jesus shook his head.

"No. I'd like to hear what she means about you being a God. Are you nuts, lady? This is Jesus of Nazareth, my best friend!"

Jesus looked at me with wide, sad eyes.

Angrily, I looked back at Sarah, "There's no such thing as God," I shouted.

"Finally!" said Sarah, "Something we can agree on!"

I looked jealously at Sarah, and for the first time I thought this woman really had seen something. Whether there was a God or not, I didn't really much care, but I wondered how she seemed to know so much about my friend.

* * *

Of course everything would have been greatly simplified had we listened to the books on tape version of the New Testament back in the motor home. I guess Jesus was still in the process of discovering some things about himself. If he already had the clarity he'd been seeking out in the desert on that rock, he didn't let on. Still, something weird was definitely going on; how else would he have known Sarah Benton's name?

It rained. It rained and rained and rained some more. It rained ten times more than it rained in the time of Noah. It seemed all the molecules of H_2O locked in the clouds, the glaciers, the polar ice caps, trapped in shale and in every other mineral on the face of the earth, above and below the earth turned out for the rain.

7. Day One

It was the evening of the seventh day since our departure from Nazareth. That particular day we slept back in time a billion years. My loud snoring woke the others and someone told me to "shut up," and we rolled over and slept back another billion years. After that we more or less just lost track of time.

During the long night of rain, it seemed the water level of the river began to rise so that our craft was buoyed up higher and higher along the canyon walls. The effect of the river had been reversed with time so that when we awoke on the morning of the first day, what had been "the river" had ceased to exist. The canyon, that mile deep trench in the ground, had yet to be scoured from the earth. As we awoke at the dawn of creation we had other thoughts to occupy us.

"Man, have I ever got to take a piss," I announced. To my amazement, the rain had stopped. When I opened my eyes, I had to ask whether or not I was dreaming, because we were in absolute and total darkness.

"No, you're not dreaming," said Jesus.

"We're all aware that you have to take a piss." said Sarah.

"Can you guys see anything?

"Nothing," said Jesus, "Absolute darkness."

"Why don't you use some of those super powers of yours and get us a flashlight, for Steve!" said Sarah sarcastically.

"I was holding onto the gunnels of the boat, finishing my business over the side and staring into the profound blackness when I saw, to my amazement, an array of lights far to starboard. I was so surprised, I lost my balance and toppled backward into the canoe with a crash.

"What is it? What's wrong?" cried Sarah.

"Nothing!" I shouted, "Lights! Off the starboard side!"

"Light?" asked Sarah, and I heard her shout, "Hey, over here."

Blinking, coal red lights wheeled toward our craft like demon eyes in a fun-house amusement ride. There were other, smaller lights, more distant and as they passed, or as we passed them, we could hear a metallic clicking and high-pitched whirring sound.

"Buoys…" muttered Jesus.

"What?" I asked.

"Nothing," he said, "Just a thought."

"No, go ahead," said Sarah, "What did you say?"

"Buoys," he repeated.

"But who…" I trailed off.

"Hang on," said Jesus sharply in the darkness, "Look up, everyone."

"What? Where?" I stammered, wheeling about blindly in the canoe.

I looked up in the dark and much to my disbelief I noticed something moving high above us. The random firing of retinal cells had drawn patterns in my mind's eye, but now I saw dim streaks of a faint, distant light – grey and diaphanous and growing with intensity. Soon, like an aviator from the future, flying through a dense cloud bank, I was looking into the vault of a grey, overcast sky that stretched from one horizon to the next.

We were on an ocean, an interminable ocean of slate, gray water. The clouds were suffused with light, but we could not detect its origin, only that everything, everywhere was illuminated and for the first time we realized the white mist slipping around the craft had encapsulated us within some sort of protective shield.

"We're inside a bubble," said Sarah, her voice quaking with awe.

"The atmosphere is still too dense for us to breathe, but only now, for the first time, light is able to penetrate to the earth's surface," said Jesus.

"Let there be light…" mumbled Sarah.

She smiled, closed her eyes and slept. We all slept. For one day or a million, I don't know, only that when I awoke, we were again in total darkness. I dozed again and when I woke to Sarah's shouting, I had something to see. There was a normal ocean now, and a real sky completely filled from horizon to horizon with bright, white clouds. For the first time, despite the overcast, the sea around us held a hint of blue and I heard the sound of gentle surf. When I turned in the direction of the sound I beheld an island of black sand. We glided forward and the long low waves deposited us on a beach. We were high and dry. Sarah turned to Jesus who had a broad beaming smile on his face.

"Is it safe?" she asked.

He nodded and she threw off her sandals and scampered out of the canoe and ran like a little girl up along the beach. I looked at Jesus and he nodded, with a smile. Together we got up and climbed out of the canoe. I kicked off my sandals and he his other tennis shoe and we proceeded barefoot up the shore. There was absolutely no wind and the overcast sky, grey with its diffused light, cast no shadow as we walked the black sand beach following Sarah.

She had turned inland and was climbing up an enormously steep dune of black sand. It was fine and dry and cool between our toes but difficult to climb. She dwindled in the distance above as we struggled upward. I was gasping for breath as we approached the summit where Sarah had stopped in her tracks staring at something half buried in the sand.

It appeared to be a machine of some sort, the height of a man, buried to its waste at the crest of the black mountain. I was convinced that, up until that point in my life, I had never seen anything like it, but then I looked at the rows of flashing lights, like glowing gems inset along the cone shaped object, as though recalling a memory from a dream, I shouted, "The buoys!"

The faintly humming contraption shuddered slightly, and we felt a faint tremor rumble across the dune. Black sand grains danced on the surface and heavy machinery groaned from somewhere beneath our feet. Suddenly, a cylinder, perhaps fifteen feet high and ten feet in diameter broke the sandy surface. Sand cascaded off the large structure which literally rose up out of the earth. The cylinder rose some fifteen feet above us and stopped, immobile, as though it had stood there a thousand years.

As though in response to the appearance of this silvery cylinder, the conical buoy began to vibrate. From seamless ports in its sides, emerged two metallic tentacles. Segmented like the concentric bands of a centipede's body, each slowly snaked about the tumbling black sand at its base, and the mechanical apparition rose out of the sand. Sarah and I had retreated several yards down slope, but Jesus only stepped closer as the buoy employed its tentacles to free itself from the sand entrapment. Jesus held one of the tentacles and it looked to me as though he was helping lift the thing up on its thick, jointed legs. Stepping from the pit on convex oval pods the creature stood upright eight feet tall on the summit beside Jesus. The thing reminded me of the clockwork toys for sale at the Jerusalem Market on festival days. It approached the cylinder and its tentacles moved along the surface, tapping a strange sequence of ringing, metallic tones.

I looked back over my shoulder, down the dizzying height of the dune. Far below, just above the surf-traced line of sea foam on the beach, was our aluminum canoe, so distant it looked no bigger than a finger of silver shinning on the black sand.

Sarah returned to Jesus and the machine man where they stood beside the cylinder. A vertical seam had appeared in the cylinder and a door opened, sliding away into the adjacent wall. Illuminated in the interior sat a red clay pot from which grew a beautiful orange tree. The mechanical man motioned my companions forward. Jesus nodded to Sarah who stepped inside and approached the tree. She parted the leaves and picked an orange which she offered to Jesus. He smiled, shook his head, and looked back toward me.

"You hungry?" he asked.

"Am I hungry?" I cried and scrambled back up the black sand to the summit. I was startled by the mechanical creature whose tentacle had snaked into the branches and snagged an orange. In an instant the bright fruit was bobbing up and down on the wavering tentacle before my face.

"Take it, "advised Jesus. "It may be a couple billion years before we see another one."

Sarah was crouched down, picking big black berries from a potted bush and gobbling them up as fast as her hands could move. I followed her inside where the room nearly overflowed with vegetation, some familiar and some the like of which I had never seen before or since. Sarah and I ate greedily as Jesus stood by with the mechanical sentry. A smile played across Jesus' lips. He seemed content, even happy, but he did not eat.

Light faded from the sky. Soon, only the white light inside the cylinder shone out like a beacon from the black dune island. In the doorway Jesus stood beside the gleaming monstrosity and spoke as though addressing an old friend.

"And there was evening and there was morning, a third day," he said. Ever so slightly, and almost imperceptibly, the creature dipped forward, perhaps a centimeter or two, as though to nod in agreement.

* * *

I awoke with a start and found myself wrapped around the base of the red clay pot that held the orange tree. The heel of Sarah's bare foot knocked me in the head. I pushed it away, pulled myself onto my side and squinted in the dimness. Sarah stirred, and resumed her slow, heavy breathing. I realized we were in the dark. The band of white light that had illuminated the interior of this small circular room had been extinguished. I detected a faint outline marking the open door of the cylinder. I crawled slowly along the smooth, polished floor until I felt sand on my fingertips.

I stood and saw to my right the triangular silhouette of the machine man, brooding silently like a strange, illuminated pyramid. It had retracted its jointed legs and sat solidly in place as though once again half buried in the sand. The array of crystals at the apex of its cone shaped body flashed a mosaic of light, and through their luminance I saw Jesus. The attention of this odd pair, sitting on the crest of the island dune, was fixed someplace above the eastern horizon. The low, sonorous murmur of the nearly invisible ocean below sounded in the background and I heard Jesus speak excitedly.

"Steve," he said, "You're just in time."

"Time for what?" I said, shuffling in the sand and sitting down with the motionless machine man between us.

Jesus pointed upward. Light dimly outlined a cloud bank of salmon sky that seemed to envelope the entire world. As I searched the mottled clouds I felt a faint wind stir against my cheek and a window opened in the sky and we gasped at the sight of a million stars blazing against the jet black field of space. A tentacle of the automaton stirred and extended skyward, glinting reflected starlight and pointing in the direction of a particularly brilliant star glowing among the others. In a continuous exhalation the breeze transported the dwindling clouds so that the window soon stretched from horizon to horizon. Starlight poured down for the very first time illuminating a swath of waves undulating from the base of the island out to a vanishing point on the rim of the earth.

We gazed upward, thrilling to each instant and now, without turning my head, I was aware that Sarah had joined us on the summit.

"Where are the constellations?" she asked no one in particular.

The question had crossed my mind, and I wondered where on earth we were that not a single configuration of stars seemed familiar. As alien as they seemed, the stars never again seemed as bright as they did that night.

"Look," said Jesus, pointing straight ahead down that first avenue of reflected starlight on the waves receding to the horizon. Simultaneously, the machine man's raised tentacle pointed in the same direction.

Faint highlights of blue shown far back in the sky overhead. The blue grew in its intensity and the faintest stars slowly faded from view. Minutes past and for the first time the ocean was clearly visible. A dark blue horizon surrounded us and changed in color to emerald at the foot of the island to blue green to brilliant blue as a burning ember of white light appeared on the horizon and the yellow orb of the sun slowly rose in the east.

"Look," cried Sarah.

"We see it," I laughed.

"No, look," she said.

We looked in the direction of her excited shout up and slightly back behind us and into the sky directly above, where the brightest stars still shone. There, pale white and blue and distant, yet looking larger than I had ever seen it before, hung the moon. We remained where we sat, fixed on the mountaintop sharing the joy of that sunrise as though we had never beheld such a beautiful sight in all our lives.

Soon the sun was warm and blinding as it climbed up out of the ocean and slipped into the glorious sky. I turned from my friends and looked back at the cylindrical room. The light was pouring directly into the open chamber and the orange tree blazed with brilliant green and the promise of its myriad orange fruit. The mechanical man rose slowly on its metallic legs and Jesus followed the machine to the open doorway of the cylinder.

Looking back over our shoulders at the sunrise, Sarah and I followed and stepped inside. The white bands of light were once again illuminating the chamber's interior. The three of us looked at the machine man to see what it would do next. Both of its tentacles had emerged. One swayed rope like before our wastes as though to bar us from the open doorway. The other appendage reached above the doorway to a console of glittering crystals and tapped a single, lighted gem. The cylinder's door slid from its recess in the circular wall and sealed us within. Lights flickered. We heard the distant drone of machinery from somewhere far beneath our feet and the structure slid down and disappeared into the mountain of sand.

8. The Workshop

The branches of the orange tree swayed slightly. I picked an orange, and began peeling it. Like the others I'd peeled earlier, this one's covering came off easily in strips. I held a bunch of it in my fist.

"Are we waiting for something?" I asked.

"Yes," said Jesus.

Sarah glared at me, "We're in an elevator, you blockhead."

I shrugged my shoulders and noticed the large clay pot that held the orange tree. I dropped the orange peels inside at the base of the trunk and looked up at the machine man beside me into what I imaged was a face: horizontal slots where a mouth should have been and an array of crystals flashing in complex patterns. Crystals near the apex of its triangular body suggested eyes, and they seemed to observe me.

"Care for some orange?" I asked good-naturedly, expecting I might raise a smile from Sarah or Jesus.

"No thank you," replied the mechanical man. I did a double-take and accidentally dropped my orange on the floor.

* * *

Back in the days when I was employed at Joseph's Carpentry in Nazareth, the workshop had room for maybe four or five guys. On the big wedding table project we were working on the night our adventure began, it could get pretty crowded. Now, as the elevator car came to a halt and the door slid away, I saw an incredibly large workroom stretching out in the perfect blue light of an illuminated cavern that stretched for miles. Each the size of the temple in Jerusalem, generators protruded at 70 degree angles from each side of the enormous passage. They gleamed from behind scaffolds, steam pipes and conduits running from the floor and disappearing overhead in the dark recesses of the ceiling hundreds of feet overhead. These pairs of dynamos were replicated, one after the other, spaced a hundred yards apart as far as I could see.

The mechanical man stepped out of the elevator, followed by Jesus and the girl. I walked behind and noticed the network of catwalks, and stairways that outlined the gigantic generators. I saw something move along these spidery traces of girder work in the reaches of the vault above, and detected motion on the central floor some half mile distant. They were men, or beings nearly the size of men, moving to and fro, some with burdens, and all monitoring the enormous complex of underground machinery. Our mechanical escort had broken off from us. He moved swiftly away on its jointed legs, waving its tentacles.

"He's calling to them," said Jesus.

"Calling?" asked Sarah.

"He's announcing our arrival to the others," said Jesus.

A shadow fell over me, causing me to jump and I accidentally bumped into Sarah. I was about to apologize when the expression on her faced made me look up. The shadow was cast by one of the mechanical men. This being was similar to our guide in every respect but one; it descended on wings, razor sharp plates of metal that fanned out on either side of its back. Cool air stirred from the slow wing beats as it dropped lower and lower. A second mechanical man sailed down to the floor and was joined by others until four of them stood beside the elevator door. The wings on the first mechanical man beat twice more, and came together like the perfectly matched wings of a butterfly at rest. This automaton disappeared into the open elevator and re-emerged with the orange tree. It held the red clay pot in a single tentacle, returned to its winged companions and the four ascended back into the expanse overhead.

I wondered where they were taking the tree when I realized our guide had gotten away from us. Jesus had followed after him so that Sarah and I were now behind some fifty yards. The mechanical man had hailed several others of his kind. These came waddling from work stations and machinery along the walls. The whole thing began to make me feel a little creepy and I took a step next to Sarah.

"It's like Santa's Workshop," she said, marveling at the commerce in the busy cavern.

"Whose workshop?"

"Santa's."

"Who's that?"

"Nobody."

"No, who?" I insisted.

"You've never heard of Santa Claus?"

I shook my head.

"Santa Claus and his elves?"

"Who's that?" I asked.

"An excuse parents use to explain presents under the Christmas tree."

"They're making presents?"

"It's a metaphor," said Sarah with exasperation in her voice. She stopped and took another look at me. "Steve," she said, "I was only trying to tell you this place reminds me of something we used to believe in when I was a child, a story about a workshop at the north pole where this old man had all these tiny helpers making toys for all the good little children in the world."

"Really?"

"Steve, it was a just a story!"

"And did you believe it?"

"Me?"

"When you were a little girl?"

"Sure. I don't know. I suppose. Everyone did. Who wouldn't?"

"What happened?" I asked

"We grew up," she said and looked up ahead where a conveyance was moving rapidly toward us.

Several of the mechanical elves stood on this gigantic metal cookie sheet, hovering inches over the floor, speeding along the cavern's central thoroughfare toward Jesus. Soon, they had all met, and Jesus turned back, waving us to approach. We came alongside our companion and found ourselves in the midst of a dozen converging machine men. The object of their labor in the underground catacomb remained a mystery. For all I knew they could have been making toys for all the good little children of the world at the behest of a mysterious "Santa Claus." Never-the-less, it became apparent the scintillating crystal eyes of a legion of automatons had trained their attention on our party.

The floating platform came to a stop and I lost sight of the machine man whom we had first encountered, but then, scanning the crowd, I saw one of them and somehow knew it was the same being we had met on the island. Sarah must have sensed the very same thing, and she approached the mechanical man who had fallen back behind the others.

"Is it you?" she asked.

"Yes," replied the machine.

"What's going on? What's happening?"

"The angels are here to welcome you and your friends from the future."

"The future?" said Sarah.

"I thought you said they were elves?" I said.

"Would you knock it off with the elves already?" Sarah cried and she turned back to the machine.

"There are only two possibilities," the robot angel continued, "Either you and your companions have journeyed here from the future or else you are from another universe entirely, the existence of which we in this installation are, for the moment, completely unaware."

"Another universe," exclaimed Sarah. "You mean there's more than one?"

"Preposterous…" chimed in a second machine man who had turned its attention from the fanfare surrounding Jesus and the arrival of the floating platform. The voice of the second being was quite distinct from our guide's. It sounded feminine, and for the first time I wondered whether these "angels" were of different sexes.

The second automaton continued, "All things have been revealed to us. There is no undiscovered universe. These three humanoids are from this planet's future."

Our guide registered no response and the other continued in a haughty, human sounding tone, "You sentinels have been alone on the surface for too long. Five hundred million years up there have left you addled, to suggest something could be overlooked or unexplained."

At this remark, our guide rose up on its joined legs. "Then explain to me the flaw…"

"The flaw? What flaw?" replied the other, and before Sarah and I could protest, the second being leaned into us and did a number on our faces with its blinking lights. Our guide seemed vindicated, because the other machine sort of dropped back like an old accordion with the wind knocked out of it.

I was about to speak, when our attention turned to the floating platform and its passengers. These machine men were larger than the others. I recalled from what little I had read at temple school that there were different types of angels. I knew for a fact that Jesus read those scrolls end to end. In fact, even from the time he was a boy he had them pretty much committed to memory, but there was something more, something extremely important that would involve him, hanging out there in the future. If Jesus knew, he wasn't letting on, and that's when I first started to wonder about Sarah. Something had happened way out ahead of us, something in the future which she alone knew, because she was looking back at it. Of course, the way she looked at us, I suppose we were just two crazy guys from a convenience store.

"Greetings," boomed a voice from a hidden device on the flying platform. It sounded like a PA system and the voice echoed up and down the cavern walls for miles and high as the rafters.

"Greetings, children of future earth. Forgive us this humble welcome, but your arrival was…" The voice trailed off as the gigantic machine man on the platform conferred with the other two. He turned back to his audience and started on a new track.

"We have labored in these mines for five hundred million years, even before that, waiting, some of us, adrift in the cloud of this dawning planet, with every iota, every particle and spark of energy calculated, organized and directed to such a day as this!"

"Yes, but it's about four billion years early," shouted an angel in back.

The big robot monster on the podium raised a tentacle and tried it again, "Let us not question the hand of Providence in this event confirming our sentinels' report. Behold three specimens of our handiwork. The product of four billion years of evolution and sub-atomic engineering yet to unfold from this day, but here in evidence of our ultimate success. I give you… Mankind!"

It blew me away, but the robots were cheering. Had there been balloons and confetti in the rafters I'm sure they would have dropped. I'm glad Jesus was the front man on this part of the welcome. They were up there glad-handing and back-slapping him with what looked to be genuine affection. I suddenly felt a whole lot better about what was going on and what lay ahead, until I heard a shriek beside me.

"Watch it," scowled Sarah. The angel who had disparaged our guide had extended a tentacle up beneath the fabric of Sarah's tee-shirt. Sarah knocked it away and smoothed her shirt back over her exposed belly.

"You possess a second skin?" said the angel.

"It's clothes, you metal pervert," she snapped.

These words caught the attention of the other machine men, and the commotion caused Jesus and the big shots on the platform to look our direction. At the same instant I felt a tug at my leg and looked down to see a dozen writhing tentacles snaking up under the hem of my robe. I heard a boyish voice from somewhere in the crowd, remark, "This one's a male!"

"Thanks for reminding me," I yelled, swinging and kicking at tentacles recoiling back to their respective owners.

"Steve," called Jesus as he strode back from the platform through the crowd, "These beings are our friends. They mean no harm."

He motioned me toward the platform, and taking Sarah by the shoulder, indicated the way ahead. Almost as an afterthought he turned to our guide, and said, "Why don't you come along with us, too?"

The three large mechanical angels on the platform regarded both Sarah and me with what we interpreted as a deferential nod as we boarded the hover ship. Sarah and I walked to the back and held a polished handrail that partially enclosed the platform. The craft rose above the floor, wheeled slowly in place and skimmed off down the avenue.

* * *

The three large angels stood perhaps twelve feet tall and were of a different sort than our friend, the angel whom they addressed curtly as M-2500. These beings were of the XL class and represented an entirely different sphere in the angelic hierarchy, one responsible for harmony in the galaxy. They were part of the "Second Sphere," what a generation of theologians would later term the Virtues or Strongholds. As such, this roving band of angels was tasked with management of the heavenly bodies to ensure order in the cosmos. Some billion years earlier, these three angelic beings, XL-5000, XL-6000 and XL-7000 found themselves in the Milky Way Galaxy to shepherd development of a medium-sized yellow star whose first appearance, viewed by an observer on the surface of the earth, had occurred less than an hour earlier.

Our unanticipated appearance had thrown a celestial monkey wrench into the works. XL-5000, the angel to whom the younger XL-7000 had deferred during the press conference on the hover platform, had a lot on his enormous mind. Here they had spent five hundred million years preparing a planet for the "miracle of life," and the carefully orchestrated sequence of developments that would eventually produce a man out of a veritable lump of clay, when out of the blue, report comes from an M-class sentry, that three human beings have already popped up on the planet.

That sure wasn't supposed to happen!

Someone up the command at central was yanking his big chain. It's likely this gigantic being was having similar thoughts as we slipped down the wide concourse. What I've learned since probably explains a lot. This big bully acted like he was in charge, but he was only middle management, which may explain why he was a whole lot meaner than the facility's real supervisor. For some reason that guy was nowhere to be seen. In fact, XL-5000 and his two younger reports were probably trying to tie everything up in a neat bow before the REAL SANTA CLAUS caught wind of what was happening out on his factory room floor.

A guy, even an angel, I suppose, is entitled to his own thoughts, and right now if he was thinking such things, XL-5000 was keeping it to himself. He hung back and let the youngster, XL-7000 do the talking. It reminds me now of a bus tour I took through Chinatown, when we were living in Oakland in the spring of '68. One of those big, double-decker buses with the open air platform on top.

Our young guide XL-7000 really did seem to enjoy his work. Sarah was mesmerized from the get go. She hung on his every word, which got pretty technical, as far as I could tell. Of course, she had been studying this stuff all through prep school and college at M.I.T., wherever that was, and was even planning to learn more stuff in a 'graduate school.' I was just trying my best to see past the fact that she was just so attractive. I was just trying to look at her as a regular person, which was pretty hard to do.

"Praise the Creator," began our guide as we passed beneath the shadow of the first overhanging dynamo, "It is to his glory that we dedicate our labors and we thank our powerful Supervisor for guiding our work on our Creator's behalf, today and every day. And we especially thank the Creator for sending us these three magnificent examples of his handiwork: Jesus, Sarah and Steve."

That sounded all right to me, and I guess it was some sort of a robot angel prayer because Jesus had his head bowed the whole time, while Sarah and I continued to look around.

"I see that the generators have caught your attention," said XL-7000.

"Huh? Oh yeah! Is that a generator?" I said.

"They convert energy from one form to another," said Sarah.

"Very good," said XL-7000. "In this instance we harness the earth's geo-thermal energy to produce electricity. Our boilers produce steam from sea water, which drives turbines to turn the coils in these large dynamos."

"There sure are a lot of them," I said.

"We require substantial amounts to sustain an operation like this. Yes, indeed, I remember it as though it was yesterday," he said with a momentary quaver in his amplified voice and he pointed to an enormous pipe, rising out of the floor and turning at a right angle into a port in the generator.

"That conduit leads to one of five thousand boilers stationed at intervals five levels below this avenue in a sub-basement. Only 1,000 feet below that basement, conduits tap a robust magma chamber, but over here you may see where our Life Unit begins. These tanks and those directly opposite across the concourse, contain primitive seawater. These are the vessels out of which our S and M-Class comrades have generated amino acids, enzymes and now..."

I leaned against the handrail, actually, I kind of slumped against the handrail. After a while I got on my knees, crossed my arms under my chin, and dozed off. It was all very interesting. I awoke, with a start. I think Jesus was the only one on board who noticed, but he looked down to his side, smiled and looked back out at the sights as XL-7000 droned on. I know I missed a bunch, but I heard something about complex molecules, and DNA and RNA and some other weird things. I remember looking up at Sarah; she was like in a freaking trance looking from XL 7000 to whatever gigantic aquarium tank he happened to describe, when somewhere along the way she exclaimed,

"Oh, can we stop? Jesus, can we stop and take a look?"

The crew obliged and soon she was jostling my arm. I was flat sprawled out on the platform sleeping amid the tentacles, robot pods and human feet.

"Steve! Steve, wake-up! You have to see this. Here's the place where they produced the very first living thing. Steve, you need to see this!"

Jesus, Steve, and the angels had piled off the ship. I rolled over and I was alone on the platform but for Sarah. Evidently, something had really impressed her, but by the time I understood what she was saying I was just annoyed. What caught my attention was the distance we had traveled. The far end of the cavern where we had started from the elevator shaft looked no bigger than a silvery dot. I pulled myself up on the handrail and squinted in the other direction, where the cavern continued on again for miles, "How big is this place?" I said to myself and shook my head with dismay.

"Come on now," said Sarah, and again I felt her tugging on my arm.

"For crying out loud," I whined, "Who cares?"

"What?"

"Who cares how life started?"

Sarah looked shocked and a little hurt, but I was tired and angry.

"God created the heaven and the earth! Blah, blah, blah. End of story. Let's move on. I'm hungry."

"But aren't you in the least bit interested in how he did it?"

"Wait a second," I said, suddenly. "I thought you didn't believe in God?"

"What?"

"You said 'he.' How 'he' did it. Don't shake your head. I just heard you!"

"No, you didn't," Sarah snapped.

"I most certainly did!"

"It's just an expression."

"Everything is just 'an expression' with you! Everything is just a 'meta...' whatever! Get real!" I yelled. On second thought, I probably didn't yell, "get real," at her. I probably picked up that expression in Oakland in the 60's the year before my favorite cola manufacturer came out with its famous slogan. Anyway, I thought she was just hiding behind all her education and stuff and I yelled something mean at her that's for sure.

She glowered at me and jumped off the hover platform. Eventually, when I realized no one would be joining me anytime soon, I shuffled my way from the platform to where Jesus, M-2500, Sarah

113

and the three Strongholds were inspecting a big TV monitor. The Stronghold named XL-7000 explained we were viewing the interior of a chamber where the S-Class angels had brewed the first molecules on earth capable of reproducing themselves.

XL-7000 boasted that the view screen was connected to a gadget which, given enough energy, was capable of "infinite magnification."

"But that's impossible," said Sarah.

"You are familiar with our technology?" interrupted the old Stronghold XL-5000.

"I've worked with machines capable of incredible magnification. We call them electron microscopes."

"Electrons?" he repeated, and I swear the other two big units chuckled at the word.

"Yes, electrons!" said Sarah, doing her best to hold her own with the big robot.

"Quaint, but of little more power than optical microscopes. Do you have those in the future?"

Now, I know I heard the other two laughing. Although I'd never heard of a microscope, electron or otherwise, I could tell the guy was being sarcastic.

"If your race is using electrons to discover the Micro-Worlds, you must have a limited understanding of your universe," said XL-5000.

"We know lots about the universe," said Sarah.

"Do you?"

"We know when it began, how big it is, and..."

"And you are aware there is more than one?" interrupted XL-7000.

That shut-up her for a minute while the enormous being turned to the third Stronghold, who had yet to utter a word, and said to him, "Zoom in."

XL-6000, touched a panel on the side of the view screen. Instantly, the image on the monitor pulled back from the gently drifting molecules, as though a camera was zooming out, and we had the sensation of traveling rapidly along the spine of a long string of molecules. The speed increased, the view rolled up and down and the sight produced a sense of motion so intense that I lost my balance. The scene was rushing faster and faster and became a dizzying blur and then, suddenly, the movement ceased. We were viewing another magnified section of molecule, but there was something new, something else was slowly moving, deep among the glowing atoms. The camera zoomed in, and we plainly saw two angels at work at the controls of a small machine. They paused, looked back over their shoulders, and waved at us.

"Oh my God…" mumbled Sarah.

"Yes, indeed," said XL-5000, "Oh my God…"

Sarah noticed I was looking at her from the corner of my eye. She cleared her throat.

"Are they really so small?" she asked.

"For the moment. Our diminutive comrades, S-Class Angels, are in that tank beside us." He pointed at a clear, rectangular container on a pedestal just to the left of the view screen.

"But I sense your reference to the Creator is hollow."

Here's where Jesus stepped in.

"He's working with this one," said Jesus.

"Is he?" said XL-5000.

"Oh he is, is he?" said Sarah, "That's news to me, Jesus. I'm so glad you brought that to my attention."

"Yes…" continued the Stronghold, suspiciously, and the array of lights which streamed across a panel where a face might have been, flashed in a new pattern and the giant robot leaned in only a few feet from Jesus' face.

"Interesting," said the Stronghold, and its array of lights resumed their original configuration. He turned slowly and the silent one, XL-6000, gave me the once over with the lights. Having finished, it looked over at its boss.

"And what of this one?" said XL-5000 as though I were an inanimate hunk of wood.

"Steve is my friend," said Jesus, stepping between us, "There is no need to worry about him."

"But he is dead inside," said XL-6000.

That did it. Good night folks. I dropped back and headed toward the hovercraft.

"Dead inside," I heard XL-5000 repeat. "Dead like the female of your species."

Boy, that didn't go over very well with Jesus, or Sarah, for that matter, but the three Strongholds were getting mighty worked up themselves.

"Are these two creatures of a separate species? Has there been a miscalculation?" asked the quiet one, XL-6000.

Our old buddy from the sand dune, who'd more or less been standing there like a potted plant, suddenly spoke up,

"Perhaps we should continue the tour?"

"Silence," thundered the Stronghold and his companions leaned toward M-2500.

"But the schedule?" protested the smaller robot.

"Higher powers have intervened," interrupted the giant and his tentacle snaked through the crowd and coiled up under my armpit as I was drifting away. There was a tense moment as he turned me around and I more or less started back. The big robot boss seemed to crouch down a smidge to address me, and his voice suddenly became very soothing,

"Now, my little friend, since you are the lowliest of your companions, I shall speak in terms that even you may understand."

"Hey, wait a minute, buddy…"

"No…" said the robot softly, "The time of waiting has elapsed. We have tilled the soil of this solar system for eons untold and planted a seed that in three point eight billion years will yield a new race of beings. The Creator has seen this, and made it so. That which the mind conceived, the hand hath wrought."

"God?" said Sarah, "Is he…? Are you talking about…?"

"You speak his name, yet know him not," replied XL-5000.

"How do you know what she knows or doesn't know!" I said.

M-2500 put a tentacle out in front of me, as though holding me back from a precipice. Even Jesus put a hand on my shoulder.

XL-5000 raised up to full stature, and his twelve foot bulk cast a long shadow on us, "We are a perfect race, incapable of error, executing the Creator's perfect will since our own beginning nine hundred trillion years ago. There are undoubtedly others of the heavenly host, far older, far wiser, far more powerful, but I assure you that no one on my team has committed a miscalculation!"

"I'm real happy for you, but what's that got to do with us?" I said.

"If you really are from the future. If you are not some heavenly decoy beyond our station sent to test our loyalty or faith, but are just as you represent yourselves to be, then we have failed."

This seemed to bother the other two units immensely, and I noticed other robots of different sizes and shapes were more or less gathering around, like munchkins coming out of the weeds and more and more elves were walking away from their workbenches. I guess you'd say a crowd was gathering around the old tour bus.

Now, the big goon XL-5000 seemed to sink down so low and gloomy that his lights went dark blue and purple and his two big buddies looked like they had just caved in as their boss continued,

"When your angelic companion M-2500 sensed your presence on the Primordial Ocean he relayed his report to our command center in the Eastern Wall. Much later, when he reported your arrival on the beach, his earlier report was confirmed. Now, I have beheld it with my own eyes!"

"You have eyes?" I grinned and looked over at Jesus, but he wasn't smiling.

"Time travel is a very, very, dangerous activity."

"Okay..." said Jesus. He sounded impatient, and I seldom detected that note in his voice.

"Only those in the Creator's inner circle, those of the 'First Sphere,' are granted the authority to employ it," continued the robot angel. "The remaining orders of the angelic host, of which I proudly number myself -- the Dominions, Strongholds, Powers, Principalities, Archangels, and Common Angels of the various ranks and classes, inhabit our being in the eternal moment of NOW. We are grateful and content to do so. It is not in the divine plan, as far as I know, that anyone outside the First Sphere should journey into the future to see the outcome of our work. Evidently, someone or something, the identity of which, we are presently unaware, has elected to do so. At the very least, someone has employed time travel to carry you from the future and deposit you here on this date, which, for the sake of convenience, we have named Day Four."

"It wasn't me!" I said. "I don't know how we got here, and that's the truth."

"I believe what you say, my little man. And I believe your companion, Sarah, has no idea how you came to be in this place today."

"You got that right, mister," said Sarah.

"But as for you," and here the creature turned on Jesus, and the other big units hung on their boss's every word.

"You are, indeed, what we had in mind when we created this facility. You are precisely what we <u>had</u> in mind: a perfect man."

There was applause from out in the crowd that had gathered between the two dynamos and angels were spilling out into the concourse. At this point, XL-6000 stepped over to his boss and whispered, "If we go over to the hover platform I could turn on the PA system."

XL-5000, pushed the junior stronghold back with a tentacle. The boss was on a roll, but after that he punched up his own volume a notch so that his voice boomed a bit louder.

"Here is the type of creature we intended, the legacy of four billion years, the generations of soulless beings yearning for survival, toiling up from oceans, through the streams, swamps, jungles, forests, and savannahs yet to be, yearning toward that supreme moment when the Creator would breathe eternal life into a soulless physical body."

"Well, something's gone wrong," said M-2500, who stepped forward and turned up his own volume a notch. Come to think of it, he jacked up his telescoping legs a few feet so the angels way in back could see him.

"Silence!" said the big stronghold.

"These beings are mortal!" said M-2500.

You could have heard a pin drop. I looked out at the crowd and somehow I recognized the pushy angel with the lady's voice from back at the elevator. It was kind of nodding to the others standing around it in the crowd. We heard a low moaning sound from way in back. I think one of the robot angels in back was "booing."

"Perhaps they are apes?" whispered XL-7000.

There was a long silence after that remark. It was a tense moment. We looked to Jesus. I guess he figured it was his turn at bat and he marched up in front of our tour guides and addressed the crowd.

"We are none of us apes," he said in a loud voice, "In our design we are each exactly as the Creator intended. Celebrate in the success of your enterprise, that all three of us are, indeed, mortal."

XL-5000 did a double take. I guess he was getting rusty, because he'd evidently missed something when he'd given Jesus the once-over with the "mortality" scanners.

"I repeat," Jesus continued, "We are mortal beings. That each us will one day suffer physical death should be of no concern to you. It is a choice that we have made, a choice that is none of yours. You have done all the Creator has asked of you. We come from the far future to testify that you have succeeded in your mission here, and for that you should rejoice."

The crowd had quieted down. There was a tense moment where it might have gone either way, but then, one of the angels way in back shouted,

"Way to go, dude!" or something like that.

And then, all of a sudden, the angels out in the crowd were cheering again. Cheering and shouting and chanting and I guess they were pretty happy to get this sneak peak at three models off their assembly line, even if two of them were low end. They probably figured upper management had set this all up, and they were feeling pretty good about themselves and their mission as they started to drift away back to their work stations. Some of them even came up to shake Jesus' hand with a tentacle and there was no denying he had really impressed the heck out of them, well, a lot of them, anyway.

Meanwhile, over where Sarah and I were standing, the biggest Stronghold still looked mighty pissed. Maybe he was questioning himself for once. He had given Jesus the treatment and somehow or other got a reading that Jesus had an eternal soul, one with super-high energy like him and his pals, although the amazing fact was that Jesus was just a person like Sarah and me. Why Sarah and I had souls that were "dead inside," I don't know. It was complicated. Maybe XL-5000 was only worried about the fact that he had failed to check with his immediate supervisor about holding the impromptu rally out on the factory room floor. He'd be getting in trouble for that soon enough.

"And upon who's authority do you speak?" demanded XL-5000.

Jesus stared calmly into the big ugly face.

"We are on a journey to the east and must be on our way."

The word "east" honestly threw them for a second. The three Strongholds conferred.

"The sun rises in the east," said one of them.

"It has only risen once in all eternity and that was three hours ago."

"Well, then, if you have your bearings…" said Jesus.

The three strongholds pointed in the direction we had been traveling down the main concourse.

"East," said XL-7000.

Jesus nodded and he walked away toward the hover platform. It was pretty freaking cool to see him walk over to the platform with the three Strongholds left looking at themselves and then following after him like all of a sudden HE was the supervisor.

Sarah and I were left with M-2500, who turned to us and spoke in what I could have sworn was a whisper. "Their race is responsible for order in the cosmos. They view your arrival as an affront to their authority and their privileged relationship with upper management." Then, as he turned toward the hover platform, he added, almost as an afterthought, "And just who is this fellow, Jesus?"

It seemed like a strange question, but I answered.

"He's my friend," I said proudly.

Apparently satisfied by my response, M-2500 seemed to wait for something from Sarah.

"I don't know him," she said.

"You know nothing at all about him?"

M-2500 seemed almost desperate for a reply as we approached the hover platform.

"No," said Sarah. "I only met him the other day."

9. The Eastern Wall

We glided down the concourse for another hour, veering into this alcove and that for the local sights narrated by the young Stronghold, XL-7000. He'd gotten back into the swing of his delivery and I had a second wind so it didn't seem all that bad to listen to his spiel. The facility was pretty much in place to simply monitor developments on the planet above. A half billion years earlier they had chosen this particular three hundred mile swath of rock in the earth's crust to set up shop due to its close proximity to an underground magma chamber. The angels had replicated conditions planned to unfold on the earth above. They tested and retested every step in the long parade of life to follow on the planet's surface from molecule to cell to organism, including the myriad leaps from species to species.

"We shall monitor the progress of life as it naturally occurs on the earth's surface in real-time. Our loyal and hardworking M series of angels are in a unique position to provide support or affect any possible course corrections." said XL-7000.

The subterranean robot angels had gotten well into flowering plants, which were pretty darn complex and the crowning achievement in the plant world. They'd been planning to send an orange tree along with some other plants to the surface to see how they did in the atmosphere which had only recently resolved itself out of a stew of otherwise noxious gases left over from formation of the oceans.

Our old pal M-2500 had been on the planet with another five thousand M-Class comrades bobbing about in the primitive ocean in total darkness keeping their collective eyes on things. The Strongholds themselves had only recently taken up more of less permanent residence on the earth. They dropped in every hundred million years or so to check up on progress at the facility and to sign off on detailed reports transmitted back to headquarters. One of them bragged how their quick action had averted an errant asteroid strike which might have delayed the timetable by fifty million years. Again, it got pretty technical, but by the time Jesus, Sarah, and I arrived, all things were "GO" for life on earth. Early in the third millennium I spent some time in the Pacific Northwest. Jesus was bartending, Sarah was working as an aerobics instructor and I was getting ready to start undergraduate school at Lewis and Clark College. Forty years earlier I had held down some part-time hours at a record store in Oakland, but found an hour or two on Tuesday's and Thursday's to take a biology course at the local community college. "Biology 101" it was called. I learned a lot about biology and evolution. For the most part the textbook and the professor had it right down to the letter, but, as you can see, they missed out on some of the important stuff, too.

* * *

We were almost at the end of the cavern and we saw some super primitive amphibians flopping around trying to breathe air through their gills, and I guess the angels were confident everything would work out according to plan on the planet's surface. The hover platform picked up speed after that. For the first time I was glad for the safety rail and the feeling of security it lent as we raced head. At some point or other I noticed the aquariums and tanks were in much less abundance and given over to cages and big stone enclosures with iron bars. Although at one point I distinctly remember a gigantic squid the size of a bus shaking its suction lined tentacles at us from an Olympic sized swimming pool, it seemed we were leaving the water park behind us. At about the two hundred mile mark, Sarah spotted a gigantic aviary draped in steel mesh that housed some leather winged monsters the size of small airplanes, and I swear I saw some weird and monstrous looking creatures, like from a nightmare, pacing back and forth in their fortified pens.

After a while our craft slowed down a bit and I caught sight of some fearsome animals I had once seen in a traveling menagerie in Jerusalem, and there were others, more familiar, right down to goats and sheep, and oxen, and baby kittens. It was only at the end, when we approached the end of the cavern, with the last five of six pairs of the temple sized dynamos on either hand, that we beheld the low cages with the most troubling sight.

"They are soulless animals," remarked XL-7000.

"They're people," stammered Jesus. "You have people in these cages?"

"Easy, my friend," said M-2500, "And the reassuring touch of its metal tentacle actually did bring him back a step to listen to what the Stronghold explained to us.

"The beings housed here in the shadow of the Eastern Wall, represent the crowning achievement of life on earth. The genetic code is complete and our molecular engineering is at an end," said XL-7000.

Sarah turned from the site where naked men and women peered out from a nearby enclosure, "And you mean to release them onto the earth?"

XL-7000 looked back from the bow of the platform, "No," he said, "These specimens will remain here to live out their natural lives unhindered, their number dwindling, generation to generation until the last prototype passes into the oblivion of death, one hundred million years before the first fish-like amphibians venture out onto the surface of dry land above."

"So, all of this is really, just a test?" said Jesus.

"A trial run if you will," said XL-7000. "We leave nothing to chance."

Sarah's eyes locked with the gaze of a small girl and she stammered, "But they're people," protested Sarah, "They look like people – don't they?"

"They sure do," I agreed.

"And with all the native capacity and potential of real people," said XL-7000, "But they are without souls." XL-7000 looked down at Sarah and me, thought better, and stepped away.

We had pulled off to the side of the road and parked in one of the alcoves to listen to XL-7000 embellish the story, and I noticed

Jesus again, standing calm, resolute but opaque as he could sometimes be. I wondered what he thought of this incredible subterranean beehive. The robots were assuring us that the naked animals milling around in the pens out there were no more human than cats or dogs or razor clams. I wasn't buying any of it, but I couldn't read Jesus.

I really wish I had learned more about it all from him when we were back in Nazareth. I remember waiting for Jesus until he was finished with temple for the day; late at night under the stars we'd look up at the heavens. He'd start off his all too familiar conversation with something like, "Do you ever wonder how all this came to be?" Or, "Steve, tell me, do you ever find yourself asking 'why was I born or where do I come from?'" I guess, nine times out of ten I was more interested in getting something to eat. I don't think I ever got around to answering him, much less bothering to think about such things on my own.

* * *

We came, finally, to the cavern's eastern terminus, a huge wall of black basalt towering up five hundred feet into the darkness. Stretching at intervals from the north side of the wall to the south, were cut a half dozen twenty-foot portals through which robots of the M class and many other odd shaped machines and "super-natural beings" were moving.

Unlike the Western Wall three hundred miles behind us, where only that single silver elevator doorway broke the uniform surface of rock, the eastern bookend was dotted by lighted apartment windows laid out against the black rock like a mosaic shinning in an artificial night. And I mean, night too, because somewhere, someone was dialing back the rheostat on the track lighting way up in the rafters. The cavern's artificial sunlight, at least in this neck of the woods, was quickly fading away. I think I heard a wolf baying from its 'environmentally controlled habitat' in the distance as we climbed off the hover platform and were intercepted by a dozen robots angels of different sizes and shapes. As we mounted a long, low marble stairway leading to the Eastern Wall's central portal, Sarah walked like a tourist in a crowded downtown, her neck craned up for a view.

"It looks the New York City skyline at night," she said, and wonder of wonders, there was a New York City street vendor selling hotdogs with sauerkraut and pretzels by the doorway.

"You guys hungry?" asked Jesus, as though we were about to step through a turnstile to see a major league baseball game.

"What is the meaning of this?" demanded XL 5000 of an obsequious L class angel, L-77, who was clearly handling the swarthy New York busker and his stand.

XL-5000 continued, "You've butchered beef, pickled cabbage and made these – what is this? Wheat?"

"I believe they're hoagies, sir," replied the lowly angel.

That bamboozled the big guy for a second. "By whose authority?" he boomed and he stopped and took another look at the guy selling hot-dogs, "Who authorized construction of this humanoid mockery?"

"What's it gonna be, mister?" said the android street vendor taking no offense and sounding as though he had just stepped off a subway from lower Manhattan, "You like it with onions?!"

"Onions?" boomed XL-5000, "Who authorized the use of these organics?"

"I'll take one," I said with a grin, stepping up and instinctively reaching for the coin purse on my belt. I stuck my finger in and dug around and remembered the road map from the desert.

"Put up that dough, ya' bum," continued the vendor, "These dogs is on the house!" he smiled, "Right, Mac?" he said to Jesus as he handed my friend two enormous hot dogs smothered in kraut and onions all wrapped in two white paper liners.

"Boy, oh boy, do they ever look good," said Jesus handing one to Sarah and then inhaling a great steam filled breath of the other before handing it to me.

Until that moment, and never again in my entire life, did I ever taste anything so good. I looked up as I munched on my hotdog, and saw chaser lights spring to life over head on a small section of the Eastern Wall, advertizing the final days of a long-running Broadway Musical about cats.

Of course, at the time I had no idea what any of this meant, and it probably was only by the power of the Holy Spirit or some such thing that I could read anything at all, but the significance was not lost on Sarah.

"It's a revival," she said, as though in a dream, "Before he died, my father took me to see this musical in New York when I was a girl."

The real life baying of wolves and the guttural shouts of pre-human guinea pigs, soulless and without guile and no more human than guinea pigs or the android street vendor placed on the corner for our comfort and amusement, were soon drowned out by a lively audio sound-track replicating the street sounds of downtown Broadway.

Meanwhile, the L-class angel, L-77, who had organized the "street-side festivities" at the Eastern Wall was backpedaling up the marble steps to the wall itself, surrounded by three of the most powerful beings presently in the solar system.

* * *

When you stop and think about it, it's pretty amazing what a hundred angels can pull off when they put their heads together for a few hours. The austere anteroom inside the Eastern Wall's main portal, designed primarily for L-Class angels, had been redecorated to approximate the lobby of a five-star hotel in downtown Manhattan visited by the recently divorced, soon to be deceased, Wallace Benton and his thirteen year old daughter, Sarah, in the summer of 2000.

Angel First Class L-1, known affectionately as "Jerry," by those of the First Centurion Guard who had served in the first mission to the solar system and who saw the "Life on Mars Project" abandoned in favor of the "Earth: It's the Natural Choice" campaign, had long been involved in observance of daily worship services.

Indeed, up until very recently, at least in the angels' way of reckoning, the Terrace, high above on the 17th floor of the Eastern Wall had been a main portion of the angel's Temple and worship sanctuary. Now, the opportunity to mount an angelic production of an award winning Broadway Musical, some three point eight billion years before its premiere, was a task that Jerry relished.

Orders came down from the office of the Ophanim (variously known as the "Thrones") through back channels. It was not unheard of for the time spanning Thrones of the First Sphere to send messages predicated on some future event, but even for someone like Jerry, who would live for eternity, it was pretty unusual. He found himself in possession of the score, libretto, set and costume designs and program copy in addition to architectural plans of the Broadway theater exactly as they would appear in New York City in September of 2000, some three point eight billion years in the future! The plans encompassed structural elements to the subatomic level and an exact record of every newspaper and print magazine on display in town during the month of September in addition to a sound track of all ambient noise in the vicinity of the Benton's three day visit.

Such minutiae fanned the flames of Jerry's flare for detail. He and his ninety nine centurions along with the help of old friends from the "Moon Days," remodeled and redecorated the main entrance of the Eastern Wall in homage to the façade, lobby, restaurant, bar and grill, and several suites of the five-star luxury hotel where Benton had tried to get reacquainted with his daughter. An entrance portal, fifty yards to the north, was hollowed out and outfitted with a re-creation, or as Jerry termed it, a "pre-creation," of the actual Broadway Theater including its lobby, auditorium, stage, scene house and dressings rooms.

With more than two hours to spare, the angels had everything in place. There was no need to rehearse, having memorized in three seconds every element of the material sent back to them from the future. Jerry's troop of players was nothing if not adaptive. A characteristic of the angels, well known since ancient times was their uncanny ability to blend in with their surroundings, to render themselves effectively "invisible," or to assume the identity of any person, place or thing. This may explain how a single L-Class angel, one of Jerry's old roommates from the interregnum following the "Life on Mars" debacle, was able to single-handedly impersonate an entire 30 piece orchestra, including the musicians, clothing, instruments and the actual music.

Indeed, at the moment, as Jerry and the Centurions were putting the last touches to a "perfect evening on the town," it was Jerry's own flare for the unexpected which had led him to contact L-77, an old buddy from the start up crew on the Earth's moon during the interregnum where L-77 was first assigned to work with the then unheard of "Human Genome Task Force." As Jerry reviewed the secret, back channel information from the First Sphere, and planned the event for the three humanoids from the future, he had naturally thought of L-77 to provide "emotional ambiance" outside the Eastern Wall. Who better than a guy with experience building real human beings to throw together android mock-ups at the last minute? With only hours until "show time," L-77 and some M-Class angels from the old HG Task Force fabricated a retinue of androids to populate the street scene at the Eastern Gate; these included school kids, hookers, businessmen, families from the American Midwest with strollers, and children in tow and military personnel on leave.

With ambient noise tapes blaring out from floating loudspeakers, almost as an afterthought, L-77 threw in "Tony, the street vendor" and a yellow cab. The particular angel at work on the automobile mock up of the taxi-cab made no connection between the bumper sticker, the plastic icon on the magnetic dashboard pedestal or the belief system of the actual taxi-driver whose future livelihood had served as a basis for their bogus car and driver.

One can hardly blame Jerry, his Centurions or the L-Class veterans for their failure to "connect-the-dots." Given an amount of information which would have instantly crashed the entire 21st century's world-wide web, and the fact that no one was particularly looking for future references to something called "Christianity," the team would be forgiven a few over-sights and opportunities lost that evening. Had a real angel impersonated the taxi cab or its driver, it's conceivable such a connection might have been drawn. As it was, the android in the driver's seat had no speaking part, and the angel at work outfitting the taxi had no understanding of spoken or written English. At that stage in the universe, a bumper sticker proclaiming that "Jesus Saves," meant no more to a common angel than it did the animated mannequin sitting in the driver's seat.

* * *

I was munching on my big fat hot dog and a piping hot pretzel, as I followed Jesus and M-2500 up into the lobby of the fake hotel. I say fake, but it was a whole lot nicer than any of the real inns I'd ever stayed at on trips to Jerusalem. This place boasted big high ceilings, fountains, chairs, sofas and tables for people to sit and talk and relax, and it was remarkable how many people there appeared to be.

I waited with Sarah beside a rack of travel brochures while Jesus and M-2500 went up to the hotel desk. By this point it was impossible for me to tell who was an android, who was an angel in disguise, and if so, whether an angel was playing more than one part at once. Nor could I discern the true nature of the furnishings and accoutrements.

Was that sofa a real sofa? It, too, might have been an angel disguised as a sofa, and the uncertainty continued even as we made our way to the bank of "fake" elevators. In that large hallway we caught sight of that loveable trio from the hover platform: XL-5000 and his two apprentices. We'd left them outside with the mechanical street vendor and the L-class angels arguing about protocol. Evidently, someone, or something had gotten back to old XL-5000 and set him straight.

* * *

It was well understood that the Creator's inner circle pretty much did as it pleased. That the Ophanim was sending orders and information through back channels did not necessarily reflect adversely on the Strongholds or any high ranking beings of the Second Sphere, including the cavern's strangely absent supervisor. But now, big old XL-5000 was ducking down so as not to hit the chandelier and he waved one of his big tentacles and attempted to convey a smile with the light array on his main panels,

"Maybe you folks would like to come down for a drink before dinner?" he said, as the elevator door slid closed.

"Something sure changed his tune," said Sarah as she leaned against the cool metal wall of the elevator car.

Jesus smiled contentedly as M-2500 stabbed a circle of light on the elevator control console. At the same time M-2500 reviewed the informational brochure that I'd perused in the lobby. M-2500 scanned the photographs with its crystal arrays. There was one particular photo of a young, full-bodied woman, leaning forward in a low-cut red evening gown. She was evidently a patron in this promotional material from the distant future. Maybe the angel had noticed my momentary fascination with that brochure, how I had somehow allowed a glossy piece of paper to influence my metabolism.

A tiny bell tone sounded in the upper recess of the elevator car. We were on the seventeenth floor of something. The door slid open revealing a room of elevator banks adjoining a long carpeted hallway containing myriad hotel room doorways. Sarah, Jesus and I stepped off the car. At that moment the brochure fluttered to the floor. By the time the tentacled lower extremities of M-2500 had crossed out of the elevator car, they had transformed into two long muscular female legs, tan in sheer hose all the way down from the evening gown to where the plate-like ambulatory pods had metamorphosed into red, opened toed high heeled shoes.

M-2500 was reaching into his silver clutch purse for room keys when I called out to him.

"Hey, M-2500 do you have the key to the…"

My mouth dropped open as I looked at the creature standing beside me in the hallway. Apart from the photograph on the brochure, I'd never seen that much exposed skin on a woman in my entire life and I wondered whether we would be sharing a room at the Inn. As it turned out, our hosts had provided separate rooms for each of us. But then I remembered that good old M-2500 was not really part of our party, but merely an employee. Evidently, the news and information which had filtered down to the angels from the future had simply overlooked separation of the sexes as a given condition of our human existence. I guess this was all happening before the angels realized that sex is dirty and must be accomplished in secret. Obviously, as it happened that evening, it was clear the whole story was not yet in. As for M-2500, protocol had definitely slipped up somewhere; as Jesus and Sarah each disappeared behind their separate doors, I suggested that M-2500 join me in my suite for some "coffee."

* * *

I saw a fresh suit of modern clothes on a large bed. After some investigation, trial and error, and nearly knocking myself out with a blast from the "shower head," I figured out how to operate the controls on the bath, and climbed into the steaming hot tub. I about screamed bloody murder when the bathroom door swung open, and but for a string of pearls daggling from her neck, M-2500 backed into the room naked as jaybird.

"Hey, wait a minute!" I cried at first in real fear, but then, I suppose, in mere humiliation.

"Let's not waste any of that bath water," said M-2500 in a sultry female voice.

I was unsure whether I should stare or turn my head as she stepped fully into the room. And now she was holding a support railing, raising a naked leg, and lowering a big toe, with its red painted nail into the water.

"Ooohhh, perfect!" she said, climbing in.

"Perfect?" I cried, "Not perfect! Not perfect! We're not married M-2500! I mean, not that I want to marry you, but we should not be together."

"We are not together."

"Well, we need to keep it that way," I said scooting back up against the wall of the hot tub.

"Were you not planning to mount me like one of the human creatures outside in the pens?"

"Mount..." and here I cleared by throat, "Of course not. They're beasts. You heard that yourself from the big robots." I paused and watched my bath mate slip down into the water. M-2500's breasts, heaving beneath that shimmering string of pearls, slid below the water line. I choked, "Are you a guy or a girl?"

"I am an angel."

"Well, yeah, I know, but the hardware, which do you normally have?"

"Hardware?"

"Down there," I indicted a point where her torso disappeared below the waterline of the steaming hot tub.

She looked up, "I have female reproductive organs, if that's what you mean."

That was it! As she looked down into the water, it was suddenly all too much for me; I reached out and grabbed down a bath towel, staggered to my feet. I climbed out of the tub and began drying myself off.

"Too weird, too weird!" I cried.

The expression on the woman's face was sad. "Downstairs in the lobby you seemed delighted by the photograph," said the being in the bath, but now the edges of its body began to blur and shimmer and in an instant the bath room was filled, not with a beautiful naked woman, but with the giant, slightly nightmarish, robot-looking body of M-2500. Displaced water flowed over the rim of the tub and splashed onto the tiled floor.

That cooled me off in a hurry. I was pulling on my clothes from the bed and as I looked back into the open bathroom and saw the familiar form of M-2500, I sighed with regret.

"What's wrong?" said M-2500. "You seem even more upset than before."

"Never, mind," I said, "Grab your purse, I mean, get the room key and let's find Sarah and Jesus.

Tying my tie in the mirror at the vanity, I could see M-2500's reflection sitting on the bed, slumped down, holding the red dress and red, high heeled shoes in a limp tentacle.

"Oh, never mind, you can dress up in it if you like!" I said.

I was fastening my old leather money pouch with its strap around my waist when I felt two soft arms drape across my shoulders,

"Here, let me help you with that, honey," said the beautiful being.

I turned. Beyond the pearls on the woman's bare shoulder, I looked at the red dress and shoes still lying on the bed.

I felt something stirring down below.

"Why don't I help you with your neck tie," said M-2500.

I took a deep breath and looked up at the ceiling, as she took hold of the neck tie. She knew what she was doing, that's for sure. I think she was tying a Windsor. Now, she explained how she'd gotten filled in a bit on the evening's activities from Jerry. I guess the angels could communicate with mental telepathy or some such thing. Who knows? Just keep talking while you finish up with the tie and get dressed. Just keep talking, and everything will be fine. I managed to find out that the angels had some trouble long ago on the planet Mars and how everything had to be started over again on earth and how mad the supervisor was about getting "blind-sided," or some such thing, and I was about to ask her whether we would ever meet the supervisor and whether or not he wasn't really the mysterious Santa Claus that Sarah had mentioned when the phone rang. I'll admit she tied one hell of a Windsor.

The beautiful, dare I say "sexy" creature by the night stand answered the phone and brought it to my ear. It was Jesus at the front desk, asking me to drop whatever I was doing and that we had reservations at the hotel restaurant.

* * *

We were a hot looking couple as we made our way across the lobby to the restaurant, and we turned more than a few heads, although I had to remind myself from time to time that most of the heads were not real heads, or if they were, belonged to S, M, and L-Class angels who had no interest in the sexes – at least not in ways that had always interested me. No, I suppose the entire evening was pretty much a make-believe deal. On the other hand, Sarah and I sure didn't mind the food. It was real enough. She had salmon and asparagus and cheesecake and wine and water. I had the same and so did my erstwhile "date" M-2500. I don't know, but any kind of romantic feelings I might have developed for the angel were partly cancelled by my memory of its original, masculine voice. I sure wished I had met her under different circumstances. While we had come to the conclusion that he was neither male nor female, but something altogether different, it had nothing to do with human procreation. Still, every so often, I'd look over and forget who she was and see what part of me wanted to see, and that was pretty cool. At one point, as our waiters cleared the dinner plates, I asked my incredibly hot date to run outside and check to see whether the street vendor was still there. If he was, M-2500 had orders to bring me another dog with onions, sauerkraut and mustard.

As soon as M-2500 was out of ear-shot, I leaned forward to my two friends. "You'll never guess who that is?" I said, "It's M-2500. Our angel from the black island!"

"Listen, Jesus, is it safe to talk here?" interrupted Sarah, ignoring me as though I were no more significant than her desert fork.

"I believe so," said Jesus, "Why do you ask?"

"None of these guys know who you are."

Jesus didn't seem particularly moved by Sarah's revelation.

"Hell, your own best friend doesn't seem to know who you are," said Sarah.

That last remark didn't make a whole lot of sense to me, but I let it slide.

"Hey Jesus," I said. "Are you going to eat that roll?"

"The roll?" Jesus looked at his place setting and seeing the roll on its dish in the corner, passed it on to me.

"Sarah can you spare any butter?" I asked.

"Would you knock it off, you two!" said Sarah.

"Knock what off?" I asked.

"What's wrong, Sarah?" asked Jesus.

"You act like two total idiots."

"Idiots?" said Jesus and he and I looked at one another.

"Don't you know by now you're supposed to be Jesus Christ?"

"Jesus who?" I interrupted, looking from Sarah to Jesus and back to Sarah.

"The son of God!" she snapped angrily.

I stood up, simultaneously knocking over my water glass, "The son of, whoops…"

This was so loud the entire dining room went silent. You could hear pots and pans and dishware from beyond the swinging doors to the kitchen hidden in the back of the room behind the waiters' station.

"Let me get that," I said and began dobbing water off Jesus' place with a napkin.

"So, why doesn't anyone recognize you?" asked Sarah.

"I thought you didn't believe in God?" said Jesus.

At this she threw down her utensil and pushed back in her chair, "Don't start in with me again," she snapped, "What I believe isn't important!"

"No? That's an odd thing to say. So, you're willing to admit that you might not have all the answers?" asked Jesus.

"I may be insane! I know that much," she said, "I'm still not convinced this isn't some sort of crazy dream or that I haven't lost my mind."

That shut us up. Jesus looked down at his uneaten food.

"But I'll play along, OK?" she said, leaning back across the table and kind of speaking in a hush because some of the patrons were looking at us out of the corners of their eyes.

"I'll just 'let go,' for a minute like I'm with my therapist and I'll grant that you're the historical Jesus. How's that?"

Jesus nodded.

"Well?"

"It's a start, I suppose," said Jesus without looking up.

"Then why don't the angels seem to recognize you?"

"I think the higher ups know I'm here."

"Higher ups? You don't mean those big XL units on the hover platform," she said.

"Higher."

"The supervisor?"

"Santa Claus," I said. If they were playing twenty questions, I had decided to go all in.

"Would you please shut up about that?" said Sarah.

"Who's Santa Claus?" asked Jesus.

"Forget it. Just forget it! I was just making small talk," she replied.

"Is there such a thing?" said Jesus and he took a sip from his water glass.

Sarah gave him a rueful look.

"I don't believe the 'Supervisor' knows we're here," said Jesus leaning across the table toward Sarah. "That's troubling because it may indicate a break in the chain of command." And now his voice had dropped to a whisper, "For whatever reason, no one at this little outpost has ever heard of us until today. That's fine. We can hang out and relax, rest up for the remainder of the journey. No one here needs help."

Sarah rolled her eyes.

"Steve, do you need any help?" asked Jesus.

"I'm good," I replied, although I didn't know what on earth they were talking about.

"I haven't really been able to figure it out yet," said Jesus kicking back in his chair with his water, "But at some point, life will unfold up above on the planet's surface and the earth will produce creatures like those humanoids out in the holding pens.

"But that's evolution!" said Sarah.

"Is that what you call it?"

"Isn't that supposed to be a nasty word with Christians?"

"If I knew what you mean by the word 'Christian,' I might be able to answer that, but will you let me finish?" asked Jesus.

Sarah nodded and Jesus took a breath.

"One day, in the far future the Creator will provide one of those creatures with a soul and breathe into it the spirit of eternal life. I don't know which one it will be, only the Creator knows, but I suppose it will be the one called Adam."

"You mean from Genesis?" I said, wanting to impress Jesus with my knowledge of the ancient texts.

"Exactly! And when Adam gets lonely, the Creator will pick out another of the herd and provide her a soul and breathe his spirit into her and Adam will have his mate."

"Whoa, now that IS a trip!" I said, "Adam and Eve, just like in the story," but when I looked over at Jesus expecting a high five, he was sullen, staring at the table's centerpiece. I don't know what he saw in that glass pot, just some moss and tiny ferns and a few flowers, like a miniature garden.

"What?" said Sarah.

"What is it, Jesus?" I asked.

"I don't know. It's like layers; with each passing day, they keep peeling away and I get closer and closer to the truth."

Jesus really started to open up and I noticed for the first time the little smirk that Sarah always wore on the corner of her mouth was nowhere to be seen.

"Ever since I was a little kid, I've always wanted to know more about God. You know, Steve."

"Sure…" I said. I could testify to that.

"I was really into it, and I just loved God and going to temple and I really started thinking of him as my spiritual father, from the time I was three. Three years old and I had his Word memorized and could recite it all to the letter. I hope you realize that I say this in all humility, but that is very uncommon in a child."

We nodded our heads in agreement.

"No," he continued, "I started to think he was REALLY my father, my ACTUAL father, and ever since the other day, I guess now about two weeks ago, Steve was there, with Cousin John back at the Jordan… Well… There's just a whole lot going on in my life right now, so we decided I should get away for a minute to sort things out."

"You said, 'we.'" said Sarah, "You mean him?"

"No," he sighed, "Someone… Someone else… The 'Entity,' I suppose you might call him."

Who was he talking about? At the time, I hadn't a clue. I was about to ask, when, for once in my life I simply shut up and listened as Jesus looked earnestly at Sarah and she returned the gaze.

"And have you? Sorted things out?" she asked.

"I remember when I was a young teenager going to my mom to ask her about it when she was alone one day in the kitchen, but when I had her attention, I just couldn't bring myself to ask. I suppose it was the way I was raised, not to talk about such things. But the other day out on the desert listening to the radio with Steve, I had this thought that I really was the son of God, I mean the actual SON of GOD."

"Well, great!"

"But there was something else!"

"What?" asked Sarah.

"I don't know how to put it into words."

"Try me."

"I don't want you to take this the wrong way, but through the static this idea came to me, from a long, long time ago."

Sarah nodded for him to get on with it.

"No, way before the beginning of the earth. I mean this voice was coming from the very beginning of this universe…"

"And…?" said Sarah.

"It was MY VOICE. It was ME!"

"That's freaking nuts," I said.

"I know, isn't it?" replied Jesus.

"No, I mean 'freaking nuts' in the bad way," I said.

"At least it's consistent," said Sarah, and Jesus gave her a funny look, almost like she'd hurt his feelings, and I could see that little smirk on the corner of her mouth again.

"Are you even listening to me?" Jesus asked.

"I am." I said.

"Sarah?"

"Look, I already know the whole story, do you mind?"

"What story?"

"Every year we celebrate Christmas where I come from."

"Christmas?" said Jesus, suspiciously.

"The Jehovah's Witness kid and the little Jewish girl in my class would draw clowns, but the rest of us made pictures of Santa Claus and we'd cut out strips of green and red construction paper with our round tipped scissors and paste them together into chains to decorate the class room. Everyone would make ornaments to decorate the Christmas trees all over town, even in my folk's house when they were still together."

"Christmas?" said Jesus.

"You didn't need to believe any of it. You just did it."

"That odd."

It didn't sound odd to me. I'd done lots of things back in the temple in Nazareth I didn't understand, much less believe in.

"My dad would get a few days off from traveling and he and mom would go out to parties together during those two weeks around the holidays and all my grandparents would come in from out of town, and I'd get money to go shopping with my grandmothers to buy presents and wrap them. There were so many great things to eat and candy and pie, which my parents could certainly afford, but which I'd never get to eat that often, and there were cool old black and white movies and Christmas specials on TV that we'd all sit around together and watch and then that night..." she paused and took a breath, but then her eyes seemed to tear up and she stopped.

"What night?"

"Christmas Eve…" she said with a bright smile on her face.

God, she's beautiful, I thought.

"I don't think anything ever was more exciting than going to bed on Christmas Eve," she continued, "There's a great poem about the night before Christmas. It doesn't have anything to do with you, well, not directly, but in the morning we'd wake up and I'd run downstairs to the Christmas Tree."

"What's a Christmas Tree?" asked Jesus.

"It's a tree cut down and raised up in memory of Christ."

"Who?" asked Jesus.

"Christ."

"The Messiah?" he asked.

"Bingo!" said Sarah.

"You mean like from Isaiah?"

I guess Sarah didn't know the story all <u>that</u> well. Her face kind of went blank. I knew Isaiah was a prophet, but I couldn't help her out so all I could do was look at her.

"Do you even know what's going to happen to you?" Sarah asked. "Have you any idea what's going to happen when you reach your mid thirties?"

"What?"

"Do you know what's going to happen?"

"Well, I never much thought about it."

"Well, you better start. Don't you think?" Sarah looked at me for support, but I was looking around the room for my date and another of those delicious hot-dogs.

"I know I have to do something," said Jesus, "Something outrageous, something that's never been done before."

"That's it?" asked Sarah, her voice full of disappointment, "That's all you've got?"

"Since you're from the future and evidently know something that I don't, why don't you just tell me what it is that I have to do?"

"Yeah, just tell us!" I said through a big mouthful of buttered roll.

"He's here to save humanity!"

"Humanity?" I laughed.

"I mean in the future! In the future he's going to become really famous, I mean like one of the most famous people in all of history, and one day he'll have followers all over the earth."

"Even in Rome?" I asked.

"The Jews that follow you won't call even themselves Jews any longer. They'll sail all over the Mediterranean and call themselves Christians and even the Roman's will worship you!"

"The Roman's worship a Jew!?" I laughed, "That's crazy!"

"So, how do you know all of this, Sarah?"

"In the future it's common knowledge. It's part of history. Everyone knows it."

"And are you one of my followers?"

At this point I stopped munching on my roll and looked across the table at Sarah. This last question from Jesus seemed to have come to her like a shot.

"Sarah?" asked Jesus again. Evidently he expected an answer, but Sarah's face was getting beet red and she stared down at her place setting.

"I don't know what I believe, anymore, if I ever believed anything," she said, "I keep hoping that I'll wake up and find myself back out at the convenience store with Larry. Who am I kidding? I didn't even like Larry! Not that I wanted him dead or anything weird like that but, sometimes, I think I've lost my mind. None of this can be happening. None of this can be real. It's just too fantastic."

"But if it were real? Would you believe it then?"

"If it were real? That makes no sense."

"If it were real," repeated Jesus, "If you just pretended it was real, could you believe it then?"

"I don't know," said Sarah, "These creatures, these angels, they all seem to agree that Steve and I are dead inside. That's a terrible thing to say. How do they know? How do they know whether we're alive or dead inside? What does that even mean?"

Jesus shook his head, "I'm sure I don't know."

"But how are you ever going to get people to follow you if you don't know anything?"

"Tell me," said Jesus with a smile, "Do you believe in a creator?"

"Huh?"

"In God?"

"God?" she replied.

"Something greater than yourself?" said Jesus, "That always seems like a good place to start."

At that moment, one of Jerry's waiters arrived with a silver brocaded desert cart. My mouth watered as I surveyed the spread of cakes and ices and concoctions which I had never imagined. Meanwhile, Jesus passed up desert and waved the waiter on, but the angel waiter had fastened its attention of Sarah.

"Miss?" he asked, "Have you made a decision?"

Sarah looked up slowly at the waiter, "I'll have the pecan pie," she said slowly and glaring the whole time at Jesus.

I was helping myself to a couple of the deserts, so I didn't catch a lot of the conversation that continued sort of "hush, hush" between them. They talked a lot about God and this and that and stuff that seemed a little boring and really not all that important to me anyway, and I guess not that important to Sarah or a lot of other people from the future. After a while the waiter returned with our bill. I guess here is where Jerry's make believe world finally broke down. The waiter had left a little tray with some paper on it for Jesus. Jesus couldn't make any sense of it and passed it to me.

"That's the bill," said Sarah with a little pride in her voice. "We'll have to pay."

Instinctively, I reached for my money belt but remembered I didn't have any coins left in it, but just an old road map of a place I'd probably never visit.

"I don't think we have any money." I said, "Jesus?"

Jesus shook his head absently, but his attention had fastened on Sarah. She moved uncomfortably in her chair as she held the tiny tray with the bill. She reached up and adjusted the strap of her evening gown. Her hand was trembling and the plastic tray clattered on the table top.

"What is it? Is it a lot?" I asked, nervously.

"Do you know where we are?" Sarah asked of no one in particular.

"I think we established that we're on earth at the dawn of life," Jesus replied.

"No! I mean here! Here in this bogus restaurant. Do you have any idea what they've named it?"

I suppose that was the oversight, a little, almost inconsequential thing on the back of a stupid check. In keeping with the evening's artistic unity, Jerry would have named the restaurant in line with the five-star Manhattan hotel. Whatever angel, thinking itself clever, or privy to an inside joke, actually printed on the backs of the bills, the actual name of the supervisor's three-hundred mile, subterranean factory. Sarah dropped the check on the table and called out to a waiter in a loud voice to get his attention while I leaned over and grabbed the check that so troubled her.

"Madame?" asked the concerned attendant.

"This place, this restaurant. What's the name of it?"

"The name?"

She nodded her head and he said something or other. Then she shook her head and pointed at the printing on the bill.

"No, I mean there," she corrected, "The name printed there on our bill?"

"Why it says 'The Pandemonium Bar and Grill,'" he replied with a smile.

"Pandemonium." The word meant nothing to me; hell, I'd never heard of John Milton or Paradise Lost until my 17th Century British Lit. class in undergraduate school, but Sarah dumbly mouthed the words over and over as I handed the tray to the waiter, who actually turned out to be the maitre de. He assured us that we did not need to trouble ourselves about the meal as the entire evening was a gift of his supervisor and the Pandemonium Angels.

After the angel had disappeared back into the crowded restaurant, Sarah turned to Jesus.

"So, much for Santa's Workshop," she sighed.

It was just then that M-2500 came up in her high heels holding a large hot dog smothered in sauerkraut, onions and mustard. To tell you the truth, I had half forgotten that she was a robot angel and I'm sure I had forgotten what Sarah and Jesus were talking about.

I let my imagination run wild. I suppose it was the wine. Yep, it was the wine. Apparently, our robot angel handlers thought it time for us to move on, and I remember being out in front of the hotel throwing up my hot dogs, salmon, asparagus and everything else onto a fake street corner.

Jesus took Sarah to see "the Broadway Show." Let's face it. She was the real babe, and I suppose I was just some dork as far as she was concerned, hurling my guts out beside some fake New York City hot dog vendor with a fake hot Hollywood sex bomb and a bunch of robot angels. Yeah, Debbie and I (I called M-2500 in her sexy human form "Deborah") she and I found our way up the fake block to the fake Broadway Theater and the musical.

What I remember of it was all pretty spectacular. Jerry, who actually came out from behind the curtain to introduce the piece and dedicate the performance to Jesus and Sarah and Steve from the future, well, Jerry got misty eyed and choked up, and a search light wheeled through the auditorium and spotlighted Jesus and Sarah who stood to thunderous applause, and then me and Debbie, not where we were supposed to be, but way up in the balcony. I was actually in the process of trying to get my hands up under her dress, feeling her up, I admit, but I had vowed to go no further.

Well, the show started and we were in the dark for a while, and then I just had to get out of there entirely. I remember shouting at Debbie to leave me alone, even though I was the one who had been groping her, and I stormed out the back door of the balcony and staggered up some flights of stairs and trudged down a long hallway and through some doorways and past some robot angels of one kind or another and up some stairs and down a hall or two and then I stopped.

I was panting heavily and had a stitch in my side. I took a deep breath and started down a hallway to a tall narrow doorway. I opened the door and peered into another adjoining hall. This corridor was long and high ceilinged and illuminated with the same type of luminescent bands we had seen inside the cylinder on the summit of the black dune. Still, the lighting was low, green and cool blue and I walked briskly along the hall, looking left and right. I came to an open doorway, entered and stopped at a blank wall. I looked left and right, headed to the right and came into a large amphitheatre.

I slumped against the back wall and looked down the aisle to the main floor below where a beautiful man-shaped being sat on a high stool beside a podium and an operating gurney. Behind him, illuminated on a huge television screen struggled the biggest, blackest, ugliest looking fly I had ever seen. The voice of the beautiful being and the buzz of fly wings sounded over a concealed PA system. It seemed that everything on this world was recorded for posterity.

"The question before us," began the beautiful man-shaped being, "Is whether our specified improvements are best rendered through chemical or mechanical means."

He applied forceps and surgical tweezers to the tiny patient. The huge metal pincers wheeled into view on the gigantic television screen. The buzzing intensified and now the seated man began to laugh.

"Hang on there, little guy," he said and tore off a wing.

"Is that better?" he laughed.

"Hold still," shouted the surgeon as his tweezers closed on the remaining wing.

The sound of tearing muscle and chitin roared over the assembly room loudspeakers. The beautiful being leaned back and lifted a glittering syringe from the table beside him. He put a thumb to the plunger.

"Why wait three billion years?" he said and leaned forward, applying the needle. "We'll grow better wings, wings infinitely more powerful."

He sat back and stood and I finally had a good look at him. He was super human, nearly twenty feet tall, like the statute of David by that famous Italian artist from the future. Muscles rippled over his body as he walked from the operating station to a small panel.

"Report."

The beautiful being waited for a response.

"Report..." he repeated.

My eyes widened as I watched from my secret alcove, the visage of the Stronghold, XL-5000, whose image filled the screen. A quavering voice sounded from grooves in a panel beneath the screen and then boomed over the hidden public address system.

"Yes. Please forgive our delay."

"I thought perhaps you had forgotten me, tucked away in my study?"

"No, sir."

"I might as well ask for an explanation."

"The Ophanim..."

"Yes...?"

"They have sent information from the future..."

"I'm waiting to hear why I missed my daily report. And now I hear you go on and on about some business with the Thrones and information from the future...." The being's paternal, ironic tone of voice grew severe, "What 'information from the future?'"

"Three human beings washed up on the shore of the Black Dune Island."

"You've let human beings escape?"

"These creatures are not from the facility."

"What do you mean, 'not from the facility?'"

"Our human stock is accounted for. These three creatures are unlike any we have manufactured – they possess human souls!"

"Silence!" thundered the beautiful being with a volume that startled me. It looked up at the ceiling, at the operating gurney where

156

the fly writhed against restraining bands, and then, back at the view screen.

"Souls, you say?"

"The trio was first observed by an M-Class sentry. We thought its report erroneous."

"Erroneous? Is there such a word?"

"We are hearing rumors from workers on the floor. With human souls already in play, we suspect the First Sphere must have a hand in it somewhere. Naturally we assumed they had informed our supervisor."

The beautiful being cleared its throat, pulled off heavy green surgical gloves and lay them on a basin beside the operating gurney. I saw that the wingless fly had grown to the size of a dog. It had re-grown its wings and the image of its master reflected a thousand times in the iridescent lenses of its compound eyes.

"Daddy will tend to you soon," said the beautiful being who looked back with a scowl on his face at the image of the giant robot angel.

"Meet me at outside the main portal of the Eastern Wall at once."

"Yes, your Excellency," replied XL-5000.

The image on the view screen went dark and the supervisor strode up a short set of steps at the back of the hall and disappeared through a doorway.

10. On the Terrace

Stealthily I left my hiding place, skipped carefully down the amphitheater steps, skirted the yawning thing on the operating table and exited through the rear. I stood on an enormous covered porch and saw the beautiful being as it walked swiftly across the black stone floor of the patio onto a terrace, framed against what looked to be the night sky, although I knew it must be the enormous empty vault of the cavern.

The being climbed up on a low barrier of stone that ringed the edge of the terrace and raised its arms as an enormous pair of wings unfolded from its shoulders. For an instant, the creature paused on the precipice seventeen stories over the cavern floor. It seemed to look back at me and grin, and with that, leaned back and dropped down from sight.

I swallowed hard and raced across the flagstones to the stone parapet and peered over. Far below, where klieg lights wheeled in front of Sarah's fake Broadway Theater, several fake cars inched along the thoroughfare at the foot of the gigantic wall.

"Good Evening," thundered a gigantic voice as the creature on beating wings suddenly swept up before me.

I gasped and fell backwards, the wing beats sending wind and bits of dust stinging into my eyes. I squinted, shielding my face with a forearm as the creature returned to the terrace where it hung in the air above me.

"No need to hear rumors repeated by a Stronghold when I can meet one of my creations in the flesh," it said.

I could only manage to stammer, "Who... are... you?"

It laughed at this, whether at my question or the fear in my voice, but the incessant beating of the wings was un-nerving. I worried one of the blade-like appendages would strike me, and, as though in response to my secret thought, the creature reclined on an invisible cushion of air, and allowed a beating wing to strike the parapet. A shower of sparks flew up and a chunk of basalt, dislodged from the wall, bounced, and spiraled away.

"Heads up!" bellowed the creature to the phony city scene below.

Like an asteroid from outer space a two hundred pound boulder raced down and slammed into the roof of a New York City Cab. The android within exploded in a shower of sparks and blue flame.

"I bet old XL-5000 is down there right now, wondering what's keeping me?" said the creature, "Do you think? I said, 'do you think?'" it repeated.

Again, I didn't know what the creature wanted me to say. It began to glow. The skin, which was sort of a pale flesh tone seemed to pulse alabaster, and then, all of a sudden, like someone had turned on head lamps, I was knocked back by wind and a blinding light that exploded from the creature. I shielded my eyes and tried to catch a glimpse of the thing, but the light and wind were too intense and suddenly I wished Jesus was there beside me and not downstairs watching some Broadway Musical.

"Well, well, well…" said the being as it glided down to sit cross legged, European style, on the rock wall. Its wings vanished behind its back and it leaned down where I lay sprawled at its feet on the flagstones. It spoke in a tone that was suddenly familiar.

"I have to tell you that it's a little humbling, because, just between you and me, I really didn't notice you hiding in my operating theater a moment ago. I should point out that you're not what we had in mind. I mean, there's nothing inside you to trip the celestial radar, so to speak."

He paused and stretched his long muscled legs, "That is, you talk, and you have thoughts, and a soul, which is something, I suppose, although how you've come to it, your particular existence, is cause for concern. How may I put this, delicately? I've been blind-sided. It really is beginning to feel as though someone doubts my ability. Someone thinks I'm incapable of following though. Someone thinks I've nothing better to do than make appearances at Jerry's little worship services every Sunday morning when there's real work to be done. Have you any idea how many wasted Sundays can go by in five hundred million years?"

I looked up at the beautiful being, afraid to move, afraid to answer, afraid to say a word.

"I suppose there will be consequences," it said and shrugged its enormous shoulders; "I suppose someone will have to take the proverbial 'fall.'"

The creature was about to continue when it stopped and looked up, its eyes scanning the wide terrace and back to the covered portion of the patio.

"Hello? M-2500? Are you there?" He looked down at me and pointed at the temple of its skull, "You see? Radar."

At that moment my beautiful dreamboat in her red-dress and pearls and holding her red, high-heels, so as not to give up her location on the sounding stones, slipped from behind the portal and looked at us.

"They're in the last act, Steve. Jesus and Sarah are going out for drinks," she said in a spritely tone, as though the scene before her was absolutely common, "Care to join us?"

The being on the precipice chuckled. Next, it lowered its head and through its light brown hair the scalp glowed white hot and I gasped at the sight of a pattern, both foreign and horribly familiar. It raised its hand in the direction of my girlfriend, and a beam of light or some kind of energy but looking like a bolt of lightning, exploded from its finger tips, arced across the terrace and grabbed hold of Debbie. In lighting flashes, I saw her in the form of the Mechanical Man from the Black Dune, and then, like the skeleton of a human being, and all at once the light disappeared and the creature sitting in front of me smiled.

"I have learned exactly nothing by plumbing the memory of my lowly associate, M-2500. I won't even ask why our comrade is dressed like a woman. I suppose it has something to do with your obsessive desire to replicate yourselves. And Steve, if I may call you Steve, I sense that you're very concerned about this whole procreation business. Angels, for your information, are really neither male nor female. Sexuality is really pretty far down the scale of attributes in a sentient being, but I do understand your predicament. Without reproduction, all trace of you will disappear. With mortal death, your flimsy soul, weak and malformed as it is, will simply dissipate through the cosmos."

To illustrate, the creature raised its index finger. The tip burst into a flame, and leaving trails of smoke it traced the letters, S T E V E in the air. Even after the flame on the finger tip extinguished, the smoke hung there, floating slowly away, like a sign, drifting in the empty space between us.

"You will linger, no more than a puff of smoke, dwindling away, adrift for all eternity," it laughed, and putting its lips together, blew softly on the disintegrating letters until my name had disappeared and the air was clear.

The creature stood and stretched, "What concerns me is that your unfortunate condition may reflect poorly on the quality of our product. I hate to say it, but I suspect there is a faction among us who will hold such failure against me, their beloved supervisor. But let me tell you something, Mister," and it spun in its tracks, raised its arms and strode out across the terrace indicating the enormous benighted cavern, "The aim of my endeavor was to produce life, which, thank you all very much, I shall bring forth abundantly from the hidden places of this earth, and as its crowning achievement a new race of beings to befriend the Creator."

It spun around and spoke in a tone of resignation, "Evidently he has grown weary of his archangels. I don't know. He didn't consult me. One thing led to another, I suppose. Oh, well..."

The being paced a few steps back and forth, and for a moment I thought I felt sorry for that fly on the operating table having its wings pulled off it, and I had finally managed to pull myself to a seated position when the creature turned to Debbie.

"Come this way, M-2500," it ordered, "We must have an audience with the female from the future and her much heralded companion."

"And what of that monster in the other room?" asked Debbie.

"What monster?"

"That creature you have cobbled together!"

"Beelzebub?"

"You've named it?"

"You know M-2500, I believe I may have kept you up top on the ocean, for one too many millennia."

"That creature's genetic code was not in the plans sent us by the Ophanim."

"What I do in my spare time, is my own business! Is that clear?"

"You are infinitely more powerful than I, but we are both equal in the eyes of our Creator."

"The Creator? You've dare evoke the name of the Creator?" it laughed and glanced back and forth, mockingly, "I don't see him anywhere, do you?"

"How dare you say such a thing."

"How dare I? How dare I?"

"We are the agents of God!"

"Are we?"

"Have you forgotten our place?"

"I glean from your feeble mind that you encountered three humanoids adrift on some shielded aluminum skin at the foundation of the earth. And again, on the dry land test area above the Western Wall as they came out of the ocean. Why was I not informed at the time?"

"You _were_ informed!"

"I most certainly was not!"

"You did not answer."

"Irrelevant."

"A thousand angels called out to you, and you were silent!"

"Where is the memo?"

"Memo?" asked the humble angel, suddenly confused.

"You say I was informed? Show me the memo!"

"Memo? There is no memo!"

"Ah ha!" said the beautiful man. "Take us to the other human beings. XL-5000 and his Strongholds are of no use to us."

Debbie and I were talking about the strange fly creature we had seen in the amphitheatre and we followed the Supervisor down through a series of enormous hallways and stairwells evidently designed for beings over twenty feet tall. In stolen bits of conversation, she let me know this guy with the familiar tattoo had a whole bunch of weird experiments going on in back rooms of the Eastern Wall behind the Terrace.

"His research would be an offense to the Ophanim."

"Research? Is that what he calls it? It looks like a chamber of horrors!" I whispered.

"Oh, please, you two," said the being in an exaggerated voice, as he pushed through a massive bronze door ahead of us into the fake theater lobby, "It's all just a harmless bit of fun. I might even make some improvements. But see, here. L-1 and his little worship team have been up to their old shenanigans."

We stood in the lobby, just outside the doors of the auditorium. "Never say I'm not one to mingle with my subordinates," it said and its twenty foot tall body began to glow, the visible edges of its form, shimmering, and the beautiful man-shaped being slowly shrank in size and proportion to that of a profoundly fit man of thirty dressed in a black tuxedo.

We stepped into the back of the theater. The fake New York theater goers were gone, reorganized into M and L-Class worker angels or checked into the android rehab facility, five doors down for refurbishing. Even Jerry, his cast, crew and orchestra had departed. We saw Jesus and Sarah, beside one another, their backs to us, sitting and talking in the empty auditorium.

Suddenly, along the perimeter of the auditorium, heavy double doors slammed and locked shut in succession along the three walls of the auditorium facing the stage. Sarah and Jesus, wheeled toward one another, jumped from their seats and looked back over a dozen rows to the figure or our handsome host.

"Hey, Sarah, Jesus!" he called in a friendly voice that reverberated through the theater, "Look who I bumped into." He had taken hold of me, with Debbie on the other side and I'm sure that M-2500, under my girlfriend's skin somewhere, could feel the crushing power of those two arms thrown with such apparent affection over our shoulders.

"Give me an introduction," he whispered out of the corner of his grinning mouth.

"What's the name?" I asked, almost afraid at what I might hear. He answered in a hissing whisper that made me shudder, but I felt a sharp elbow in the ribs and like a parrot, under no power of my own, found myself calling out in a flat, otherworldly voice: "Ms. Sara Benton and Mr. Jesus of Nazareth, I'd like to introduce you to the…"

An up-tempo fanfare sounded over my intro on the house PA system. "…the being who needs no introduction, supreme ruler of the Powers in the Second Sphere, Heaven's Evening Star, The Prince of Air and Darkness, Supervisor of the Pandemonium Angels and our Creator's right hand man, the archangel, Lucifer."

There was thunderous applause. A spotlight pierced the dim hall, bathing the smiling archangel who waved for the benefit of some imaginary audience, because the applause was a taped applause, and aside from one lowly M-class angel and three frightened human beings from the future, the cavernous auditorium was empty.

We walked down the aisle and our host extended his human looking hand to Jesus.

"I don't believe I've had the pleasure. And you would be…?"

"Jesus," he said shaking the phony man's hand.

"Jesus? Okay, that's interesting."

"And you would be?"

"Her name is Sarah," said Jesus, but Sarah had stepped up and extended her hand, "I can speak for myself," she said, "The name is Sarah Benton."

Debbie and I held our collective breath as they met and shook hands.

"And Ms. Sarah Benton," the being smiled broadly, revealing two rows of sharp, white, perfectly formed teeth, "It is an honor to meet you. You represent something of a departure from the original plan. I say 'original.' There was going to be only the one, but the Creator must have seen something, and changed his mind. Hey, that's his prerogative. We certainly planned for contingencies every step of the way. I remember those long walks with him back on my blue sky island, where we talked it all out. We can put a billion females up top if he needs them. But maybe you could explain something, how this one…" and he reached back, without even looking, to indicate me, "You see, the human soul is like a battery. If your energy level drops below a certain point, you still have a battery but it doesn't do anyone much good. You can't really go anywhere or do anything. You're basically 'dead inside' like this one back here, which is troubling because you were all designed for fellowship with our mutual Creator. I understood, in the numerous memos I've received, and kept on file…" he continued, glancing at Debbie, "…that you were to represent some kind of improvement over us – which would be a remarkable accomplishment. The trouble is -- the trouble is -- I just don't see the improvement!"

He looked back and forth between Sarah and Jesus for some sign of acknowledgement.

"You're skeptical. Hey, you are looking at the original skeptic," he reached over and slapped Debbie hard, on her back, "Am I right? Aren't I the original skeptic?"

There was no answer and he pushed us both aside and stepped down the aisle closer to Jesus and Sarah.

"As a matter of fact, I'm not getting much out of this little lady either." And with that he turned from Sarah as though he had just been talking to a piece of furniture.

"You, on the other hand, and no offense, Sarah, but Jesus, I'm getting some vibrations from you, like you really have something going on, which is great, which is like the plan. But still, I keep getting the feeling that even you are missing something, as though, if I were to extend my hand just now..." he reached toward Jesus, "...and were to put my fingers around your throat and simply squeeze..."

His hand had wrapped around our friend's neck. Jesus reached up slowly and put his hand over the creature's wrist. They looked deeply into one another's eyes. The being smiled and nodded, withdrawing his hand.

"So, tell me, Jesus, in the future, are most of the people like you? Have things turned out the way we planned or not, because I'm kind of guessing right now, that they haven't. I mean just looking at the percentages here."

Jesus took a breath. He seemed to search for the right words, "It didn't turn out quite the way one would have liked."

"No?" said the handsome looking man.

"There may be a course correction down the line, but I believe that ultimately good shall triumph," said Jesus.

"Good?" asked the beautiful being.

"A concept from the future, a concept which has meaning only in relation to its opposite," Jesus replied.

"I haven't had the luxury of traveling into the future. Only the Creator and his 'inner circle' possess that technology, at present…"

"I can't help you," Jesus interrupted.

"No?"

"No."

"So, you just kind of showed up here? Just accidently dropped in from three and a half billion years in the future?"

"I guess so."

"Well, give me a couple billion years down here and I'll crack that nut too. You just watch."

"Time travel?"

"I'm one brilliant angel," he said with a smile.

"I'm sure you are."

The handsome man nodded. "Speaking of time travel, I scanned your little friend's memory upstairs and found nothing by way of explanation. But there was another, one whom you failed to mention. A being of some rather unique ability from the future. You did not mention him, Jesus. Why is that?"

"Who?"

"Someone you met on your travels through the wilderness?"

The two adversaries exchanged a long, silent look.

"Well, here," said the creature producing from his tuxedo vest pocket a business card with a black logo embossed on its surface. "If you ever run into him again, be sure to give him this."

Jesus took the card and looked at it, suspiciously.

"If he ever figures out how to travel through time..." the creature continued, "...perhaps he can get back to me. We'd make a great team."

Jesus let the card drop. It fluttered to the floor.

"Hey..." said the handsome being, who looked as though his feelings had been wounded. "That's a pretty rotten thing to do!" he said as he stooped down and retrieved his business card, but as he rose he moved even closer to Sarah.

"Have you anything to add?"

Sarah shook her head, and to tell the truth she looked scared to death. The handsome guy started to glow and through the hair on his head, we saw the black tattoo, the same symbol as the logo on the business card, the roiling pattern in intricate negative relief against the white light blazing from his skull. From his out stretched hand a beam of light leapt out and struck Sarah in the face. It threw her head back and lifted her an inch off the floor.

That's when Jesus stepped in. Oh brother, I tell you what! He'd really been holding out on us, because he stepped right into the light, so that Sarah suddenly relaxed and staggered back.

"I was getting around to you," called the spirit, his head still lowered as though he was now in a contest of wills.

An arc of energy crackled about both their heads and a wind was stirring in the empty theater. Debbie and I slipped past the creature in the aisle and with Sarah, made a break for the stage behind Jesus. We met close to the orchestra pit and looked back at the tableau of the two beings. Just when we thought the sound and pyrotechnics had reached their climax, there was a massive explosion midway in the power stream between Jesus and Lucifer. The archangel cried out in amazement with a shock it had not experienced in all of its existence. It was thrown back ten yards, tumbling, head over heels. Curls of smoke and steam wafted up from the skull and shoulders of the being on the floor.

"Never..." it said, sitting up on the carpet and running a hand through its smoldering hair. "I think perhaps that I am finally out of patience."

In the next few moments, all hell broke loose. He pointed a finger up above our heads and an explosion tore a hole in the ceiling and a mass of plaster, steel and stone crashed down. Debbie threw herself into Jesus, and amazingly, her outstretched palm diverted the plummeting debris.

"Take them to safety," Jesus shouted to Debbie as the masonry crumbled to the floor around them.

"What about you?" she shouted, grabbing Sarah and me by our collars like we were shopping bags at a department store.

Meanwhile, Lucifer leaned to his side, tore a row of four theater seats from its moorings and hurled it down the aisle. Jesus jumped out of the way and the seats tumbled toward Debbie, Sarah, and me. Debbie pushed us over the lip of the orchestra pit.

"Hang on," she cried.

"Hang on to what?" I shouted, falling over the edge, when, in the next instant, the hurtling theater seats tore through the orchestra pit guard rail, sailed over the pit and crashed onto the stage.

Jesus picked himself up from the floor between two rows of seats. He wiped a trickle of blood from his mouth, and smiled. From the orchestra pit, Sarah and I emerged from beneath a ruined banner of purple velour. Debbie had her arms around us. She held us suspended by the powerful wing beats of razor sharp wings which had sprouted beside the red shoulder straps of her evening gown.

"The canoe," called Jesus, "Meet me back at the canoe in exactly four hours,"

"Four hours," I thought, but the black sand island and the canoe were three hundred miles to the west. I clung tightly to Debbie's shoulder and had my arm crossed over Sarah's arms. She clung for dear life on the other side as we were carried up toward the proscenium arch. Another bank of seats flipped through the air and exploded beside Jesus as he rolled away and raced down the row to the far aisle way. Debbie tacked to the left dodging a blast of cold blue energy from Lucifer's open palm.

* * *

I tell you for a fact that Jesus was as surprised as I was by what happened next. It's funny, given his extraordinary background and his future role in human history that he should have been so much in the dark about stuff. He'd been totally blindsided about Lucifer. I guess they both had been. Lucifer was pretty pissed off by our surprise visit, but I got the idea he'd been pissed off by a lot of things. Then there was the business with his weird experiments and basically blowing off Jerry's Sunday worship services for a couple hundred million years and turning the angels' worship sanctuary into a chamber of horrors – well, that was a lot of Sundays. It was no wonder that the Ophanim had

172

dispatched a major posse from the First Sphere to bust his ass. His messing with Jesus was the last straw, but I suppose sometimes a guy, even the Lord of Evil, has to take a stand.

We didn't know any of this as we flew up through the curtains into the scene house. Crap was flying onto the stage from the auditorium where Lucifer was throwing furniture like an angry theater patron who had really hated the performance and didn't care whether he ever got his money back. We were already up in the catwalks. Deb had set Sarah and me down on a steel gantry, seventy feet over the stage floor and now she led us along through a side door into a narrow corridor. The hallway looked familiar and after a while we were back in the upper rooms of the Eastern Wall. Somehow, perhaps because she had already been there, earlier that evening Debbie led us to the amphitheatre.

"Come on," cried Debbie.

Debbie raced down the aisle to the operating station. The gurney was abandoned. The creature that had occupied it earlier in the evening had evidently freed itself. The thought of possibly running into it made be shudder. Sarah and I followed Debbie through the long low doorway at the back of the podium and out onto the broad terrace. We moved quickly across the black basalt flagstones to the parapet.

"End of the line," I said peering over the edge. "What are we doing back here, anyway?"

"This is where I have been instructed to wait."

"Instructed by whom?"

"The Ophanim."

"The Ophanim?"

"They have contacted all the S, M and L class angels in the facility and have advised us of the pending arrival of the Messengers."

"Messengers?" I repeated.

"Well, great. Let's roll out the red carpet," cried Sarah. "If they hurry they can get a ring side seat and watch us all get annihilated by that flying monster with the tattoo."

"Lucifer will not be pleased."

"No... He doesn't seem much pleased by anything today," Sarah replied.

At that instant there was an explosion from behind us at the entrance to the terrace. From the low doorway we saw a burning flash of light followed by the sight of Jesus running for his life across the basalt flagstones.

"Run!" shouted Jesus.

"Run where?" I cried as he joined us up against the parapet.

"There's no place to go," said Sarah.

A ball of blue flame rolled from the distant doorway and exploded in a shower of yellow sparks only ten yards from where we stood pressed up against the low wall on the precipice.

"Well, we can't stay here." cried Jesus as another explosion rocked the night and Lucifer emerged from the doorway.

"And just where do you think you're going?" he snarled, and he bent low in an apparent spasm of pain, writhed to his left and re-emerged at his full twenty-foot height.

Without a word, Jesus pushed Sarah and me toward Debbie,

"I thought I told you to get them to safety?"

I saw Debbie take off her string of pearls from around her neck and lay them carefully on the ledge of the guardrail. In the next instant her feminine arms had changed into the thousand jointed tentacles of M-2500 and the three of us were airborne, leaving Jesus in the distance. The terrace seemed to fall away, dwindling to a narrow cleft in the enormous facade of the black Eastern Wall.

Deborah's warm, fleshy arms had turned into cold metal tentacles, but the loops and coils were infinitely better suited to the transport of her human cargo. Sarah and I clung to our M-Class angel as the being's powerful wing beats took us west, further and further from our friend whose troubles were only now just beginning.

* * *

It's probably a good thing we weren't around for what happened next. It is unlikely we would have survived. It's a wonder that Jesus did. He was just asking for trouble up there on that patio with the freaking ruler of the world. On the other hand it may have been a good thing that we traveled back in time and found ourselves in Santa's Workshop. It gave Jesus a chance to look at Lucifer in a new light. He had read of the archangels in what later came to be known as "The Old Testament," so he knew the guy could be a creep, and a party crasher, and sort of a Gloomy Gus, but until our little trip, he had never imagined.

M-2500, Sarah and I were in mid-air, no more than a mile from the black faced Eastern Wall, which basically filled the entire view over our shoulders. We were flying a hundred feet over the concourse when the entire underground cavern became to tremble.

"Don't let it worry you," cried M-2500 against the wind in our faces and the fury of his wing beats, "The Ophanim have visited in the past. The cavern was built to survive such a shock, but you should not look directly into the vortex. The seeing crystals I left behind will document the event. Here," she continued, and in amazement Sarah and I, both clinging to the triangular torso of M-2500, watched a small slot open in its chest and a circular panel slide out. It looked like a rearview mirror on a metal stalk. We stared into a tiny view screen and gasped with horror as we witnessed the events unfolding, further and further away, back on the terrace.

When Jesus saw Sarah and I were safely in the grip of Debbie, he looked back in time to see Lucifer come up fast from the dark recess of the patio. This outdoor terrace extended out from the Eastern Wall by as much as fifty yards along the 17th floor so that when Lucifer cleared the obstruction above, he was able to raise himself to full height. At once he let loose a blast of cold blue flame at Jesus. For a man, Jesus was probably the greatest natural athlete to have ever lived. Even in a tuxedo and black dress shoes he was able to move with near super human speed and avoid the shattering bolt of energy. Ultimately, of course, Jesus the man would prove no match for the archangel. The bolts flew fast and furious, and Jesus was finding less and less room to navigate. He came at last to the edge of the terrace and climbed up on the parapet searching in the dim light for some means of escape as Lucifer drew near.

M-2500's string of pearl lenses on the parapet tracked the combatants and zoomed in to the distorted expression of rage on the face of the giant angel.

"Well, then," he thundered. "Come to the end of the line, have we?"

"Perhaps not," said Jesus, defiantly.

"No?" laughed the other and looked back over his shoulder in the direction of the doorway. He made some sign, and the crystal pearl lenses tracked another figure, obscene and horrific as it emerged from the dark recess of the patio. It shambled along on segmented legs, lurching one side to another. We heard a buzzing sound from the view screen speakers as the creature tested damp and oozing wings on the dark air. It was airborne and dropped down, and scrambled forward, and took to the air again and soon it had come close to its master.

"Jesus of Nazareth," boomed the giant angel, "I give you, Beelzebub!"

"What foul science have you practiced here?" Jesus replied.

"None fouler than was taught us by our father!"

The creature had come to rest only ten feet from Jesus, and stood, looking at our friend through the iridescent lenses of its enormous, spiny head. Oozing mouthparts worked to fashion audible speech as this amalgam of insect, man, and super-human spirit came close to Jesus.

"Good evening, Jesus," it chortled. And its rotten breath was close and Jesus back pedaled on the brink of the precipice.

"Well, then, Jesus. Whatever will you do?" asked the archangel.

"There will be a reckoning for this, Lucifer."

"Will there, be?"

With that the giant angel dropped to one knee and with an enormous arm carefully, almost tenderly moved the insect monstrosity to one side and brought his face down level with Jesus.

"Now tell me, once and for all. Who are you, and why have you come?"

"I am not absolutely certain, but I believe..." and here Jesus took a step forward so that his face was almost pressing against Lucifer's, "I believe I may be the Son of God."

"Yes, well then aren't we all."

"No, I mean the actual, one and only son."

"The son?"

"That's me."

"Impossible."

"No, really, listen..."

"You listen!" Lucifer roared, and the sound waves were so great that Jesus stumbled back and lost his balance on the precipice and fell. The shock waves rebounded to the string of pearls and sent them sliding to the terrace floor.

Our view wheeled wildly on the tiny view screen.

"What's happening up there?" cried M-2500 who continued to fly west, but who looked down at us in terror.

"Has he fallen? Did Jesus fall?" he asked.

The tumbling images on the screen came to a halt and resolved into a picture of the giant and the insect monster leaning over the parapet.

Jesus held onto the ledge with his arms. His torso and legs dangled over the edge into the abyss.

"The son of God, you say?" laughed Lucifer.

"Yes, it is a definite possibility," said Jesus looking up as the giant walked up and sat beside him on the guard wall as one might sit at a park bench. The insect monster, shambled up and sat, as best it could, on the opposite side. The forearms and head of Jesus were still visible between them.

"Very well, then Jesus, if you are indeed the son of God then surely..."

"No," said Jesus, "Let me add something to that list... There's more..."

"More?" said Lucifer.

"I don't mean to sound prideful, but I've been thinking a lot about this and I've coming to the conclusion that I just may be..."

Lucifer seemed confused as he looked across the makeshift stone bench at his monstrous lieutenant.

The fly creature rasped, "What does he mean?"

"Well," said Jesus, "I think, yes... Let me amend that. Yes. I believe I am the Creator himself."

Lucifer and the insect-man looked down at Jesus who was struggling to keep himself from losing his grip on the wall and falling to his death. Lucifer laughed a short burst and the fly-like monster gave what approximated a laugh and quickly, almost reflexively, brought up its front legs and rubbed them together prayer-like over its head and eyes. Now, Lucifer was really laughing.

"The Creator himself!" he laughed. "The Creator? Oh, yes. Of, course, what other explanation could their possibly be?" He stood and wheeled angrily, "Son of the Creator, or the Creator himself, or whatever or whoever you really are: your existence is an affront and a mockery, more so than this little beast's could ever be. I, Lucifer, have created a race of immortal beings to populate the planet. Well then, All father, save yourself!"

"What's he doing?" shouted M-2500.

"I'm not sure," cried Sarah, "We should go back. Steve, we should go back!"

Dumbly, I could only rivet my attention to the screen and do my best to listen to the amplified voices against the wind as we continued West despite Sarah's protests.

"If you are as you say, then cast yourself down. Surely the Creator has given his angels charge of you. On their hands they will bear you up lest your foot strike against a stone."

"You will not tempt..." Jesus gasped, pulling himself up onto the ledge, "You will not tempt the Lord your God."

"No?"

Lucifer motioned the fly creature toward Jesus, but Jesus rolled to his left, and swinging a leg over the wall, sprung back onto the terrace as the monster lunged. Jesus side-stepped and brought his fist down on the creature's back so that it tumbled headlong over the edge.

"No!" cried Lucifer peering over the wall, and in that moment, Jesus dashed toward the covered patio of the terrace. But now a smile was on Lucifer's lips.

Just as it was about to smash into the pavement far below, the insect creature gained control of its new wings and with renewed, buzzing vengeance, soared back up the side of the great wall towards its master. The monster reappeared above the parapet to Lucifer's delight and they both returned their attention to Jesus.

No sooner had they moved in his direction than the entire cavern shook with a deafening roar. Jesus picked himself off the black flagstones. He looked back. Even Lucifer had been thrown down by the tremor and he rolled to his side on the pavement. The fly creature had been similarly tossed to the terrace floor. It flopped about and looked back with Lucifer in the direction from which the sound had traveled.

We were looking too, and not at the tiny view screen, but back the ten miles we had flown. We stared at an enormous glowing orb which suddenly appeared like a miniature sun suspended three hundred feet above the cavern floor. From every nook and cranny, every apartment portal, doorway, workroom, laboratory, pen and cell, all eyes lifted up at the light. A sphere of beryl colored metal a hundred feet in diameter and spinning madly in the vortex appeared, resolving itself from the glowing, flashing globe of light. The darkness in the cavern was gone for miles in every direction. The whirling thing slowed so that one saw not a single, solid sphere, but two concentric wheels spinning one within the other in opposite directions. As the gigantic wheels took up a slow, rhythmic spinning, there appeared, affixed to the perimeters of the wheels, a thousand crystal lenses, each flashing with blinding intelligence.

"The Ophanim," quaked M-2500 and our forward progress came suddenly to a halt.

We were losing altitude, as though somehow, in response to the appearance of the otherworldly wheels in the fake night sky, this angel had no choice but to park it and bow down.

Down at ground level in the vicinity of the fake Broadway, the three XL class Strongholds were reconsidering their options. They were under strict orders from The Prince of Air and Darkness to await his arrival at the main portal on the Eastern Wall. They had been waiting nearly a half an hour, and if they had been overly concerned about their superior's delay, the conflagration erupting above their heads and slightly to the West now totally consumed their attention.

Likewise, our reliable angel had brought us to a landing on the shoulder of the cavern's great, central thoroughfare. As the enormous orb pulsed in the expanse above, all the angelic conveyances had come to a halt. Thousands of angels, Small, Medium and Large had landed or stopped in their tracks to look up in awe as the whirling wheels slowed their steady pulse. The cavern shivered with a shower of crystalline sparks and a figure emerged mid air from the sphere of light, and now other angelic beings, clad in armor, winged, and of a stature three times the height of normal men. The celestial beings glided down, effortlessly from the point of light where they had entered our dimension. They drifted east and disappeared into the stone cleft some seventeen stories above the streets in the side of the Eastern Wall.

Sarah and I stood spellbound, but our attentiveness was nothing compared to that of our companion. M-2500 had come unhinged and just stood, stock-still, watching, vibrating slightly and a low whirring voice emanated from its casings.

"Raphael. Uriel. Gabriel. Michael..." it droned.

"Those are angels. Angel names," I said excitedly.

"Archangels?" said Sarah.

The lights on M-2500's array blinked in affirmation.

"Here," said Sarah, turning around in front of M-2500 and grabbing the view screen. It swiveled out from the angel's chest and we watched the images tell their story across the small crystal screen as four enormous forms sailed down from the heights and touched lightly down on the black flagstone pavestones of the terrace.

Lucifer was all smiles.

"Greetings, comrades. You travel with a member of the Ophanim so I understand this an official visit?"

Floating there, high above the ground, but now less than a hundred yards from the terrace, the whirling concentric wheels slowed even further. One of the two wheels had stopped entirely and its thousand crystal eyes riveted on the person of Lucifer.

"Hello, up there," waved Lucifer in his most charming voice. He bowed courteously to the four heavily armed messengers who stood ranged before him.

"Where is the human?" barked the spirit called Uriel, who looked, for all the world, like an Amazon princess clad in golden armor.

"Human?"

"Where is he?"

"I'm not expecting any additional humans here for another three point eight billion years, so I think you've come early. I hope you don't mean the little pre-human colony out on the lot?"

The archangel named Michael stepped forward, "You know who we are talking about and why we have come."

"I most certainly do not," replied Lucifer.

"There were three visitors from the future. One in particular whom you have detained."

At that instant from the terrace doorway Jesus tumbled head over heels into view pursued by the giant fly creature. I guess that was the last thing Lucifer needed. Hell, it just hadn't been his day. The archangels stepped back, freaked out by the sight, as the fly man pounced on Jesus. It had pinned our friend on his back to the pavement and was atop him, trying to piece him with a lance-like mouthpart that protruded from its hideous head. Jesus squirmed, turning his head side to side, dodging the errant death jabs. The creature's dripping stylus sent up sparks from the stone.

"Call it off," cried Uriel.

"Call what off?"

"That monstrosity," shouted Uriel, "Call it off. We know you are its master!"

The archangel, Uriel, strode across the flagstones, grabbed the fly creature by the back of its neck and yanked it off Jesus. The being hoisted the wriggling monster up into the air like a rag doll and shook it in the direction of Lucifer, "This apparition!"

Uriel tossed the fly creature, no bigger in size to her than a dog is to man, onto the pavement where it tumbled end over end and landed in a shuddering heap beside the precipice wall not far from Jesus who had slowly pulled himself to a seated position on the flagstones.

"Have a care," warned Lucifer stepping toward Uriel, "Do not threaten me on this world."

"This is NOT your world," replied Uriel.

"It is mine! I am subject to no one here!"

"Blasphemy!"

"You have no authority here," Lucifer shouted.

"I speak not by my own authority."

And here is where the angel in the golden armor, tipped her head back in the direction of the glowing wheels. Lucifer, followed the gaze, lifting his head and addressed the thousand eyed apparition.

"I am Lord of this world," he said.

It seemed to take the Ophanim a second to digest this statement. And for an instant, in what Sarah and I could detect from M-2500's feeble view screen, a thousand eyes seemed to blink.

Haggard, Jesus climbed to his feet slowly, resolutely toward the two archangels. He seemed no more than a child standing before giants.

"Lucifer!" cried Jesus. "You are at the crossroads!"

The beautiful angel looked down from the witness of the glowing wheel and regarded the feeble being of flesh and blood at its feet. He looked across the terrace at his shuddering creation, the fly man who had regained consciousness and who looked back with its own thousand lensed eyes, recording the moment.

Lucifer began to tremble, and a deep, guttural cry started up in him as he glared down into the face of Jesus. He raised his fist and brought it down to obliterate the man. The blow never landed. A stream of energy poured from the crystal lenses of the Ophanim and fastened on Lucifer's forearm as it descended. Lucifer let loose a bellow of frustrated rage, so intense that it knocked Jesus and the archangel, Uriel to the pavement.

It was a mighty struggle. Actually, it looked like an arm wrestling completion. As Lucifer opposed the beam, the Ophanim began to diminish in size. The flashing wheels began to move steadily closer to the terrace. Smaller and smaller, closer and closer they descended toward its combatant. In the space of ten seconds, the wheeling orb, which had been roughly a hundred feet in diameter, had diminished to the size of a bowling ball. Its power beam still held Lucifer's arm in its grip as it glided down to the terrace, and when the wheels had come within striking distance of the archangel's free hand, Lucifer swatted at them.

But now a second beam burst from the second concentric wheel and fastened its hold on Lucifer's left forearm. Lucifer wailed in an agony of frustration, shaking back and forth to free himself, as the orb shrank still further, now no larger than a baseball, and Lucifer's wrists were both held in its blinding grip. The archangel's fingers worked liked those of a mad man trying only to grasp what hung directly before him, to grip and choke the life from the glowing, revolving bands.

The cavern rocked with the struggle. We looked up from the view screen, back east. The terrace appeared as a band of blazing light etched in the cleft of the cavern wall. Lucifer dropped to one knee with a crash and then to the other. Jesus and Uriel had come to their feet and watched with amazement as the glowing orb shrank still further. It was no bigger than a marble, whirling an arm's length from Lucifer's bowed head.

The light in the wheels flared out. Lucifer's arms dropped to his sides. The Ophanim had been reduced to the size of a bauble of light grey metal, smaller than a child's toy gyroscope, miraculously suspended, spinning inches from Lucifer's sullen face. Lucifer groaned and with what seemed his last remaining iota of strength lifted his heavy right hand and batted at the tiny whirling wheels. He hit the tiny object and knocked it down. It bounced on the pavement, skittered across the pavement and came to rest at Jesus' feet.

We held our breath. Uriel and Jesus exchanged a long look. Jesus reached down and picked up the tiny object. The tiny concentric wheels had frozen, the tiny eyes closed. Slowly, carefully Jesus held the object in his palm. His fingers closed over it. He shook his head sadly, closed his eyes and looked skyward, beyond the cavern's fake sky, and the tons of earth above and beyond the earth.

The horribly deformed fly creature had crept on its spiny legs to the spot where its master knelt, head downcast. It raised a thorny, clawed appendage toward its master's lowered brow, for Lucifer's stature had been diminished in the apparent contest and he was now no larger than a man himself.

"Is he dead?" I whispered.

"Quiet," said Sarah.

We saw that Jesus was walking. His figure seemed to grow larger and larger and fill the view screen so that we suddenly realized he had crossed the terrace to the point where M-2500's strand of pearls had slid off the parapet onto the terrace pavement.

Before the screen went dark, we caught only one last view of the scene transpiring far above and away. It was the terrifying visage of Satan's first lieutenant, bent back horribly from the drooping head of its master.

It called past the silent form of Uriel to Jesus, "You will pay for this Jesus of Nazareth," croaked the monster. "You will pay."

Sarah and I looked at one another and back at the view screen. We caught only one last image before the transmission ended. The hand of Jesus came down over the crystal viewing pearls. The image tumbled as he gathered up the strand and we saw his face one last time.

"Sarah. Steve" he said, "If you are watching. If you can hear me, run. Run for your lives!"

11. Escape

Back at street level, things got ugly really fast. One of the hover platforms careened off the side of the road not more than a hundred feet from where he stood. It exploded in a fireball up against the side of one of the gigantic dynamos. A group of angels, who one minute had been silently staring up at the confrontation on the terrace of the Eastern Wall along with the rest of us, started quarreling and throwing punches at one another. I heard Sarah scream, and the next instant felt her slam into me, pushing me out of the way as two angels, tentacles flailing, spiraled out of the sky, locked in a death struggle. M-2500 helped us to our feet and we ran toward the shelter of a portico that extended for a mile along the side of the road. Debris rained down from the cavern roof and the peaceful commerce of the underground laboratory erupted into violence. Everywhere in the sky, groups and pairs of flying angels suddenly turned on one another in a horrible ballet of aerial dogfights. As we passed a compound where prototypes of the creatures destined for the Cenozoic era were housed, we saw a tiny angel on a flying machine speed past, knocking open the padlocked doors with a metal pipe. Wild eyed monsters sprang into the street. Further along the portico a Stronghold of the XL Class stumbled from a portal covered with four smaller S-Class angels smashing its crystals arrays with chunks of basalt.

"We've got to get out of here!" cried Sarah.

"You're telling me!" I shouted as I dodged the talons of a flying pterodactyl unleashed from the wire mesh enclosure of a smashed aviary.

"Run!" she cried.

I did my best to navigate the ruined walkway as a fissure unzipped a zigzag gash across the concourse. The columns and roof of the porch collapsed. I back-pedaled in horror at the sight of a steaming crevice that opened in my path. An orange glow welled-up through a half dozen sub-basements.

"Jump!" Sarah screamed on the opposite side of the jagged crevice, which was widening and creeping rapidly up the side of a nearby dynamo. There was an explosion in the bowels of the cavern beneath and a scalding blast of steam and smoke erupted between us. I lost my footing and was falling forward when I felt a metal tentacle coil about my waste and pull me across the abyss. M-2500 had us both in its grip as its wings engaged the dusty, choking air and carried us aloft. These scenes repeated themselves with horrible variation over the next two hundred and fifty miles of our desperate journey west.

As we neared the elevator shaft that would lead us back to the surface, we were horror struck by the sight of the aquariums bursting and primitive oceans of sea life tumbling into the submerged concourse. Giant squids mixed in the turbid depths with giant fanged reptiles and everywhere angels of every size and shape fought one another for dominion: pounding, blasting, beating one another beyond the point of madness.

As the Western Wall came into view, a five mile section of catwalk from the cavern ceiling let loose in an ear splitting scream of rending, twisting metal and rasping stone. Shock waves tossed M-2500 off course a dozen times in that last hour as we finally neared the elevator. We looked back into the bogus sky to see Ophanim orbs blossom like miniature suns at intervals along the skyway: three, four, five and perhaps a dozen more as far back to the east as we could see along the ruined concourse. As the whirling wheels resolved from blinding luminescence, we saw legions of angels tumble forth from distant dimensions already locked in combat across time and space and joining the battle in the three hundred mile trench below the surface of the planet.

Sarah and I babbled incoherently as our angel guide tapped out the code on the elevator control panel. Choking, spitting and weeping, Sarah and I collapsed into the cylindrical car and watched the door close on the scene of chaos, rebellion and war. There was a spasm in the elevator shaft and for an instant we watched M-2500 enter a code on the interior control panel. There was another, even more violent tremor and Sarah and I flew up and smashed back down on the hard floor. The luminescent bands of the interior lights, flickered, went dark and then returned dimly, and I sank down to my knees and closed my eyes and waited as I felt the car stir with life and surge upward.

We came to the surface of the earth only moments later and found ourselves again on top of the black dune island, exactly as we had left it. We scrambled out of the cylindrical elevator car and looked back at M-2500. It stepped out of the car, tapped a code on the console, gathered us in its tentacles, and ushered us down the slope as the door slid shut and the car slowly slid back down into the sand.

We quickly recalled Jesus' last words and waited not a second longer to pitch ourselves headlong down the great black dune toward the shore. Leaping ten yards at a gallop and tumbling head over heels we flew down the mountain toward the white line of surf below. The glint of sunrise on a cloudless morning reflected off the aluminum skin of the canoe. It had not moved an inch from where Jesus and I had left it two days before.

We were in the surf with the canoe between us, Sarah and me, pushing out into knee deep water with our faithful friend, M-2500, in the bow scanning the sand mountain of the black island. The angel began waving its tentacles excitedly. Seeming no larger than a thumbnail held up against the blazing blue sky, the silver elevator car had re-emerged on the summit. A mixture of tears and sea salt stung our eyes and lips as a lone figure dressed in black vaulted from the car followed by a plume of smoke that drifted skyward. Like a raindrop on a window tracing an erratic path to the sill, the lone figure descended the face of the enormous dune. It was Jesus, and if we had leapt ten yards at a bound, he covered twenty.

The sea bed trembled beneath us. An explosion of smoke and fire and house-sized boulders erupted from the throat of the elevator shaft. The island shook violently. Sarah was thrown backwards into the surf. M-2500 slammed forward, face down, capsizing the canoe. I watched in horror as white steam and molten bombs exploded on the beach and in the low sonorous waves about us.

With every ounce of strength we fought to regain control of the canoe, flipping it upright in the waves and we waited in a rain of ash and hot stones raining from the sky, as Jesus bounded down the last fifty yards of dune to the beach and dashed out into the surf.

"Go! Go! Go!" he cried, and Sarah, back at the side of the canoe, pulled herself aboard. I piled in and reached over the side for Jesus' outstretched hand. He grabbed hold and Sarah took hold of his shoulder and we pulled him in and he smiled and immediately looked up at M-2500.

"Can you get us out of here in the next thirty seconds?" asked Jesus.

"Yes," said the machine man clamoring into the canoe and swiveling back in the stern so that it faced the shaking island. A light began to glow in its chest and then, suddenly, a blast of cold blue energy streamed out, peeling the water back to the wet sand. The bow of the canoe shot up almost vertically and we hung on as the craft rocketed forward at a hundred and fifty miles an hour toward the open ocean.

Jesus had not exaggerated. Even when the sight of the island had receded from view and Sarah and I found we had been holding our breaths and started to breathe again, Jesus remained intent on M-2500's efforts. Jesus was counting the seconds and did not break his concentration or his countdown: "Five, four, three, two, one…"

The black island disappeared in a cataclysm of light. The shock wave reached us an instant later, but like harmless mist, the ash, rock and scalding hot steam streamed over us as an invisible pocket of other worldly force enveloped our fragile craft. It was the same protective power which had shielded us in the white water canyon and cradled us in our four billion year journey back to the dawn of creation on earth.

Our aluminum craft slipped through the remains of the black island like an unerring knife. And now the pace of our apparent headlong motion slowed to a calm, steady swaying.

"Hold on, M-2500," shouted Jesus.

The rest of us knew the drill and braced ourselves as we watched the clean, white mist stream past.

BUMP. The craft flew up and rebounded, and we each looked to the other and smiled.

We traveled this way for some time. I dozed off and when I awoke, our craft was illuminated only by the dancing lights from M-2500's array. In the dimness I half listened to Jesus, Sarah and the angel speak in low whispers, apparently in consideration so as not to wake me. I smiled to myself, comforted by the low voices of my friends, and the slow steady rocking of the canoe. I scratched an itch on the back of my right hand, rolled to my side and slept deeply.

12. Red Clay

When I awoke, three point eight billion years had slipped by. Life had grown up out of the oceans, ventured onto land and taken to the skies, just as the angels had planned. The dense mist peeled off our craft and we found ourselves on a big, lazy river. The water was green and slow and wide and we were way out in the middle. On either hand the distant shores were lined with dense green jungle. Far behind us and beyond a bend in the river, blue and mighty in the distance, a white capped mountain range rose into the sky. I supposed the protective envelope of force that shielded us during our miraculous journey had slipped away because we could feel a light breeze blowing in the direction of the current. Jesus was in the bow of the boat scanning the horizon. I half expected him to turn and wish me "good morning," or "how did you sleep?" but he turned instead, and looking beyond me and the still sleeping form of Sarah, addressed M-2500 in the stern.

"We're headed the wrong direction."

Without a word, M-2500 extended two of its tentacles to a length of ten feet from its torso. They curved back behind the canoe. The last four feet of the left handed appendage flared out like a paddle and dipped down into the water behind us. The tailing four foot section of the right hand tentacle suddenly bent at a right angle from the main stalk and began to whirl like a propeller. M-2500 set this spinning fan blade into the water and suddenly the craft shot forward and our vessel soon approached a speed of twenty miles an hour. Steering with the rudder of its left tentacle, M-2500 brought the craft in a long sweeping arc in the middle of the river, so that we were pointed against the current, heading upstream in the direction of the mountains and a rising sun.

"What's going on?" asked Sarah, sitting up beside me in the mid-section of the canoe and rubbing the sleep from her eyes.

"Good morning, Sarah," I said, cheerfully, hoping, through three simple words, as best I could to convey my concern and genuine affection for her.

"Good morning, Steve," she replied and leaned back toward M-2500. "Where are we? Where are we going now?"

"<u>When</u> are we…?" replied the angel, "Might be the more essential question."

Jesus turned in the bow of the boat. He had taken off his black tuxedo jacket, rolled up the sleeves of his dress shirt, unbuttoned the top two buttons and untied his bow tie. The ends flapped in the breeze as he spoke. His long hair was blowing back in his face and catching here and there on the stubble coming in on his chin. He took a hand and pulled back the lock and shook his head. He leaned forward and the sun, breaking over the distant mountains gleamed in his hair like a halo. I shrugged my shoulders, looked over the gunnels and watched the distant river bank speed past. We headed east into the dawn until the sun was bright and high in the sky above us. The broad, placid river brought its own relief from the tumultuous events of the past few days.

Not long into our voyage we went ashore on a low, wooded island no more than a fifty yards from shore. Here the island formed a small inlet where the water was shallow and clear so that the sandy bottom glimmered with undulating wave patterns. We had pulled up to the sandy beach to relieve ourselves, and we each headed off in a different direction, leaving M-2500 to tend to our miraculous aluminum craft. The angel's bodily functions remained a mystery. I wondered what joy it might derive from an existence requiring neither food or drink nor the sun's warmth, or even the cool clear air to breathe. I found a secluded spot and gratefully emptied bowels and bladder in the shade of a low boulder and stood. Fastening my trousers, I headed back in the direction of the beach. It crossed my mind as I came from behind a screen of bushes that my body was exceedingly dirty. The grim and dust hung heavy in my matted hair and beard.

The thought of taking a bath evidently had been on Sarah's mind. When I returned to the inlet where M-2500 waited with the canoe, I caught sight of Sarah up to her waist at the far end of the lagoon. I saw now her tattered blue evening gown and white under garments draped across the over turned bow of the canoe.

She was twenty feet out in the water and crouched in the shallows at the end of the island. The thought that she was entirely nude made me jump and I glanced back in the direction I had come and nearly stumbled. When I decided to continue to the canoe, I couldn't believe my eyes when, stealing a second glace in Sarah's direction, I saw Jesus even further out in the lagoon floating languidly on his back. As I arrived at the stern of the canoe and hunkered down beside M-2500 I flushed with embarrassment when I noticed the black trousers, suit jacket, white shirt and under garments spread out over the hull.

"Well, what do you think about that?" I asked.

"About what?" asked M-2500.

"Them!" I replied.

"I believe they are bathing."

"Oh, is that what they're doing?"

"I believe so," continued the angel, "We had predicted the life process would lead to an accumulation of unwanted by-products. The sloughing off of dead skin cells, the build-up of natural oils, perspiration. Much as they evacuate digested food matter and liquid, they bathe because it is necessary."

"They could do without."

"I imagine so, but would that be wise?"

"Just look. They seem to be having an awfully good time!"

"A good time?"

"Yes!" I said.

"What else could it be?"

"Where I come from, men and women just don't do that sort of thing."

"Bathe?"

I thought we'd been over this before. "We bathe, but not together," I said, "Well, maybe they do in Rome, but not where we come from."

"Rome? What is Rome?"

Oh, this was not at all what I wanted to be talking about, and I caught sight of Sarah's naked shoulders out there across the shimmering water and I went all hollow inside. I saw Jesus out there laughing about something or other she had said and I picked up a rock. For some reason I was mad at him for being out there and I threw the rock toward the shoreline on the other side of the channel.

"It's a city," I said.

"Where men and women bathe together?"

"I don't know, Debbie," I said, shaking my head. "For an angel, you sure seem to be..."

"To be what?"

"In the dark about things."

"Things? What sort of things?"

"The way of the world."

"By that, do you mean the existence of evil?

"Whoa," I thought. Where did that come from? I looked over at the robot angel and half expected it to be staring at me with the weird mosaic light show that was its apparent face, but it had not moved.

"Evil?" I said, and my hand went out among the stones. I felt for a flat one to skim, "Yeah. That's exactly what I mean: evil."

I side-armed the flat rock out beyond the inlet. It took two skips in the direction of the shoreline, cleared the lagoon, and disappeared into the river channel.

"It is a new idea to me, but I sense its presence."

That got my attention. "You do?"

Colors scattered across the crystal array and flashed. I took that as a "Yes."

"Ah ha!" I said, triumphantly. "It's the two of them out there swimming in the same water without any clothes! I knew it!"

"No, my friend," said the angel, "Not here, but ahead, beyond those low hills. Beyond the bend in the river."

"Evil? Up there?" I felt a breeze stir the low bushes on this sand bar and my hand clutched another small stone.

"It is a terrible word, is it not?"

"Oh, yeah." I said.

"I have been praying on it since we left the black island."

"Praying?"

"Yes," the angel replied.

"You pray?"

"Do not all sentient beings?"

I looked down at the rock in my hand. I'd been clutching it so hard, my hand had cramped.

"Oh, sure. Pray. Everyone prays. Every once in a while. You have to."

"And to whom do you pray?" asked M-2500.

At that moment Jesus swam up where the stern of the canoe trailed into the lagoon.

"You ought to come out for a swim," he called to me, cheerfully. He came up behind the canoe and grabbed his boxer shorts. The

Ophanim had omitted nothing in their account of 21st Century eveningwear. He pulled on his shorts and trousers.

"What's wrong, Steve?" said Jesus, grabbing his dress shirt.

"Oh nothing," I said, "We were just talking."

"About what?"

"Are we camping out here, or what?"

Now Sarah came up. She was on her belly floating along. She looked up, with a sweet smile that just about broke my heart.

"Excuse me boys," she said, "Would one of you please hand me my things?"

As I plotted some way I might possibly be the one to help her out with her request, M-2500's dexterous tentacle, like an obedient servant, coiled about the underwear and evening dress and lifted them like laundry on a clothes line and extended them twenty feet past where we were sitting to where she had propped herself up on the shore.

She didn't seem particularly modest about getting dressed over there, and I found the chit-chat between Jesus and M-2500 annoying as they went on about plans for the afternoon and our supposed destination. When Sarah had finished putting on her things and tying a headband across her hair and forehead with a strip of blue cloth from the hem of her evening gown, I got mad and stood up and walked away toward the opposite end of the island.

"Where you going, Steve?" Sarah called as she sat down beside Jesus and M-2500.

"Nowhere," I called back without turning, "I'm just going to have a look around. I'll be back, if it matters!"

Well, there really wasn't any place to go. Still, I walked along the lagoon to where she and Jesus had just finished their great "morning swim" and crossed over a low rise until I came to the end of the island. I sat down beside an outcropping of reddish looking clay and looked out across the long tract of river to where it curved into a low set of dense, green hills.

I was there not more than five or ten minutes and getting hungry when I saw something stir faintly along that distant shore. Suddenly, a flock of beautiful pink birds took flight. I'd never seen so many birds before and I wondered where they might be headed. I had been leaning back against the embankment with my left hand when it slipped and went out from beneath me and I toppled over on my side. I looked at my hand and rubbed my fingers together and smiled. Now, using my hand like a claw I dug into the soil and pulled out a clump of grainy, red clay. I pulled out little twigs and bits of wood and worked the lump over and over in my hand as I stared out over the river, past the hills to the towering blue mountains in the far distance.

"How's it going, Steve?"

The voice startled me and I dropped my clod of clay and looked back over my shoulder.

"Oh, hi," I managed to say as Jesus came alongside and sat down.

"Are you all right?" he asked.

"Me?"

"You seemed upset about something back there."

"I'm okay."

"Mind if I sit with you a while?"

"Are we camping here, or what?" I asked.

"We're going to have to find some food pretty soon," said Jesus, absentmindedly reaching down and pulling a clump of clay from the embankment. I picked up the lump I had been working over in my hand and looked at my friend.

"Why?" I said.

"Well, you're hungry aren't you?"

"What about you?"

"I'm okay."

"You know, Jesus, we've been gone almost two weeks and I don't recall I've seen you take a single bite in that entire time."

"Oh, I don't know…"

"No. No, you haven't had anything to eat in two weeks. Are you fasting or something?"

"Look at all this clay," he replied.

"Yeah, pretty neat. Too bad we can't eat it."

Jesus laughed, and for a while I watched his long fingers working the clay, over and over. He had already succeeded in kneading his lump into a smooth, palm size ball and was pulling bits of it into a star shape as we sat and watched the river flow past us on either side of the island.

"M-2500 says there is evil up ahead," I said.

"Did he?"

"He sure did."

"And what do you think?"

"I don't know. It's hard to imagine anything evil in a place like this."

No sooner were the words out of my mouth, than I felt I'd misspoken. I really did feel sort of confused all of a sudden and was about to speak when Jesus put a hand on my shoulder.

"Don't worry about it," he said.

"No?"

"Hey, now, this little fellow is coming along."

I looked over at the clay in his hands. He had fashioned the star shape into the figure of a man. Jesus bent forward and used the nail of his little finger to sculpt a tiny, sleeping face.

"That's pretty good," I admitted and looked down at the round ball of clay in my own hands.

In the next instant we heard Sarah's voice.

"Hey, what are you guys doing?" she said happily and she and M-2500 appeared on the crest of the embankment behind us. We looked up at Sarah who stood in the shadow of M-2500 who was carrying our twenty foot canoe in its superhuman tentacles daintily over her head like a parasol.

"You guys might want to think about getting out of the sun you know," said Sarah.

I laughed, "We could smear some of this on our faces," I said and held up my ball of clay.

"I just took a bath, silly," replied Sarah.

I'd noticed, I thought to myself, but said nothing.

"Wow, what do you have there, Jesus?" asked Sarah and she scrambled down between us and looked over at his little clay man, "Oh, he is just too cute," she said.

M-2500 set the canoe gently down in the reeds at the shoreline and hunkered down beside Jesus.

Sarah had taken the little figurine from Jesus and held it carefully in her outstretched hand, "I used to throw clay pots on a wheel back in prep school art class, but nothing this cool. It almost looks real."

I began compressing my clay ball, rolling it back and forth between my palms when M-2500 reached over to Sarah with a tentacle. The tentacle's silver tip came close to Sarah's hand and the end of the tentacle began to glow.

"Oooh, that tingles,' she said and looked over at M-2500, "What are you doing?"

Jesus smiled, shaking his head, and we were all for a moment bathed in a glow of blue green light emanating from the angel's crystal arrays. A thin beam of light touched the chest of the clay figure in Sarah's palm. Her eyes widened with wonderment as the beam from the tentacle bathed the figure in a cone of light. The lump quivered like jelly, rolled to its side, climbed to its tiny brick colored feet and stood. The tiny man drew its hand across its face and waved its arms, jumped up an inch, walked in a small half circle and sat on the ball of Sarah's thumb.

I don't know, but I'd seen tiny clockwork men for sale in the dealer stalls at the Jerusalem Market, more convincing than this. I had finished rolling out my ball of clay into a long noodle.

"What do you think?" I said, holding my creation up alongside the tiny man in Sarah's hand.

"What is it?" asked Sarah.

"A snake!" I said.

"Well, that's interesting," said Sarah, but she turned to M-2500.

"Is this little man really alive?"

The light from the quivering tentacle went dark and the tiny man slipped from the seat of Sarah's thumb back into her palm like a marionette whose strings had been suddenly cut.

"Getting him to move is the easy part," replied the angel.

I could see that no one was particularly interested in my clay noodle, and I tossed it down in the weeds and looked back jealously at the little clay figure.

"So, when are we going to get something to eat?" I said loudly and before I knew what I was doing I had reached over, snatched the little clay figure from Sarah's hand, and crushed it in my right fist so that clay oozed out between my fingers.

"Hey you jerk!" shouted Sarah, "What did you do that for?"

"Show's over!" I said, letting the smashed clump of clay slide off my hand into the weeds.

Sarah backhanded me in the side of the head, and I raised my hand to give her a little swat of my own, when I felt the lash and icy grip of M-2500's tentacle on my wrist.

Jesus gave me a stern glance and the tentacle uncoiled. I looked down at the ruined figurine at my feet, and rubbing my wrist, longed to be anywhere but where I sat.

"Let's get out of here," said Jesus and he and M-2500 stepped over to the nearby canoe and guided it into the water. Sarah followed and climbed aboard.

"Come on Steve!" she called. "I forgive you!"

Forgive me? She's the one who smacked me, I thought, but I watched my mouth, and taking a deep breath, followed after and jumped aboard our aluminum craft.

* * *

The current immediately seized hold and drew us down river past the lagoon almost to the opposite end of the island where we had started. By the time M-2500 had repositioned itself in the stern and applied its powerful tentacles to the water, the river had carried us out of the channel a hundred yards below the island. Now, with M-2500's rotor engaged, the craft turned in a sweeping curve away from the island, picked up speed, quickly regaining the several hundred yards we'd lost and headed out onto the broad back of the river.

We traveled along the middle of the river for some fifteen minutes until we came into the enormous river bend where the current had cut into the long hillside and scoured out a broken series of fifty foot cliffs. The afternoon sun dropped down a bit in the southern sky so that the wall of cold stone on the river's southern bend offered shade.

M-2500 adjusted his rudder and our aluminum craft slipped silently into the cool, blue green shadows. From what I could tell, Jesus was asleep upfront, an arm on the bow, supporting his head. Sarah was curled up in a ball at his feet, sleeping soundly. I rubbed the fingers of my right hand together and looked down at the fingers in my lap. The remnants of the clay had dried out and left a red stain. I let my hand trail in the cool water on the starboard side of the boat to rinse it clean, but found an annoying, slippery, residue on my fingers. Maybe they were right. Maybe I should have taken a bath.

My leg had fallen asleep and I shifted my weight in the back of the canoe and felt a buzzing in my numb right leg. Reaching down to massage my ankle I accidentally banged my elbow into the metal side of the boat and I let out a howl.

The sound of my cry reverberated off the side of the cliff. I cursed out loud and then glanced over at Jesus and Sarah. They stirred slightly but slept on.

"Do you employ aluminum in your time?" a voice sounded in my head. The sound made me gasp with a start and I looked back at M-2500. I regarded the horizontal slits lined up slightly below the angel's crystal array.

"What?" I thought to myself. If M-2500 had said something to me, it certainly gave no sign that it had spoken. I rubbed my elbow with my clean hand and looked at the gleaming metal of the canoe. "Aluminum, huh? Never heard of it."

"It is the most plentiful metal on the planet, but requires temperatures approaching 1000 degrees Celsius to free it from bauxite, the most common aluminum ore."

Bauxite? Nope, never heard of that either, I thought to myself. I recalled a visit to the blacksmith's in Nazareth and the fiery furnace where he heated copper, tin, zinc, iron, and on occasion, silver and gold. I had tried to find work there one summer after a fight I had with Jesus' dad, Joseph. I remembered walking into the blacksmith's workroom where I watched a burning bowl of molten iron stream from its crucible into a plaster mold to form sharp iron rods for joining beams.

"Kaolinite, a ferrous, red clay is rich in bauxite and a common source of the element." Weird letters and numbers swam through my mind's eye, drifting into strange configurations. I rubbed together the fingers of my right hand. Once again they were dry and I looked down at the reddish stain, and back at M-2500.

"Hey," I said out loud. "Hey, you!" I said again.

The slowly shifting light patterns drifting across M-2500's crystal array resolved into a steady mosaic of white light.

"Yes?" sounded the angel's familiar voice.

"What's all this about aluminum?" I found that I had difficulty even pronouncing the word.

"Aluminum?"

"Yes, that's it."

"What about it, Steve?"

"No, you were just asking me something about aluminum!" I banged the side of the canoe with the side of my fist.

"Steve, I haven't uttered a word."

"Maybe you're using that mental telepathy of yours. Trying to get into my head?"

M-2500 only sat at there in the stern of the canoe staring at me with its strange face.

"How on earth would I come up with a word like aluminum? I don't even know what it means!"

"It is a metallic element! The most plentiful metal on the planet."

"Yeah, I know that!" I shouted, although it was news to me, and now I found I had broken out in a sweat. Water was steaming down my forehead and I was getting mighty impatient with this little joke the robot angel was having at my expense. I felt a shiver course along my spine and I looked up over my shoulder at the high shadowy cliffs, where tendrils of green jungle hung over the rim rock.

"What was that?" I said in alarm.

"What?"

"Up there," I pointed.

"Where?"

"Up there in the cliffs!" I cried, and for some reason I stood up in the canoe.

The craft dipped dangerously to the side, and I was almost thrown overboard. Jesus and Sarah woke up in a moment of intense confusion and I felt the tentacles of M-2500 coiling about me, pulling me back down into the canoe.

"Are you dreaming?" cried Jesus.

"What's the matter?" shouted Sarah.

"Get your freaking aluminum hooks off me," I spat, struggling as the exorable metallic cables pulled me into the bottom of the canoe.

"What's wrong, Steve?" said Jesus and somehow in the tumult I felt as though I was coming up from a deep dark pool and Jesus' face was only just visible through a shifting veil of water at the surface.

"Get away from me," I gasped.

"Steve!" I heard Jesus call from a very long way away.

* * *

I must have blacked out for five minutes, because when I awoke, the three of them were all looking down at me with expressions of distress and concern. Even big old M-2500, who still had its oily snake arms wrapped around me like I was going to get up and do something, acted like it was worried. Well, I'd had it with this crew. They were talking amongst themselves about something or other and they seemed totally oblivious to me and the fact that I was wide awake and watching them and listening to every little thing they were saying about me. At the same time they remained totally ignorant of the hidden eyes that were gazing down on them from the cliffs.

With those tentacles binding me, the rudder and the propeller had come out of the water and the canoe was slowing drifting back with the current. As we moved steadily back along the cliffs we had just passed, I caught sight of them, high in the trees, apelike, half human forms watching, moving stealthily. Oh well, I had tried to warn my so-called friends, but the game was up. They'd all be busy enough in a second.

That's when the first boulder came down. It was the size of a grapefruit and the air made a big gulping sound as the river swallowed up the projectile two feet from the port side. A cold spray of river water showered the canoe. I guess somebody forgot to switch on the protective envelope, because the second boulder, the size and weight of a car battery came straight down between my feet and Sarah's knees and exploded a three foot hole in the skin of our aluminum vessel.

In moments we were all underwater. I fought like mad in the dark grip of the current at the base of the cliff and when I came to the surface I saw white arms thrashing in the waves and a feeble tentacle lashing about and drifting steadily away down river to the west. Fortunately, I had not forgotten how to swim and smacking the waves for all I was worth, quickly fought my way to the black wall of the cliff and grabbed hold of an outcrop. There was a narrow ledge just above the water line. With my feet scrambling along the slippery wall beneath the waves, I brought my body up out of the river and onto the narrow sill of rock.

A raven, black and glinting blue in the sunlight beyond the cliffs skimmed over the water and brought up something floating on its surface and disappeared in the sky behind the cliffs. The first sound that greeted my hearing was the near insane whooping of creatures seventy and eighty feet above on top of the cliff and in the overhanging tree branches. A volley of rocks and boulders sailed out from above and left a staccato trail in the river leading toward the three figures still struggling out in the main part of the river.

I pulled myself to a seated position on the convenient bench of rock. My legs dangled over the ledge and I tapped the tops of the lapping waves with the soles of my black shoes as I watched the little drama of the three companions drift away and out of sight. I wondered what they were thinking of the afternoon. I laughed. It was funny, but for an instant, I suddenly thought I had forgotten something and my hands went out desperately searching my thighs, my chest, the damp insides of my empty trouser pockets. I let out a terrific, soul rending sob, a wail so painful that I doubled over at the gut and nearly fell off my perch back into the river, but then I saw the image of Jesus' little red clay man held out in his palm and my mind became clear. I sat up and wiped the stream of tears that a moment earlier had poured from my weary eyes and with a sudden clarity of purpose I reached up, grabbed a nubbin of rock on the cliff wall and pulled myself to my feet.

* * *

The next four days went by as though in a dream. With almost robotic ease I found my way to a vertical fissure in the rock wall and scaled the fifty foot height to find myself on the verge of a dense and ominous jungle. Humanoid creature in the trees scattered in terror as I made my way along the twisting roots and vines that dangled out over the cliff. I made my way, calmly, steadily until dusk when the distant western horizon swarm in a fiery red sunset and the sun sank with a dying blaze over the broad river bend. In the twilight, the land leveled off with the river bank and the jungle gave way to low hills covered with wild flowers and tall grass.

A doe and its fawn were at the water's edge and as I came down out of the jungle she looked up with bright black eyes and turned her head to watch me. I followed the river bank by moonlight as it snaked through the hillsides and I never once thought about that day or anything that had gone before.

I was fully, confidently aware that I was being followed by the humanoid denizens of the dark wood as I slipped though the evening shade, now in the light of a cold, distant moon. As I came out of the hills the next morning I found myself on the edge on an immense valley. I had come to the headwaters of four mighty rivers. The four waters meandered in the shimmering sun drenched expanse and merged at a single point in the distance where they continued as a single, slender river. I would cross this valley, following that river where it climbed the green foothills of a mountain range lining the eastern horizon. I headed downward, with each step determined to reach the source of that single river.

In those days I had forgotten who I was, and knew only that I had a destination and that I was pursued, always at a distance by that whooping, scampering horde of nether men. The stench of my own body was acrid in my nostrils, but not nearly as foul as the scent of those who followed me, always an hour's walk back in the low bushes or behind the glistening onyx studded boulders that dotted the landscape. Had I been in my right senses, I might have wept at the beauty of the scene and of the land I was fast approaching. Herds of elk, cattle, horses, and elephants moved across the sea of grass in shifting patterns mirrored by the flocks of brilliantly colored birds that traced the skyways. Low white clouds scudded across a perfect, blue sky. The day came and went and my stride did not diminish. If I slept, it was only a brief dreamless sleep near the banks of the murmuring stream that spawned the great river in my wake.

Here and there as I made my way to the axis of the four waters, I saw occasionally off on either side of my path the skeletons of these strange, unthinking men. They had come this way, by chance or driven by the same mindless curiosity that propels the worker ant or bee to scout the terrain beyond its nest. Such a one had come a year or two before me, no wiser or stronger perhaps than any dozen others of the troop of gibbering adolescents who might have come before and who now dogged my heels.

On the morning of the third day I awoke from a bottomless black sleep in a low hedge of grass. I beheld the shimmering headwater: the broad clear pool where the four rivers began. I stood on what had become a peninsula, one of three pie-shaped wedges of land that jutted into the pool. Fanning out like spokes in a wheel, the four streams babbled away from their single source.

Something stirred in the tall grass behind me. I picked up a heavy rock at my feet, turned and walked back up the peninsula in the opposite direction I had come the night before. The sound of the moving waters made it difficult to hear, but I could see the flash of something hiding in the weeds. It was the boldest of those who had been following me. When I had closed the distance to no more than ten feet, it leapt up, naked and growling. I swung once with the heavy rock and bashed it in the skull. From every roost and hidden nest, birds screamed and took flight and for a moment I was blinded by the flapping wings darting into the air. The creature which I'd struck fell back, yowling. I kicked at it and laughed where it lay at my feet, holding the gash in its brow and looking up at me with terror in its dull, animal eyes.

It had the face of young man. It was young; the face of a boy. I hesitated and slowly looked up at the sky into the bright heavens. I swallowed hard, and for the second time since my solitary flight to the east, I suddenly doubled over with an intense pain in the core of my being. The stone dropped from my right hand and thudded on the sod at my feet. I sobbed and looked back at the creature who had taken the slight hesitation to push back and roll to its feet. It scampered back away through the grass further up the peninsula and sought refuge with its fellows who rose up from behind the low bushes and waved their fists and shouted with voices that knew no words.

I turned back in the direction of the mountains where the sun was rising over the furthest peak. I strode ahead like an automaton until I came to the end of the peninsula and walked straight ahead into the pool. A shower of glistening spray shot up as I trudged ahead past my knees, to my waist and when I could no longer walk, I swam. I swam for thirty minutes until, once again, I felt stones beneath the water-logged soles of my shoes. I trudged on for another five minutes to the other side of the pool and walked into the mouth of the solitary river. I climbed ashore and roared back, defiantly, at the hundreds of creatures who now ringed the pool on the opposite shore.

I walked along the bank of the first river until noon when I hiked up out of the valley, and onto to a great white walkway of finally crushed gravel that curved both to the left and right as far as the eye could see. Before me, across the wide, empty thoroughfare, rose an impenetrable green hedge forty feet high. To my right, the river, at this point no more than a dozen feet wide, and which I might have leapt across, gushed in a torrent from a culvert of white marble below the walkway.

I turned, obeying some inner call, climbed onto the crushed gravel path and started off to my right. I had taken no more than a step when I noticed a low, dark opening in the wall of green. I stepped forward, walked below an arch of dense overhanging branches and entered the Garden of Eden.

13. The Garden

The Garden of Eden was a very big place. I remember when we were in Oakland, Sarah had come back from a weekend of volunteering at a woman's shelter with a stack of old geographic magazines. I was thumbing through them one afternoon and came upon the August 1963 issue showcasing an amusement park which had opened a few years earlier in Los Angeles. Folded up inside was this cool-looking map of the park. The place had all sorts of neat sounding attractions inside its walls like Fun City, Old Time Village, Fairyville and Future World. I spent a lot of time reading the articles and looking at the pictures, but mostly just looking at that map and wondering what it might be like to walk along those paths and see all that cool stuff.

It was kind of like that when I got to the Garden of Eden. I cleared the archway through the hedge and entered a great enclosed area, paved with glistening white marble flagstones, and open to the sky. Barring my progress into the park itself stood a row of turnstiles and abandoned ticket booths. Since no one was around I walked up to the turnstile, pushed the metal bar forward and entered the park. On the other side of a broad paved area I found a covered portico lined with park benches. I walked to the furthest of these and sat before an enormous lawn slopping gradually upward to the East. I had gained enough altitude since entering the park that when I looked back to the West I could easily see over the encircling forty-foot hedge and out across the valley where the sun hung low in the sky. I reached beneath the waist band of my tattered, black tuxedo trousers and felt for my money pouch, fastened securely against my skin by its leather thong. I loosened the pull string and dug around in the pouch with my fingers and smiled. I pulled out the map. It was damp but undamaged and I carefully unfolded it there in the garden in the cool of the day. I sat on the marble seat and studied the plan of the enormous parkway. I scanned the paths and grottoes and wide open lawns and the river that flowed down out of Eden to the now distant pool and the four distant rivers that flowed away in every compass direction to the ends of the earth and I had a mighty good laugh.

When I was done and dried my eyes, I had the unsettling thought that I had actually been crying. I couldn't remember, and I had to squint a little because the sun was starting to sink in the west and its light was slanting in, bright and golden and sharp, but I looked down at the map and chuckled. I remember stopping for a second to think about the sound my voice.

"Hello?" I said. There was no answer. I relieved myself on the lawn and looked through the map at the rose gardens, the herb gardens, the vegetable gardens and the vineyards and the different kinds of orchards, ponds and pools and a waterfall over by the center of the garden not far from the world famous Tree of Eternal Life. I would have to check that out, but first I finished my business and stood up. No need to wipe, I thought; I already smelled like a walking corpse and I walked up the path, paying little heed to the wonders of that marvelous place.

When I arrived at my destination, it was nearly midnight. The moon was nowhere to be seen but the sky was ablaze with stars and by starlight I crept along the central path until I came to a vast, open space surrounded by evenly planted concentric stands of cypress, olive and cedar around the hub of a vast array of intersecting pathways. Off to the left and slightly down the hill lay the great marble reflecting pond I had seen on the map, at the bottom of which a towering waterfall poured down out of Eden to what, I supposed, was another auxiliary stream connected by a series of underground culverts to Eden's main river far below. I crossed a circular swath of manicured lawn that surrounded a knoll in the exact center of the place. There was a low wall of stone encircling the rise, so that it would have been impossible to proceed further without a conscious decision to climb over the obstacle. I climbed over the low rock wall in a heartbeat and scampered up the mossy slope to the base of an ancient looking tree.

In the dimness, it was difficult to see precisely what kind of tree it was. The bark was gnarled and corky to the touch, the leaves were large, green and waxy and as I reached up to a low hanging branch, I felt my fingers close around something soft and fleshy. I took a deep breath and tugged. The fruit came loose with a snap. I put the fragrant object to my lips and took an enormous bite. It was sweet and juicy and tart like an orange or mango but with a consistency between that of a pear or apple. It was fleshly all through, and no sooner had I consumed one, seeds and all, than I ate another and another and another.

I slumped down alongside the tree trunk and fell at once into a deep, dreamless sleep.

* * *

I awoke to a sound of laughter. A young man and woman in their late teens were down below, beyond the stone barrier and the encircling walkway out on the enormous, green lawn. They were laughing and giggling and chasing, and tumbling over one another on the grass, and I felt like shouting at them to shut up and go home, when I remember where I was. It was a strange sensation sitting there covered in fruit juice and my own excrement, like a drunk waking up from a bender with the fruit stained map in tatters beside me, my back up against the tree and listening to the sound of my bowels. I seemed to drift up, outside myself and watched powerless as the scene played out below me.

They were talking to one another, these two. The male seemed built of no greater stuff than the soul-less humanoid I had bashed in the head the other day and who had gone about its business as thought nothing in particular had occurred. The young buck on the lawn wasn't all that different, climbing on top of the girl and rolling over and over with her in the grass. He had stumbled up here into the garden and gotten the nod from the Creator. Yep, one day a barking snapping creature with no more spirit than a monkey or a sea-cumber and the next, he wakes up Lord of the Greatest Theme Park in all the universe.

I bided my time up on the hillock the way a spider bides its time in the hub of its web. After a while the young man yawned and hugged the girl like she was his sister and climbed to his feet and galloped off like a kid pretending he was a pony.

Left alone, the woman sort of "luxuriated" on the ground like she was doing calisthenics or yoga or posing for a men's magazine. The girl was buck naked and good looking too. Watching her cavort around down there for ten minutes in the nude, I felt a surge in my lap, but I just sat there, staring, unable to look away. When the girl got up, she looked toward the knoll and was about to scamper off, when somebody pulled a trigger in my brain and strummed my vocal cords.

"Hey!"

Was that even me, I thought to myself?

She paused a beat out on the lawn, looked down and started off again.

"Hey!" I croaked.

She stopped and looked around and was about to walk away.

"Hey, up here."

She looked up. She saw me now.

"Howdy!" I called down to her.

She tilted her head to one side and took a step forward, the perfect toes of her perfect feet pressing down into the cool forgiving lawn.

"Good morning," she said.

"Jesus," I thought to myself. I sure wish you were here right now. "Oh, god!" My body spasmed and a stabbing pain shot through my gut. I was up there lashed to a tree in a pool of excrement, vomit and urine, a living, breathing, human stool. I was some monstrous pedophile stalking the mother of all humankind.

Had I no integrity? Had I no conscience? Was I so ignorant of human civilization? Had I no inkling where this was headed?

A smile split my face like a knife cutting an overripe melon and the words spilled out, "What's going on?" I asked.

Flies buzzed around the base of the tree. They had probably come in the front door with me the night before, but I couldn't help myself, and I looked down at the red clay stain in my hand and chortled.

"Why don't you come up and have something to eat?"

She stopped. "Oh, no," she said.

"How's that?"

"We're not supposed to go up there."

"Up where?"

"Up there, to the tree," she said, pointing.

"Why not?"

"It is forbidden."

"Forbidden?" I parroted. "That's a funny word." It is a funny word, come to think of it, one which, in all my miserable life I have not been particular fond, nor heeded, but I went ahead like I was reading the words from a script.

"Just get your pretty little self up here and have a look around, and if you like it… Well… I'm up here, aren't I?"

"That's true," she replied.

Now I had her, and suddenly I was thinking about Jesus and Sarah and M-2500. I knew somehow they'd managed to survive the attack of the man monsters on the river and were racing ahead at that very moment like the earth's mightiest superheroes, slogging through the saw grass, crashing through the crystal pool at the foot of Eden and charging up the hillside toward the arbor. Meanwhile, I consoled the woman-child, encouraged her, as she threw a slender leg over the rock wall and sat there looking up at me with her deep, trusting eyes.

"Great job! See how easy that was? The next part is simple!"

She was climbing up the slope and coming up to me where I slouched against the side of the tree.

"Are you all right?" she asked.

My voice had grown husky. I could barely utter the words.

"Yes... Yes, I'm fine." My head swam and I was scared and I looked up with tears running down my face, "Now that you're up here you might as well have a bite to eat from the tree. Up there. See? I've left some for you."

She looked up, and I gazed at the full, round breasts of which I had only moments earlier been so enamored and I writhed on the ground hoping to find some hole in the dirt in which to burrow and hide myself from her gaze.

"The old man in the garden warned us never to eat of this tree lest we die."

"Nonsense!" I choked, "I've been eating it all night and it hasn't hurt me any!"

"Really?"

"Really," I replied, although in that instant I really feel as though I was dying.

For a frozen moment, which I shall never forget, I saw her long, powerful fingers reaching up through the foliage in the morning light:

the digits poised and awaiting instruction from her human nervous system.

In that same moment at the bottom of the lawn, the cavalry arrived. The three of them already knew where they were and what was going on. Grimacing with every step, Jesus leaned against a makeshift walking staff of driftwood and hobbled along with a broken leg. The leg appeared splinted and I knew in an instant it was the work of Sarah who had applied a driftwood stick, lashed it to his calf and thigh with blue strips of cloth torn from the dwindling hem of her dress. Evidently, M-2500 had no powers in Munchkin Land; he could move no faster than Sarah, who led the way.

"Eve, don't do it!" shouted Sarah, "For the love of God, don't do it!"

In the text instant, I was battling against a seeming ton of weight. I pushed myself upward along the rough trunk of the tree and reached out as the naked woman plucked the first deadly fruit from its twig. My own, frail hand intercepted hers and I snared the fruit. I screamed, at the top of voice as I wrested the fruit from her grasp and with all my might hurled it in the direction of the waterfall. I collapsed on the ground at her feet but not without first seeing the fruit sail over the heads of my three friends and hit the reflecting pool with a splash. We gasped as it bobbed to the surface, tipped to one side and then disappeared over the waterfall and away from Eden.

My friends looked horror struck and I had no idea why until I looked back up at Eve standing tippy-toe reaching for another piece of fruit. Sarah hurdled over the stone barrier, scrambled up the slope and had a hand on Eve's shoulder. Sarah succeeded in wrenching away a second deadly piece of fruit from the first woman. Now, it was Sarah's turn as she wheeled like a big league pitcher and hurled the piece of deadly cargo to the reflecting pool.

All the commotion by the Tree of the Knowledge of Good and Evil had caught the attention of Eve's boyfriend. Adam appeared on the lawn looking understandably concerned. He was calling Eve's name, but the tree preoccupied her and the limbs began to sway. A breeze wafted up from the ground where we were variously standing, or, in my case, writhing about in a fit of agony on the ground. The tree branches began to shake and now, one, two, three pieces of fruit dropped from every branch and twig end. It was raining apples, and all at once they all dropped off the tree. They scattered everywhere; many rolled down the slope. Eve pranced away from the tree and with a mad look of glee scampered halfway down the hillside and snatched up a piece. She had raised it to her open mouth when Sarah executed a commando leap and landed on Eve's back. Holding Eve, Sarah managed to pull away one piece, but Eve had her hand on another. She was laughing, like this was a game with a little sister and the two tumbled over and over down the slope. Sarah crashed against the wall below as Eve stood, triumphantly, with a new piece of fruit.

"Don't do it!" cried Jesus who stumbled up on his driftwood crutch. His hand was outstretched, but another human hand, powerful in its own right, pushed him away, knocking Jesus down onto the walkway.

"Watch it," said the boyfriend as Eve finally landed a great big bite on the piece of fruit in her hands.

She looked up in a short-lived ecstasy of culinary delight.

"Oh, my goodness," she declared, "It's absolutely delicious," she said and handed the fruit to her boyfriend, "You've got to try it!"

Grinning sheepishly, the big kid took the fruit, "If you say so," he said and took an enormous chunk into his mouth.

They sat together on the rock wall sharing the fruit beside a clearly marked sign on the slope: "Warning: Eating the Fruit of This Tree is Strictly Forbidden."

Where he'd been knocked down and leaning on his crutch once again, Jesus slowly drew a hand down across his face. Sarah appeared from behind the stone wall and looked up, painfully, at the mother and father of all human kind. The naked couple was finishing the last of the fruit, when they suddenly noticed us: me, behind them on the knoll, flopping around like a beached carp; Sarah only ten feet to the side leaning on the stone wall; Jesus sprawled at their feet on the walkway, and M-2500 standing respectfully to the side on the grass like an avant-garde lawn sculpture.

"Well," said Jesus, wearily, "Don't say we didn't warn you."

Adam looked down imperiously at his distant, grandchild.

"Do I know you?" he asked.

"Here," said Sarah, curtly. She reached down, picked up one of a dozen pieces of fruit from the Tree of the Knowledge of Good and Evil and tossed it to Eve.

"Why don't you have another?" the piece of fruit bounced on the top of the wall beside them and landed at their feet.

The couple looked down at the fruit as it spun for a moment and came to rest on its side. In unison their gaze went from their feet up their shins to their knees along their thighs and stopped. They looked up at one another, as though for the first time.

"Excuse me," said Adam.

"Pardon me," said Eve shielding her breasts with her forearms. She slid off the low stone wall and holding her hands down shielding her privates, backed away up the walk.

"Nice weather, we're having," said Adam, similarly backing away up the walk protecting his groin from view with his hands.

I slid down the slope with a dozen pieces of fruit and came to a stop beside Sarah not far from where the first couple had been sitting. Sarah took a bite from a piece of the fruit that was scattered everywhere. She chewed and swallowed.

"I don't know," she said, "I can't taste how it was worth it."

We sat in absolute silence for some time, thinking our private thoughts. I was going to speak, with my own voice now, but at that moment the lawn sprinklers came on. The sound of the vibrating sprinkler heads erupted across the great, empty lawn. M-2500 raised itself up on its tentacled legs and lumbered onto the dry walkway as an old man in faded dungarees and a plaid work shirt approached from the pathway. He held a corn cob pipe in one hand, a large leather bundle over his shoulder and walked with a slow measured step seeming to inspect every inch of the pathway as he shuffled forward.

Sarah's eyes widened, "You don't suppose..."

"Shhh..." said Jesus.

The old timer stopped not more than an arms-length from M-2500. He reached into the breast pocket of his plaid shirt and produced a wooden kitchen match. Without looking, he reached out and pulled the match head quickly along the dome of the angel's triangular head. Owing to the water droplets from the sprinkler, the match failed to ignite on the first pass, and the old-timer again set the match against the metallic dome and with the deft flick of his fingers succeeded in lighting the match which he drew to the bowl of his pipe.

"Reliable model, the M-series," he muttered.

He took a long draw and flicked the match out onto the lawn. The match lighted beside a blade of wet grass where it was soon extinguished by the sprinkler. A tiny plume of blue smoke rose two feet above the lawn and quickly dissipated. The old-timer took a long draw on the corn cob pipe and exhaled a breath of smoke. On second thought maybe I only imagined he was holding a corncob pipe? Maybe that was my name drifting away on the green lawn? I sure could have used a smoke. Was I smoking in those days?

The old timer looked up at us as though only now aware of our presence on the pathway.

"Morning," he said.

"Good morning," said Sarah.

"Morning, sir," I said.

"Well, young fella', looks like you've had a rough night."

"Yes, sir." I said.

The old-timer looked up at the tree and over at the warning sign which had been knocked askew during the morning activity on the slope. He looked back up at the tree.

"E-yeah." he said with a New England inflection, in acknowledgment of the damage done to the centerpiece of his garden, but perhaps, and more probably, in deference to Sarah's childhood in

New England. She watched him intently as he shuffled forward and stopped, only a yard from where Jesus sat on the ground before him.

"I don't suppose you've seen any young folks frolicking out here on the lawn this morning?"

None of us knew what to say.

"Kind of hard to miss," he said.

"Yes," Sarah began haltingly, "I think…" she looked down at Jesus who nodded. "I think they went that way," she said and pointed down the path.

"I stitched up some clothes for them, back at the shop," he said and with a nod of his head indicated the bundle he had slung across his shoulder. He took another step and was nearly on top of Jesus when he looked down, seeming to notice for the first time, the man sprawled on the walkway in his path. The old-timer smiled a broad, beaming smile that lifted our spirits. Even across the way, the lights on M-2500's array panel flashed brightly. The old timer extended a hand.

"Here son," he said to Jesus, "Let me help you up."

They clasped hands and exchanged a long look. Using the driftwood staff, and evidently fighting the pain in his leg, Jesus stood.

"Now, let me take a look at you," said the old-timer. Leaning back and taking a hold of Jesus by the shoulders he looked up into the young man's face, "Sometimes, I surprise myself!" he said.

Jesus lowered his head, smiling.

"And how have you been getting along with that Uncle of yours?"

"Okay, I guess."

"Learned anything?"

"Some."

Jesus seemed to blush and then the old-timer looked side to side and down at the crude splint on Jesus' leg.

"He had this wild hair to send you on this little vacation before you join the working world."

"Hasn't seemed like much of a vacation," said Jesus.

"You can take that up with him!"

The old-timer crouched down a bit and looked over his spectacles at Jesus' leg. Slowly, carefully, he reached down and placed his hand over the injury and stepped back.

"There, now. How's that?" he asked.

Jesus carefully shifted his weight. He moved side to side and then bounced heavily on the splinted leg. He looked at the old timer and smiled.

"Wow," Jesus exclaimed.

"E-yeah?" asked the old-timer.

"Oh, yeah!" said Jesus with a smile.

The old-timer gave Jesus a squeeze on the shoulder and started away, "Can't have you gallivanting around the wilderness on a broken leg," he said moving away up the path. He stopped and looked down at me.

"Don't be too hard on yourself, son. Stick with my boy, over there. You'll manage."

He reached over the rock wall and with some exertion pulled out the warning sign. He banged its metal stake against the wall, knocking off clods of earth. He looked down at the inscription, and slowly shook his head. He called back, to no one in particular. He might have been speaking only to himself, "Plenty of fruit, here about. Won't do any harm, now, I don't suppose. Bake yourselves a real nice pie," he paused and looked back at us, and then, almost angrily he called to Jesus.

"Don't let your two friends help themselves to any of that fruit from the Tree of Life. They ain't right with me," he said. "Anyway, that ride is closed down, forbidden, and strictly off limits."

"No, sir."

"And while I'm thinking about it..."

"Yes, sir?"

"How are you planning to get out of here?"

"Out of here?"

"Your Uncle didn't think of that, did he?"

"I don't know," Jesus stammered, as though his dad was about to discover that he'd accidentally wrecked the family station wagon on summer break in Fort Lauderdale.

"Your boat ride's sunk to the bottom of the Euphrates. One of my cherubim's on his way from the Ultimate Universe to close down the park in about one hour. And no, Ms. Sarah, they ain't the cute little babies you post on your Internet Valentine's day cards!"

With that, the old timer disappeared over the crest of the hill and we were left, speechless, staring at one another. Sarah climbed over the stone wall to a seated position and approached Jesus who stood looking up the empty path.

"Was that who I think it was?" she asked.

Jesus nodded solemnly.

"As much of him as one could see at one time without facing annihilation," said Jesus.

"That's a pleasant thought," she said, "He seemed like a nice guy."

"A nice guy?" said Jesus, "Not really."

Sarah looked puzzled.

"He is what he is."

"So, what about your leg? Did he really heal it?"

Jesus reached down to his leg.

"Seems so."

Sarah crouched down and untied the strips of blue cloth, "Well, that was pretty nice of him, don't you think?"

"I suppose it was," said Jesus with a smile.

"So, who's your uncle?" Sarah asked as Jesus dropped his walking staff and helped Sarah up to her feet.

"A friend," he said, "I don't suppose he's really my Uncle, but he and the old man go way back. He's like family, I guess. I don't know where he'd been my whole life. He just showed up with my cousin back on the river a couple weeks ago. He used to go by another name. 'The Entity,' I think it was. He asked would I like to take a road trip with him."

"Well, your old man said we needed to get out of here and I believe him!"

Jesus left Sarah in the walkway, straddled the rock wall and extended his hand to me, "Come on Steve, we have to go."

Sarah followed Jesus to the wall, "He said we have only one hour." She looked down at me and grimaced.

"Good God! Where have you been?"

"Hell and back," said Jesus.

"I'm sorry, you guys," I said. "I don't know what got into me."

"We have an idea," said Jesus.

* * *

Sometimes when you're on a busy street corner or in a crowded department store, you get used to a certain level of noise. If the sound suddenly cuts out, it can really startle you. It's like that in the outdoors with the sound of birds and insects and wildlife; something mighty bad can be on its way that spooks them so they shut up all of a sudden, but we human's don't catch on for a minute until we notice the silence. When we finally do, it can make us jump. At that moment in the garden, it was like that.

"Listen!" I said.

"What?" said Sarah.

"It got quiet all of a sudden," said Jesus.

"The sprinklers! The lawn sprinklers have shut down," I said.

For once I was exactly right! We looked back at the wide lawns and at intervals of fifty feet the last plumes of water were receding back to the now motionless sprinkler heads.

"Maybe we could use the map." I said.

"What map?" asked Jesus.

"The map from the glove box of the driver's..." I trailed off and glanced at Sarah.

"Steve," began Jesus and he reached out his hand, but I was already scampering back up the slope toward the ancient tree. The spot where I'd been sitting was swarming with black flies.

233

"Leave it!" shouted Jesus.

"But it might…" I swatted flies from my face in the shadow of the Tree of the Knowledge of Good and Evil. The map, what I could see of it, was covered with flies and filth. I swallowed hard, squinted and reached down to whisk it away, when suddenly, it burst into flames.

"Ye-ouch," I cried and flipped over backwards and tumbled down the slope.

"Get over here, Steve!" shouted Jesus.

The smell of burned hair from my signed right arms added to my complex aroma as I looked back up the hillock. The side of the tree was engulfed in fire. Flames leaped along the trunk into the branches, when suddenly, like the robot on the old Lost in Space TV show, M-2500 began swiveling at the torso, array lights flashing, and its two primary tentacles waving in the air.

"Warning! Warning!"

"We've been warned," said Jesus to himself, and with his fingers he pressed the temples of his skull, evidently attempting to channel his absent uncle for suggestions on what to do next. Meanwhile, to make myself useful, I scooped up an armful of the fallen fruit from the burning Tree of the Knowledge of Good and Evil. The few remaining fruits in the highest branches were exploding like giant popcorns sending out blotches of what looked like hot applesauce.

"What are you doing?" cried Sarah.

I had an armful of fruit as I climbed over the wall and had taken a finger-full of beige jam that had landed on my shirt sleeve and popped it into my mouth.

"Mmm! That's good!" I reported.

"Steve, get rid of that stuff!" she said and dodged a fat dollop of hot fruit puree that sailed out of the tree and splattered on the pavement between us.

"But he said we could make pies!"

She came up to me hard and knocked the fruit out of my arms.

"He was being sarcastic!"

Suddenly, like an Internet video of a big Saturn Five rocket launch on rewind, a blazing light appeared in the blue sky far overhead. Something was approaching, and a loud roaring sound swept down over the garden. At the same instant, from hidden loudspeakers, we heard a voice. It wasn't the voice of the old timer but more like a Midwestern radio announcer's voice. It might have been the same guy who did voice-over work on a documentary I'd see one day in my college biology class in Oakland.

"Attention. Attention. The park will be closing in forty-five minutes. Please proceed to the exit turnstiles. Attention, attention. The park will be closing in forty-five minutes. Please proceed to the exit turnstiles. Have a nice day, and thanks for visiting."

The four of us came together and started off around the circular walk and down the main path leading west out of the Garden of Eden. Against the background roar of the descending "THING FROM OUTER SPACE" and in weird counterpoint, the pre-recorded voice continued its announcement from concealed speakers beneath the low branches of a cypress, the cupola of an empty gazebo, and the awning of a vacated concession stand. I looked over my shoulder at the descending object and before I knew it, we were nearing the main gates. We entered the great level plaza, passed the marble portico and approached the row of turnstiles. They had all been barred except for one at the end where an attendant occupied a lighted ticket booth and was letting people through. Actually, he wasn't letting anyone through at the moment, because there weren't any other visitors in the place, except us and a couple dressed in animal skins.

The pair stood in front of a big colorful placard, with a huge photograph of the place as a back drop, at the top of which read, "I visited the Garden of Eden!"

Dressed in a park attendant uniform, a photographer was giving them directions and finally the flash went off on his camera and he pulled out the instant film, peeled off the protective backing and handed the photo to the man. The woman snatched the picture out of the man's hand and complained that the picture made her look fat and that it wouldn't have killed her companion to have combed his hair for this keepsake, or to have smiled as thought they had been having a good time and so forth. They went out past the sullen attendant at the turnstile into the world arguing with one another, and shouting and exchanging oaths.

All this time the big light show behind us in the sky was getting brighter and brighter and its roar made it almost impossible to hear without shouting, but we could still hear the announcer's voice reminding us that we now had only five minutes to evacuate.

Up ahead we ran into a familiar face.

"Well, well, well. Look who we have here!" crowed the cameraman.

"We have to be going," said Jesus.

"Not so fast, brother," said the man, stepping directly into Jesus' path to the last turnstile.

"Maybe the little lady would like a memento of her visit?"

"Not today," said Jesus. "Thank you."

"Wouldn't you like to remember the place where I succeeded in destroying the old-timer's finest creations?"

"You haven't destroyed anything!"

"No?"

"You are a weed."

"Am I?"

"To be pulled out by the roots and discarded into the realm of nothingness!"

"Hey, not so fast," snarled the vendor as Jesus again attempted to walk past. The guy shoved Jesus back, hard.

"Keep your hands to yourself," warned Jesus.

"Yeah? And what are you going to do about it?"

Without a word, Jesus hauled off and punched the guy square in the jaw. The expensive camera flew out of the vendor's hands and smashed into the background standee toppling it over with a clatter. The camera landed in a ruin on the hard marble stones. Meanwhile, the force of Jesus' blow sent the vendor into a complete pirouette and he flew backwards end over end and landed on his back, bawling like a big bully.

"Hey, that hurt!" shouted the photographer on the ground as he rubbed his jaw. His rakishly angled park attendant hat had toppled off his head to reveal his bald skull. As he sat there cursing; we could see the familiar black tattoo etched on his scalp.

Jesus was first to reach the turnstile and he pulled a double-take as he recognized the attendant inside the ticket booth.

"Oh, not you again," moaned Jesus.

Sarah, M-2500, and I were standing just a few feet away preoccupied by the object hovering in the sky behind us. It was enormous, six or seven times the apparent size of the wheel shaped Ophanim we had seen in the fake sky outside the Pandemonium Bar and Grill. Those started out a hundred feet across. This sucker could have used the Temple Mount in Jerusalem as a park bench.

"So, that's a cherub?" mumbled Sarah.

Where the storm clouds had come from I don't know. But a big, ugly, anvil shaped thunderhead rising eighty-thousand feet into the sky had slipped in over the summit of the big snow capped peak behind the park as a thematic backdrop to the descending "THING FROM OUTTER SPACE. Lighting was flashing inside the ominous cloud and the rumbles provided a deep bone wrenching bass to the high pitched roar of the thing settling in back to the East of the Garden.

* * *

The faces of a man, an ox, a lion, and a griffin. What the hell is that? I mean, long after my adventures with Jesus were over, I met John, The Beloved, outside of Capernaum. John had been a close buddy of Jesus', part of his entourage in the days after Jesus became famous and was doing a lot of touring up and down the coast. John was a great guy, don't get me wrong, hell, he was "beloved." I got to know him pretty well before he went into exile long after my adventures with Jesus in the Wilderness had come to an end. Still, when I read John's book about the end times and his stuff about what

I was seeing come down with my own eyes out of the sky that afternoon in Eden, I think he was seriously in over his head. Okay, I may not seem like the most credible judge since I was possessed by the Devil and talked Eve into committing the original sin, but I tell you, I was over all of that. Now, I'm beginning to think John just suffered from a limited vocabulary. He just couldn't put his experience into words. I mean, what did he know about DNA and Black Holes and Cell Phones and Jungian Psychology? I suppose he was just getting it out the best he was able, like one of those court room sketch artists.

John talks about wings of the Cherubim. What in the world does a creature, who can travel across all dimensions of time and space and the dimensions beyond time and space, need with wings? This monster angel was dropping in from the old-timer's inner circle, the First Sphere. He didn't need wings. What he did have were four gigantic dark, matter panels. And eyes? Really? I suppose they were "like" eyes, but not "eyeballs" like you I have. These were more like the crystal arrays on M-2500. They could see up and down the electro-magnetic spectrum and that was just for starters. And the four faces? Come on, John! Have you ever looked up at the constellations at night? Do you really see all that crap up there? The Big Dipper: maybe. Orion's belt: I'll grant you that. But the rest of those pictures? Connect the dots and see whatever you want. And finally, the oxen feet: they were simply landing gear, my old friend.

However you want to describe it, a cherub was definitely coming down out of the sky. The Creator was totally pissed, and after he'd put all that cool stuff in the garden I think it really broke his heart how Adam and Eve had just blown him off. He was putting the whole joint off limits; that's where the "sword" came in. From what I could tell, it looked more like a mile long bolt of electricity. You would not want to be anywhere near it, spinning around in the air another fifty yards above the top of the Cherub. I mean, it took a long, sparking sweep, like the warning beam from a light house. "Keep the hell away from here!"

All this stuff was coming down on us and Jesus motioned Sarah through the turnstile and then I got stuck behind M-2500. No way was he coming out through that turnstile. The Creator could get real picayune about stuff, but just the same, even though you might not have liked his rules or understood them, you knew, about ninety percent of the time, it was just best to do what he said. It was like that with M-2500. Do you suppose he had come through the turnstile on the way in? No. He had just climbed over the top. Now, with the storm clouds gathering and the gigantic cherub guarding the mountain top and the spinning electric scimitar of death wheeling to all four corners of the compass to keep anyone from getting to the Tree of Eternal Life, the Creator wasn't letting anyone out except through that turnstile.

Fortunately, we had an answer to this and with a nod from Jesus, M-2500 did his quick-change metamorphosis and there, once again, was my buxom girlfriend Debbie from the Eastern Wall. She pushed through the turnstile with a sexy side swipe of her hip and almost at once, to my dismay and disappointment, resumed the shape of the Mechanical Angel, leaving me behind with the Prince of Air and Darkness. I guess even Satan, who had just inherited the entire planet as his personal playground, heck, the entire Solar System clear out to the Termination Shock in the Kupier Belt was getting nervous about getting back out through that gate.

"Attention. Attention. The park will be closing in one minute. Please proceed to the exit turnstiles. Attention. Attention. The park will be closing in one minute. Please proceed to the exit turnstiles. Have a nice day, and thanks for visiting."

"Let's move it," he shouted behind me.

I looked up at the turnstile operator in the attendant's ticket booth and couldn't believe who I saw. Hunkered down in brown khaki shorts, a button down shirt, and a broad brimmed ranger hat, that was way too small for his enormous head, was the obscenely deformed fly creature from the dawn of life.

"Hey, can I get a stamp?" I asked.

The creature looked at me, puzzled, and looked through the glass booth at his boss.

"A stamp," I repeated, "In case I want to get back in."

"What?" it croaked.

"In case I want to get back in? I'd like a stamp."

"Listen, we have to get out of this place, now!" shouted the photographer.

My friends on the other side of the turnstile stopped in their tracks and looked back at me in horror. Behind us, towering like some monstrous amusement ride, the cherub and the gigantic whirling blades of energy sparked and roared and a wind had whipped up and golf-ball sized hail started bouncing down on the marble pavement.

"I want a stamp!" I shouted at the fly man and I shoved my right hand through the narrow slot at the base of the ticket window. The bewildered creature reached over to a little rubber stamp. It had difficulty grasping the wooden handle in its hairy black claw. It took quite some time, given the circumstances, rocking the rubberstamp back and forth on the ink pad.

I watched the back of my red-stained hand as the creature carefully applied the stamp.

"How's that?" it asked.

I withdrew my hand and examined the ink mark. It was the same intricate web laced symbol in miniature that Satan had tattooed on the crown of his skull and embossed on his business cards. I nodded with satisfaction and pushed through the metal turnstile. Immediately, I felt the hands of Jesus, Sarah and the metal tentacles of M-2500 pulling on my arms and shoulders and tearing me away toward the low hanging opening in the hedge, but more than that, and I shall never forget, I distinctly remember hearing the last metallic click of the turnstile arm as it rose up behind me and locked in place.

Furiously, the photograph pushed on the metal bar just as the announcer's voice sounded through the dark, storming garden.

"The Garden of Eden is Now Closed."

I could see the fly man with all its arms pressed up against the glass of the ticket booth trying to exit and its master pushing and pulling this way and that on the arm of the turnstile screaming after us. The sound of his voice was drowned out as the deadly funnel of a tornado, spawned from the storm cloud, suddenly touched down where they stood. Green branches exploded overhead as we vaulted through the hedge and tumbled into a dense white mist. Locked arm in arm with my friends I remember feeling a distinct BUMP, which I remember because I bit my tongue, and then we rolled out onto the gravel walkway on the other side.

We wondered how long we had been inside the Garden of Eden, and in particular, how much time had passed between the time I made it through the turnstile and the four of us tumbled out through the now sealed entryway of the forty foot high hedge.

It was raining like mad and a dense fog sat on the hillside made it impossible to see for more than a mile or two in any direction. M-2500 had sprouted an impressive menu of hardware from the triangular apex of its head.

"The topography has changed substantially, but I'm getting too much clutter from the rain, to provide a better estimate."

Jesus nodded solemnly.

"Thousands of years or more have elapsed since we entered these grounds," said the angel.

Behind us, our way into the park was blocked by a dense overgrowth of thorns and brambles. As we moved down slope to the west, we looked back through the drizzle and realized the towering funnel cloud had long ago lifted back into the sky. For all we knew what remained of the Cherub to the east was only its deadly whirling blade, now only a beacon of light flashing steadily, at four second intervals, through the gloom. We only guessed that it was daytime, there was so little light on the mountainside.

"Where's the river?" I said, squinting my eyes against the rain and searching for what I remembered was once a marble culvert in the hillside.

"There is no river!" shouted Jesus, helping Sarah to her feet.

We were all ankle deep in rising water, as the concealing fog began to roll away like steam. But for stray, distant peaks, really no more than islands, all around from horizon to horizon beneath the gray, overcast sky, the valley had become an inland ocean. It must have been raining for a very long time. Someone shouted and we all looked across the waves.

We could see it coming a mile off.

Yep, it was Noah's Ark.

14. Hands of the Colossus

Although you might have criticized me for helping condemn humanity to a life of mortal toil rounded by the cold embrace of death and for my bearing the seal of the devil on the back of my right hand, you can hardly fault me for all the bad choices people were making in the days and years and centuries leading up to the great flood. M-2500's telemetry measured the craft at roughly three hundred by fifty cubits. Given the draft of such a vessel and estimating the weight of its cargo, it might have been, roughly 30 cubits high. Still, I did feel a little guilty about the way I'd been behaving and I was determined to help my friends out of the jam they were in.

"M-2500 can sprout his wings and fly us over there!" I shouted to Jesus.

Jesus looked at the enormous vessel moving slowly, silently north.

"That might work!" shouted Sarah through the rain.

"He can land on the roof! They'll never know we're there," I said.

Jesus stood watching the vessel move slowly north before us. By now it was probably two miles off disappearing back into a patch of fog.

"Let's get to higher ground while we still can!" he shouted.

Sarah and I exchanged a long glance and slogged after Jesus through the water that was now nearly to our knees. Fortunately, as I recalled from the driver's road map, The Garden of Eden was built on a mountainside. The old gravel pathway encircled the entire park. Following Jesus to the southeast along the overgrown hedge, we could gain at least another thousand feet in altitude. We made our way through the blowing wind and stinging sheets of rain for an hour and had almost given up hope that the trail would ever curve up slope to the east, but as we struggled in nearly thigh deep water, the grade began to gradually rise. After another twenty minutes we'd left the waves behind us.

Catching up with Jesus I called out, "What about the ark?"

"Forget the ark. We get around to the backside of the Garden. It will be dry up there. At least for a while."

"What about the monster?"

"The Cherub?"

"Are we hitching a ride out of here with him?"

"Oh, that's a great idea," yelled Sarah.

"Let's keep up the pace," Jesus said.

By the time we got to the back side of the Garden, M-2500 predicted that we had bought ourselves another hour of "dry time." We stood on the rim of a high mountain valley in the rain behind the ruin of the Garden. Through the fog I could see a sign by the side of the gravel road with an arrow pointing down a mountain path. The path led down slope into a fog-filled mountain valley and then, on the other side, climbed up the mountainside to a high mountain pass leading to:

"Nod," said Sarah reading the inscription on the sign, "The Land of Nod. It leads to Cain's village over that mountain pass!"

"Yes," said Jesus.

On the lea side of Eden's overgrown hedge, fog was rising out of the mountain valley. I was running down the trail when the sight of an enormous stone monument stopped me in my tracks. I looked up, five hundred feet through the fogbank at the gigantic Cherub, the celestial being that had once descended to bar the way to the Tree of Eternal life. What remained of the Cherub was now only a immobile, stone colossus on a pedestal of black basalt. If the tree still existed back behind us in the Garden it was submerged beneath a hundred feet of water. As I descended the mountain trail, I looked down ahead through another layer of fog and collapsed in an agony of disappointment. The high mountain valley was already flooded. The pathway which might have led us over the mountains to the land of Nod was drowned in a wave-tossed sea of rain. I fell back against the cold stone of the Cherub's pedestal and cried.

After a while, I looked back up the path and saw the beacon light of the flaming scimitar sweep above the abandoned Garden and I counted, one, two, three, four. It blinked out. In desperation I looked back across the valley to mountainside. It was a good five miles across to the other side. If only we had the aluminum raft, if only M-2500 could turn himself into something other than a hot babe in a low cut evening dress. I looked up at the others through the rain. I slogged my way back up the muddy trail. They had already seen the gigantic, stone Colossus through the fog. I was waving my arms with another great idea, but Sarah had already stolen it.

"Just ask M-2500 to turn into a boat!" she was saying.

"A boat?" replied Jesus.

"I've seen what an angel can do for a Broadway Theater!"

"It would not necessarily possess the power of our canoe," Jesus replied.

"Who knows!" she shouted, "At least it could get us over there!"

She pointed east in the direction Cain had taken centuries earlier.

"Then what?" said Jesus.

"We climb!"

"And what will you eat on a glacier!"

"Snow!" I interrupted, "There's lots of snow!"

"What do you care?" continued Sarah. "Steve and I will fish. We'll hunt for sea birds."

"Until every peak is overtopped by the ocean?"

"Listen, Einstein, there isn't enough water on the planet to raise the sea level to cover that summit up there."

She hung in Jesus' face, her arm outstretched and her finger pointing like a knife in the direction of the mountain top.

"Well?" she said, "We can't stay here!"

"What would you have me do, Jesus?" asked M-2500.

"Just a minute," said Jesus.

"A minute? You want a minute? Where was that minute when we could have flown over to Noah's Ark?"

"That ark? So, that's what this is about?" he replied.

"It's about getting out of here alive!"

"But you don't even believe in Noah's Ark!"

"I know what I saw with my own eyes!"

"Well then, you may have a decision to make!" shouted Jesus and he stabbed a finger east toward the channel and a point in the fog bank between the colossus and the mountain peak where a large, slow moving craft slowly drifted into view.

Sarah's mouth dropped open.

I looked from Jesus to Sarah and ran down to the water's edge waving my arms and shouting.

"Hey! Wait! Come back," I cried.

"There you go Sarah," said Jesus, "See, how well you do with the Babylonians."

"But…"

I didn't know what on earth they were talking about, but off in the distance there sure as hell was another slow moving barge passing through to the north. The waves lapped up against my feet down by the Colossus, and I figured it was our last chance to hitch a ride. As the enormous craft slipped from view, I raced back up the slope through the mud where Jesus and Sarah were still yammering at one another.

"Go on," shouted Jesus, "Make a decision! Debbie can put on her wings and take you where ever you want to go. This ark, that ark, it's not too late. As long as you survive, isn't that all that really matters?"

"If I survive?" she said.

"And you can live to laugh about it at a cocktail party when you're eighty years old in a high rise condominium in Florida or Cape Cod or wherever you decide to go, finally, to die."

Jesus really looked like he was going to break down after that. He turned away and walked off through the rain down to the gigantic stone monument. He dropped against the base of the enormous stair-step pedestal and stared across the slate grey ocean to the mountain pass that led to the land of Nod and I think he may have been crying. I don't know. Maybe it was just the rain. But he just hung out down there as an ark carrying hundreds of God's creatures drifted slowly through the fog and out of sight to the north.

Sarah had dropped down to her knees in the mud staring, I supposed, at the puddles and the concentric circles left by each drop and the thousand drops and the ten thousand, thousand radiating circles. Maybe she was thinking about the night Jesus had gone back for her on the highway. She stood up and walked down to Jesus where he stood, motionless, beside the Colossus.

"I'm sorry," she said. She cleared her throat, "You know, I don't think I ever stopped to thank you for what you did the other night."

"What other night?"

"On the highway. I thought I had you all figured out. That you wanted me for a ransom or some weird serial killer thing, but I've run out of possible explanations."

"You saved my life once, so I guess we're even."

"But why, Jesus… Why did you go back for me…?"

She walked to his side.

"Jesus?"

He looked at her, "That's what I do," he said, "I go back for people."

They both leaned back against the enormous pedestal and watched the water rise in the valley. Meanwhile I was having very little luck with my friend, M-2500.

"Could you turn into a raft? Nothing fancy. It doesn't have to be aluminum. Just enough to get us across that channel to the mountain? There's plenty of snow to eat up there."

Of course, I'd never seen any real snow at that point in my life. I may have over-estimated its nutritional value in terms of our possible survival on the mountain top.

"Jesus doesn't seem to think it will do us much good in the long run," said M-2500.

"I'm not worried about the long run, I'm worried about the next fifteen minutes." I stopped short. Something else had suddenly crossed my mind.

Funny how ideas can just be out there, floating around, like driftwood. You put two and two together and you come with four every time. You find somebody else with the same idea, and sometime you come up with seven or some other number you never expected. That's when I looked over at the statue of the Cherub, guarding the way against no one, the slate gray ocean creeping up along the hem of its pedestal. I'd never heard of a Saturn V Rocket, but Sarah had. As she and Jesus watched the approaching tide and looked up at the towering height of the statue, she remembered the thing as it first appeared coming down out of the sky above the garden those centuries ago and she turned to Jesus and grabbed him by the shoulder

"A rocket!" she exclaimed.

"A what?"

"A rocket ship! M-2500 can turn into a rocket ship!"

"What on earth is a rocket ship?"

"No! It's not on the earth! I mean we'll get off the earth entirely. We'll fly up to the International Space Station and…"

She trailed off.

"What's wrong?"

"I don't suppose you've ever heard of space stations have you?"

Jesus shook his head.

"All the power in the universe and we're stuck here to drown beside this relic."

"How's that?"

"I suppose we should try to climb up on that pedestal," said Sarah, shaking off her blues and looking up through the rain. "It'll buy us another fifty feet."

"No," said Jesus, excitedly, suddenly checking his pockets. "You said the relic."

"I did?"

What remained of the enormous cherub stood on a stair-stepped series of three house sized blocks of granite. The last platform was not much higher than the level of the gravel walkway where we had been standing by the abandoned garden, but it seemed the only place to go. I suppose Sarah had stolen another of my ideas as she waved to M-2500 and me. We walked down to the Colossus and listened and that's where I had an even better idea. When the end finally came, I reasoned we might be able to climb up from the pedestal and scale the body of the statue, up the legs, the torso and each of could chose one of the four heads: Man, Oxen, Lion, and Griffin, to await the final hour, each on his own private island when the ocean rose up and obliterated all trace of us. If it came to that, and it probably would, I called dibs on the Lion.

"I call dibs on the lion head," I shouted, as M-2500 helped Sarah up the side of the first enormous slab of rock.

"What are you babbling about, now," said Sarah. She was on the first slab, on her belly and she reached down and took my hand. I scampered up M-2500's back and rolled onto the pedestal beside Sarah. I explained my plan as Jesus and the angel followed us onto the first slab. In five minutes we had scaled the remaining two slabs until we were all four of us standing on the final elevation. I immediately walked to the gigantic landing gear of the Colossus and extended my hands. I cursed when they met only a smooth polished surface.

The area of this last platform where we would await our demise was roughly the dimension of a large tennis court. I left the others and continued my survey of the monstrosity's pyramid shaped landing gear, but it was all too slick and smooth and steep all the way around to offer any hope of ascent. I had pretty much resigned myself to obliteration when I came around the corner and saw my three friends huddled together.

Jesus had found the relic he was looking for in his trousers pocket. I came up and looked at the small aluminum object he held in his open palm. It was the little gray bauble from the terrace of the Eastern Wall. The relic of the Ophanim, the strange time-spanning minions of the Creator's inner circle reduced to two concentric rings, frozen, one within the other at ninety degree angles.

"I thought they'd left it as a keepsake," said Jesus, "But the voice I've been hearing ever since I met John told me to pick it up."

"Your Uncle?" I said.

"What is it?" asked Sarah.

"I'm not sure," said Jesus, handing it to her, "Careful," he said.

Between thumb and index fingers she took the tiny, metallic curiosity and held it up in the gray light of the overcast day and inspected it.

Mary Ann and the Professor never seemed to learn that Gilligan would inevitably spoil their hopes of rescue. His unerring ability to ruin things was outdone only by their unfaltering confidence in his capacity to learn from his mistakes. It was a favorite show of mine during our times in California, but I never appreciated the comparison. My fellow castaways had no such misguided faith in me.

"Hey, can I see it?" I said thrusting forth my hand, but Sarah jumped back and M-2500 tentacles shot out like iron bars, halting my progress.

Sarah held fast to the bauble, "It looks like a helium atom," she announced, "The models we study in chemistry, showing the paths of the electrons, but there's nothing inside this thing." She looked even more closely, "But wait," she said, "The bands are covered with hundreds of smooth little bumps."

"The eyes," said M-2500, solemnly.

"Eyes?" I said, trying to push in closer for a better look.

"Here," said Sarah, carefully handing the keepsake to Jesus.

He held it firmly in his fist.

"Do you mind if we pray over it?" asked Jesus.

Oh brother! That did it. Of all the million things he possibly might have said, he had to go and bring THAT into it. You could see the wind go out of Sarah's sails and she dropped back from our little conclave under the shadow of the Colossus.

"You know, Sarah," I said, "You might as well humor him at this point. What have you got to lose?"

I looked at Jesus. He didn't seem all that impressed by my efforts. Sarah stared sullenly at her feet.

"Just pray, Sarah," I whined, "Would it kill you?"

"Pray?" she said and shook her head and looked up, "I wouldn't know where to begin."

"Just do what he does! Bow your head. I don't know either!" I said.

The wind had picked up considerably and the waves were crashing higher and higher against the sides of the pedestal. The first two levels were submerged and a sheet of foamy water spread out across the deck of the third elevation as Sarah trudged back to us where Jesus and M-2500 stood examining the metal rings in Jesus' hand.

"Let's pray," said Sarah in a husky voice, "So, how do we do this?"

"Here," said Jesus again clasping his fingers over the metal object and placing his clenched fist between us. Sarah placed a hand over his. I placed my hand with the sign of the devil over that, and watched as M-2500 removed my hand with its tentacle.

"Do you mind using the other hand?" Jesus suggested.

I nodded and placed my left palm down on the back of Sarah's hand. To the pile of human fingers, M-2500 added a gleaming metallic tentacle. Jesus closed his eyes and bowed his head. Sarah smirked a little, but followed his example. I wasn't sure M-2500 could bow its head or close its eyes, but I closed mine and waited.

"All right, then," said Jesus. "Sarah?"

"What?"

"Will you lead us in prayer?

"I'm sure I wouldn't know what to say."

"Well, we should start with a prayer of thanksgiving," he suggested.

"Thanksgiving?"

"Hey Jesus," I said opening my eyes and noticing that the water had now completely covered our platform and was lapping at our ankles.

"Can we just skip to the part where we ask for help?"

"Very well," he said with a sigh, "But we have all got to mean what we say and speak from our hearts."

"Our hearts?" said Sarah, rolling her eyes.

"Sure," I said. I'd been around the dinner table at his place often enough over the years to know the drill, and so we bowed our heads and closed out eyes.

"If you like, Jesus," I said, "I can even throw in the thanksgiving part."

"That would be fine."

So at last, we had all closed our eyes and bowed our heads again, and surprisingly, it took me a long time to think of what to say. Maybe a full minute had gone by when I finally spoke.

"Dear, God," I started, "We just want to thank you for our time together here and we just want to ask you go get us all out of here as quickly as possible. Amen."

"Amen," the others agreed.

We opened our eyes and looked at one another and then down at Jesus' hand. He opened his fingers revealing the bands of metal.

"Did it work?" I asked.

"I don't know," said Jesus.

"Look! Look," said Sarah, and we stared evenly more intently at the rings.

"The eyes! Look! The eyes are opening!" said Jesus.

Well, what do you know? Sure enough, the rows of tiny eyes, or whatever they were that looked like eyes, which ringed both of the bands had opened. They glowed and cast tiny glimmers of light on Jesus' open palm.

"Well," I said. "Now they can watch us drown."

Sarah glared at me as Jesus held the bands with the thumb and index fingers of both hands and pulled in opposite directions.

"What are you doing?" asked Sarah as a big wave rolled in and crashed against the side of the statue.

"I'm trying to separate the rings." He groaned, but the two glowing bands remained fixed at right angles, locked, one within the other.

"Why?"

"I don't know. That's what I'm getting in answer to our prayer." And the muscles in this neck bulged with exertion as he pulled, "The bands must be…" He let out a cry of pain, "I can't." he said, "I can't separate them."

"If the thing would only tell us what we're supposed to do," said Sarah.

"That's it!" said Jesus excitedly, "The rings aren't for me" and he turned excitedly to M-2500, "Give me your tentacles, here. Loop one through each of these bands."

M-2500 threaded the tips of its tentacles through each of the loops and began to pull in opposite directions.

"Give him room," said Jesus, and he corralled Sarah and me off to the side of the statue, "It is going to require a super human force to separate those two rings."

He was right. The array on M-2500's face shone brilliant white and its entire frame began to vibrate. Rain drops striking its tentacles turned immediately to steam and rolled away in hot sheets. There was an explosive thunder clap as the two bands released one another. M-2500 took a step back and the colors of the spectrum raced across its brightly lit crystal arrays.

"Well?" asked Jesus, slowly approaching the angel.

We looked at M-2500. It held its two tentacles outstretched before the flashing lights of its face. The rings had each slipped down the tapered ends of its two tentacles.

"I have received a transmission from the future," said the angel.

We stood there for a minute. I had a real creepy feeling.

"We need a…" Jesus turned to Sarah. "What was it?"

"A rocket ship."

"A rocket ship. Can you provide a rocket ship to rescue us?"

"I understand what is required," said the angel.

"Make it so," said Jesus.

That sounded mighty impressive, I have to admit. The trouble was that we had run out of time; the waves were sweeping in from all sides and it looked like Jesus was planning to offer a parting prayer for Sarah and me to wind up our lives on that granite slab. Suddenly, we felt a bone-wrenching tremor course through the granite pedestal. Maybe the big giant standing over us was feeling left out of the proceedings. No sooner had Jesus let loose his rather imperious sounding, "Make it so," remark, than the gigantic Cherub stepped off its pedestal. Terrified, we grabbed hold of M-2500 for dear life as the northern most foot of the Colossus began sliding away and dropped down over the edge of the enormous base. The shock wave of the Colossus picking up its feet and stepping down to the submerged mountainside sent us tumbling with M-2500 to the edge of the platform. The ocean was crashing in around our waists.

"What's happening!" cried Sarah!

"We've awakened the monument!"

"Hey, Jesus," I shouted.

"What?"

"Do Cherubim have arms?"

"I don't think so!"

"Well, this one does!"

Through the spray of crashing surf in our faces and the downpour of rain, Jesus followed my gaze along the massive columns of rock towering above us. We watched two enormous hands, with fingers, big as railroad cars, descend rapidly toward us. Preparing for my end, I closed my eyes -- to be squashed like a beetle on the back of a damp patio square. I felt a gale like wind, but then, to my amazement, realized I was still alive. The Colossus had stepped off its pedestal, loosed the topmost slab of granite with its massive mitts and was gentling raising us up into the air like hors d'oeuvres on a serving tray. Water streamed from our legs and disappeared off the four edges of the rectangular platform as our thousand ton sanctuary rose into the air.

"What's happening?" cried Sarah.

"It doesn't want us to drown," shouted Jesus, and then, stepping back to M-2500, "Are you ready?"

"I believe so, but the metamorphosis will require all available area of the platform."

"All right, then! The three of us will move over by the giant's fingers."

The Colossus was holding the slab on each end with its enormous digits. Its thumbs were curved up beneath, providing support as its mighty arms propelled us up into the sky. We rose through the open air past the statue's legs, torso, its gigantic wing-shaped dark-matter panels and up and up into the air. We were well over five hundred feet above the waves and approaching the chins of the four motionless heads, each head as big as a small island resting on the creature's shoulders. But we did not stop there. The creature was bench pressing the granite slab over its heads, up through clouds another three hundred feet into the sky.

We broke through the first cloud deck. All trace of the world and its endless ocean had disappeared below. Across the gray field of clouds, five miles to the east and just below the second higher cloud deck of endless rain, we could see the mountain peak. It did not look nearly as tall from our new vantage point.

"Let's move" said Jesus, grabbing me by the sleeve, "Move to its fingers over there and give our angel some room."

We followed his command and hastened to the western edge of the platform, where the stone fingers of the Cherub curved up and over, their tips planted like four black redwoods in the edge of the granite slab. A hundred feet across the granite platform we saw the gigantic fingers of its right hand where it gripped the slab's eastern edge. This Cherub had not moved in a thousand years. Now, after these few exhilarating moments, it ground to a halt once more. All motion across the deck had ceased except the strong, wet breeze driving in from the west.

M-2500 had moved quickly to the center of the slab and stopped. We watched and held our breath. After a while I took another breath and held it. The knuckles of my clenched fists were white. This was going to be something spectacular, I just knew it! I opened my eyes and looked over at Sarah. Her eyes were tightly closed and her face screwed up as though she was awaiting an explosion. Jesus stood with head bowed; evidently deep in prayer, and I looked back the fifty feet at M-2500 planted in the platform's center. I took another deep breath and closed my eyes. My hands had cramped a bit, and I opened them and flexed my fingers. I shifted the weight onto my left foot. After a while, I sat down and bowed my head. I hadn't thought of home in a long while. I reconsidered my vague thoughts of one day moving to the coast of the Mediterranean or the Galilee and purchasing a fishing fleet.

I looked through the rain at M-2500. It hadn't moved as far as I could tell. I looked over at Sarah.

"What's going on?" I asked.

She shook her head.

I guess we sat or stood there for another forty-five minutes until Jesus came out of his trance, climbed to his feet and walked over to M-2500. He was over there for quite a while. I couldn't really tell what he was doing and I was about to go over and ask him, when he came back and sat down between us on the granite slab.

"Well?" asked Sarah.

"It's working," Jesus replied.

"What's working?" I said. I'd almost forgotten why we were waiting.

"Our friend is receiving information from the future."

"The future?" snorted Sarah.

Jesus looked her straight in the eyes.

"Downloading information?" she said with a little throw away laugh.

"Apparently, yes, if that's the word for it," said Jesus.

"Great!" said Sarah, "So when does he turn into a rocket ship?"

"The process has already begun."

"Process?" moaned Sarah.

She didn't like that word. I didn't like the sound of it either. If getting a rocket ship was going to require a "process" maybe we could just drop the "rocket" part of the deal, whatever a "rocket" was. I'd settle for a plain old ship.

"There is nothing else we can do but wait and pray," continued Jesus.

"More praying?" I whined.

"Be patient," he said gently.

"But we already prayed," I shouted.

"How long is it going to take?" Sarah yelled. She looked at Jesus as though she expected an answer. They exchanged a long look and she lowered her gaze, "I'm sorry," she said, "I suppose I should be grateful we weren't swept away by the ocean down there."

"That might be a good place to begin," said Jesus.

That made us think for a while, but a person can only sit for so long and the time wore on, and if there was any change in our friend the angel over on the launching pad, I couldn't see it. Later that afternoon we came to the conclusion that changing into a rocket ship was going to take quite a while and we surveyed our floating island. It was about one hundred feet long by fifty feet wide. At either side, like serving handles, the four giant stone fingers rose up in the air at a height of ten or fifteen feet, curved at the knuckles and planted their tips in granite. To our delight and relief we soon discovered that on both sides of the platform, the palms of the hands were pressed flush against the edges of our granite slab and we could get in out of the rain protected by the overarching fingers, particularly on the western side where the back of the giant's hand blocked the wind. Sheltered thus from the rain and wind and with the black stone palms pressed seamlessly against the platform, there was no danger of us rolling off the edge to our certain deaths.

I fell asleep with my arms wrapped around the tip of our giant's little pinky. When I awoke, M-2500's transformation was still incomplete. In the near total darkness it continued to rain, and out across the platform, there was no sign of the angel. I started shouting, and woke Jesus.

"Where is he? What happened to M-2500?" I cried.

When I came out from behind the fingers onto the platform I about stumbled over what was left of him. It looked as though our friend had melted: melted like a gigantic candle and flowed out like wax over the stone. I stopped in my tracks. The pool of him, it was really too big to call a puddle, was about twenty feet in diameter. Later that day as the rain clouds filled with their oppressive gray light, the pool became more clearly visible. I bent down to touch it. Jesus advised against this. While the viscous blob was plastic and flowed almost imperceptibly, it shed the rain. Through the afternoon it began to spread into more and more an oval shape growing gradually in thickness and length until it stretched nearly a hundred feet long.

It was frustrating to watch. We took turns doing this throughout the long day, sitting alone, or the two of us, or sometime all three. Like watching the minute hand of a watch, it was happening all too slowly. You only noticed any kind of change after your concentration had been broken, and you found yourself looking back at a memory or when you thought about something else for a while or returned to watching after a nap.

All we could do, all that long, cold rainy day was wait, and watch and try to sleep and try not to think about food. Night came and went. You could lie on your back with your mouth open and your eyes closed and get a decent mouthful of water, but there was nothing to eat. Several times we tried talking to our friend the angel, but it was no use. Sarah said he looked like a deflated hot air balloon, whatever that was, of red, white and chrome colored fabric.

On the third day, Sarah and I were getting mighty hungry. I thought about food every waking moment. Sarah spent a lot of time with Jesus during those times on other side of the platform in her shelter of the giant's left hand. I checked in every hour or so. At first I had assumed that he was lecturing her, the way he used to lecture the boys and young men at temple, but I soon realized that it was Sarah who was doing most of the talking.

Jesus wanted to know everything that she knew about world of the future. He was especially interested in what she had learned about history. When did civilization begin? Who were the earliest people? What did they believe? Who were their gods? She had plenty to say, and maybe it was a good thing too, because we had an awful lot of time our hands. At the end of the first day of the "Sarah Lectures," which marked our third day on the platform, she got him all the way to classical Greece. She was really impressed with the guys from those times. Some guys named Plato and Aristotle. She really seemed to have the "hots" for that guy, Aristotle. I don't know, but Jesus seemed more interested in what she said about Plato's ideas and how that guy's teacher had been some kind of martyr and died over something or other.

I think Jesus was actually looking forward to another day on the platform. That was pretty freaking weird. I suppose he and I were on different timetables. I spent most of my waking hours out on the deck in the rain. I was watching the angel for some sign that it was turning into our escape vehicle. Sarah had explained the idea of rocket ships to Jesus and me, but I still had a tough time imagining what it was going to wind up looking like and constantly wondered what to check for in the way of progress. Basically, by the morning of the fourth day, M-2500 looked like an eighty foot long loaf of bread. He was painted cherry red on the sides with a doughy white top and lots of silvery tubes poking in and out this way and that along his flanks. The whole thing was about ten feet high but was definitely rising, and that afternoon it actually sprouted silvery dorsal fins in what we supposed was the rear section.

The transformation definitely seemed to be picking up steam and that was a good thing because late in the afternoon Jesus and Sarah were coming out of one of their history sessions when I walked over to them and happened to glance over the edge of the platform. The ocean had risen up to the clouds! It had swallowed up that first lower cloud deck below. Now the waters were rising up along the uplifted arms of the statue.

Meanwhile, Sarah had managed to deliver fairly extensive reports on the Egyptian Book of the Dead, Hinduism and Buddhism. She had talked for hours about Islam, more or less skimmed over Judaism, since Jesus already knew just about all there was to know on that subject, and seemed to be "saving up" for her talk on Christianity. She was keeping the best for last and had been planning this last installment all along, building up to it, so to speak.

According to Sarah, we three were apparently stuck somewhere "in the wilderness" between the time Jesus was baptized in the Jordan River and the time that he began his so-called ministry. I guess because the water was rising so quickly, she had to leave out a lot of the details about his later life, only that after his death he would be known one day as a great prophet and the founder of one of the world's great religions. She was vague about some of the particulars. I think at one point she let slip that he would be known as the savior of mankind. That seemed to jive with what Jesus already knew from the prophets about the Jewish Messiah, and that really got his interest going. Since I actually knew Jesus, the talk about him seemed a little more interesting to me than facts about the lives of people I'd never met or even heard of, so I stuck around. It was funny, because Sarah was able to talk a mile a minute on everything else under the sun, but on this subject she kept pausing and picking her words carefully as though she didn't quite know what to say or how to say it.

"So, how exactly does he end up saving everyone?" I asked at one point.

"He makes a sacrifice."

I nodded my head.

"A sacrifice of what?" asked Jesus.

"Of something very important."

"A sheep?" I asked, although no sooner had I said it than I changed my mind and added, "A heard of sheep?"

"I don't own a heard of sheep," said Jesus.

"But you might someday." I said and I turned to Sarah. "Does he sacrifice a heard of sheep?"

Even as I waited for her answer I didn't know how giving up a heard of sheep would save mankind, and from what? Sarah seemed to be getting very impatient with us. She stood.

"I think I'll go out on the deck and see how M-2500 is doing." she said.

Jesus and I were left looking at one another.

"Man, something sure got into her," I said.

Jesus nodded.

"Sounds to me like there was something she didn't want to tell you."

"Yes, it did."

"Do you have any idea what she was talking about?"

"Some."

I smiled excitedly, "So, are you really planning to start a religion when we get back?"

"I hadn't thought about it that way."

"Well, I don't think the priests will like it if you go back and try to start your own religion."

"No, I don't suspect they would."

"Will we be able to eat pork?"

"Excuse me?"

"In your new religion, will we be able to eat pork?"

"I don't know. Pork?"

"That would be pretty cool if we could eat some pork once in a while."

"It's not really going to be a religion about what we eat."

"What about shellfish?"

"Huh?"

"You know. Oysters, lobster, some big old jumbo prawns?"

"Maybe. I don't know."

"I sure would like a mess of deep fried clams with lemon and tartar sauce."

"I'm sure we all would."

"What about rabbit in a rabbit stew?"

"Steve…"

"Crab Louie?"

"Steve, I really don't know."

"Well, it sounds to me like you haven't done much thinking about this religion you're planning to start."

"I've thought a lot about it, and I never said I was planning to start a religion." Jesus replied. "It's just that food isn't going to be the main point of it all."

"Why not?"

"It's not a religion about food!"

Whatever I'd said had gotten to him. I was quiet for a while. I could see out across the platform through a small gap between the index finder and the middle finger of the giant hand, almost like a small window below the third knuckle. Sarah was out there looking at M-2500's progress in the rain.

"Well, can we a eat lot?" I said.

"Steve, would you stop?"

"I'd like to know. It's important. Will we be able to eat any old time and as much as we can stand?"

"What do you mean?"

"I mean a lot. A whole bunch of food. Like the Romans?"

"No. Definitely not. Not like the Romans. Nothing in excess."

"Well, it doesn't sound like your religion is going to be much an improvement over the one we have now."

Jesus laughed. Actually, he laughed very hard, harder and longer than I had seen him laugh since our days in the white water canyon. It made me really uncomfortable. Of course I was already pretty uncomfortable, pretty miserable actually. If he was laughing at me – I didn't really care.

"That's right," I said, "Have a good laugh!"

I walked out from around the shelter of the over-hanging fingers to where Sarah stood.

"What do you think of the rocket ship?" I said.

"I don't know," she said.

"Do you think it will be ready in time?"

"Listen, Steve," she said, turning to me, "I may regret telling you this, because most of the time you strike me as a pretty big screw up, and I don't really have any reason to trust you, but I can see Jesus cares a lot about you and that he sees something in you of value, which I just haven't been able to see."

"Well, why don't you just save it for somebody else," I said curtly and started away from her across to the opposite shelter on the Western side of the platform as though I had important business to attend on the other side of town.

She walked along behind me, "Steve, Steve wait."

Reluctantly, I stopped and looked back at her.

"You're his friend."

I smiled, "Yes," I said. "I am his friend. So, what?"

"So, this is about Jesus."

"What about him?"

"I don't know how we get out of this, or whether you and I ever do get out of this, but he does."

"Great."

"At least I think he gets out of here."

"So?" I said with a little fake impatience in my voice. I could have stood there all day looking her over. Man, she was pretty.

"So, he manages to get back to your time and gathers a bunch of guys from Galilee and preaches for three years, and he goes to Jerusalem for Passover."

"Lots of people go to Jerusalem for Passover."

"But you don't understand!" She grabbed me by the shoulders, "He gets arrested!"

My mouth dropped open; that was the voice she used when she knew what she was talking about.

"What happens to me?"

"I don't know."

"Well, if he goes up to Jerusalem there's a good chance I will have gone up with him."

"Steve. This isn't about you. It's about him!"

What I wouldn't have done for a cigarette and a shot of bourbon whiskey.

"Anyway, you don't become famous like Jesus."

"And you read about this in your history books from the future?"

"Yes…"

"No mention of me? Steve of Nazareth?"

"Sorry."

"Well, if you're so worried about his getting in trouble in Jerusalem, why don't you tell him about it?"

"I started to."

"I'll tell him."

"No, wait…" She reached out and took my arm, "There's more. He gets arrested and put on trail and he's executed."

"Executed?"

She had my attention now. She looked kind of scared.

"What did he do?" I asked.

"That's the whole point. He didn't <u>do</u> anything. He'll be totally innocent."

"Wow…" I shook my head. "That's quite a story."

"Wait a minute. It's not just a story. It really happened, or will happen. It's an historic fact. No one disputes the idea that he actually lived. It's only the significance of his life that people argue about."

"So, what do you want me to do? Warn him never to go to Jerusalem?"

"I don't know what I want you to do. I'm sorry. I shouldn't have said anything, but just don't mention anything to him about it, all right?"

"Sure…"

"Promise?"

"Yeah."

"Steve, promise!"

"Yes! I promise."

"Thank you, Steve. I'll figure out some way to talk to him about it."

I'm not sure that she ever did, but, of course, as his best friend, I had to mention it to him. That night as we climbed into the shelter on the evening of the fifth day, I told him exactly what Sarah had told me. Funny thing was; he didn't bat an eye. Actually, he may have batted an eye. It was way too dark to see a detail like that, but he didn't seem at all concerned. Finally, as we drifted off to dream our separate dreams – me about steak, eggs and that mouthwatering hotdog smothered in onions, sauerkraut and mustard on a freshly baked hoagie handed out on the fake Broadway, and Jesus, about "whatever," I heard him say,

"A lot of people aren't going to like what I have to tell them. I won't be surprised if I get arrested. No, it's a real possibility."

"I don't know what you have planned when we get back home," I said, drifting off to sleep, "But I sure hope you make it okay to eat all that stuff we were talking about. That sure would be nice!"

The next morning brought many surprises. Chief among them was the sea foam scudding across the deck. The ocean waves were pounding the forearms of the Colossus sending up a shower of salty spray onto the platform. For half an hour it looked as though the sun would break through the dense clouds, but the sky remained overcast. Late in the morning, an island of ice, two hundred feet thick and big as a city block broke loose from a glacier on the mountain peak five miles distant sending a tidal wave surging across the drowned valley.

"Run for you lives," I warned the others, but then I realized Jesus and Sarah were over in the shelter of the left hand. As a huge wave fanned out toward us, I figured that left hand was as good a place as any to seek refuge, and I made a dash for it. Jesus and Sarah had come out looking for me when and I dove around the corner of Mr. Pointer Finger, and we each got on our knees and grabbed hold of a finger and closed our eyes.

There was a terrific crash and the wave swamped the platform. I felt cold ocean water in my mouth and a tremendous tug on my back and legs, but I held on for everything I was worth. Almost immediately the water drained away and Sarah and Jesus were out on the deck, looking at M-2500. Like a barnacle, he had weathered the killer wave. Tide pools dotted his bumpy back. I tried a mouthful of seaweed but I just couldn't keep it down and ended up retching over the side.

"I warned you, Steve," said Sarah.

And I was about to say something smart in reply, when, wiping my mouth with my forearm, we each stopped in our tracks as an iceberg breached the surface of the ocean, swirled past us like a gigantic ice cube and drifted away to the north.

After that incident, the chief object of my attention remained our bitchin' hot ride that was taking shape out on the launching pad. M-2500 looked like a cross between a sleek 21st century luxury yacht and a cherry red '57 Chevy. She sprouted some kind of lazy Susan on her belly so the entire vehicle was now slowly rotating like the needle of a compass in a ninety degree arc, or the cars of the future I saw at an Auto Show at the Expo Center in St. Louis with hot babes in bikinis and high heeled shoes splayed out on the hoods. It would take three hours, but the craft, instead of pointing east into the knuckles of the giant's left hand, would end up pointing north. When this was accomplished the nose and the tail would hang off either side of the granite platform. I wondered how we might get back to the other side of the platform.

That afternoon I received an answer as the vehicle began to rise ten feet off the platform on a set of chrome runners. The glistening skids tapered down in the rear portion holding the flashy tail section perhaps five feet above the horizontal plane. The forward struts, extending from the runners to the ship's hull, held the vehicle's needle nosed bow a good ten feet higher than the aft section. The mottled, doughy appearance of the craft's surface had begun to settle to a hard, smooth, polished gloss, glimmering with highlights even on the overcast afternoon.

I was back there looking at my reflection in the chrome trim by the tail fins when I felt a stinging, burning sensation on the back of my right hand. I brushed it off, thought it was just my imagination. Jesus was on the other side of the platform, looking up at his new ship.

"It sure is beautiful," he said.

"Awesome," said Sarah.

"How long do you think it will be until she's ready?" I asked.

My two friends turned in my direction and were about to make some disparaging remark when they noticed the object that had prompted my question. To our south, no more than a hundred yards out in the waves something was roiling the waters. All at once the submersible Black Scorpion Flag Ship of the Prince of Air and Darkness split the waves and crashed down hard on the surface like a breaching whale. Jesus' apparent nemesis had nothing, if not a flare for the dramatic. His demonic henchmen soon appeared in the sleek black conning tower on the vessels' monstrous back and hoisted their captain's standard: a black flag bearing, in white reverse, his convoluted web emblem.

"Oh my God," moaned Sarah.

I looked at the back of my hand.

"Don't tell me you're proud of that thing!" she snapped and looked at Jesus.

He only scowled at the both of us as he crossed the deck to my side where I stood rubbing my hand. I stared at the monstrous craft off our starboard side.

"I'm going to have to get some balm for that hand of yours," said Jesus.

"Do you think it's the driver?"

"Close enough."

"What do you think he wants?"

Through the rain, we saw a tall figure emerge on the conning tower. He was the size and shape of a lean, powerful man dressed in black with a flowing, purple cape. He held a microphone and spoke, the amplified sound reverberating from hidden loudspeakers. The familiar voice boomed across the white caps.

"Good afternoon people! My, my, my. Amazing how we keep bumping into one another over the millennia. Makes one wonder whether this is something more than mere, random coincidence. Imagine the odds! It's almost as though someone had invented a tracking device and planted it on a member of your party!"

He laughed at this and then went off in a new direction as arch-villains are prone to do. "So, what do you think of my Black Scorpion Flagship?"

Right on cue two ugly claws of black serrated metal, draining streams of black seawater and as big as steam shovels rose slowly out of the waves on either side of the black conning tower. They snaked alongside, on jointed metal arms and snapped like infernal castanets as the electronic voice continued.

"All those years in bio-medical research and genetic engineering for my old boss weren't a total waste! You can see that in the last twenty million years we've diversified our portfolio." He chuckled again, "But I tell you, we had to throw this puppy together in a hurry. I don't suppose you've seen primitive vessels come through here in the past few days? They have the jump on us, but we've been tracking them from our secret underground lair in the side of that mountain over there!"

"Humor him," whispered Jesus, "The longer we can stall him, the longer M-2500 will have to finish up."

"What was that?" boomed the voice from across the narrow channel that now separated our platform from the slowly approaching vessel.

"I can read lips you know! Not to boast about my eyesight, but if it weren't for these rain clouds I could read the inscriptions I've planned for your tombstones on the moon!"

Below the conning tower on the sleek black bow of the craft, three artificial eyes glowed a murderous red. From the central eye, a searing beam of energy leapt forward and exploded on one of the hands of the Colossus behind us.

"Which reminds me," the disembodied voice continued. "I don't suppose you've seen an M-Class Angel here about? About eight feet tall, triangular head, tentacles? He was traveling in your party at some time in the past. He used to work for us, you may recall. Real dependable, always did what he was told. Didn't miss a single day's work in over five hundred million years, but he ran off one day. My guess is that he sided with upper management in our little dispute. Be that as it may, I believe he has something of ours from the old shop. Something that belongs to us."

"What's he talking about?" said Sarah who had come to us from behind.

"The rings," whispered Jesus.

"Let's be clear," continued the arch-enemy, "The technology you're sporting in your show room up there is from the far future! Do you think it fair that only one side gets to go gallivanting about the time stream willy-nilly at the drop of a hat? Frankly, I'm a little upset. You've had us on our heels, I credit you that, but consider your advantage. Given enough time, we'll figure it out. We already understand the riddle of the two human beings from the future who were SUPPOSED BE IMMORTAL."

Sarah and I exchanged a glance.

"Thanks, Steve you were a big help! We'd planned to use a serpent man from our private menagerie, but then you fell into our lap on the banks of the Euphrates. Trapping us when management closed up the garden was only a temporary set-back, so now…"

He must have put his hand over the microphone. We could hear his muffled voice and others voices in the background over the loudspeakers.

"Well, as you can no doubt see, the hour of retribution has arrived. Don't you think it wonderfully ironic that the Creator's own waters should carry us to your doorstep? Now, seriously folks, stand back as we bring THE BLACK SCORPION FLAGSHIP alongside and prepare to board."

True enough, we watched in horror as the black submarine slowly came alongside our granite platform. An ominous portal opened in the side of the conning tower and five fly creatures in black battle armor scurried out onto the hull of their vessel. Two of them immediately set to work on a mechanical crank-handle engaging a telescoping gang blank that emerged from a groove beneath the threshold. The walkway dipped tremulously toward our granite sanctuary in response to the heaving ocean swells. Dramatically back lit by the red glow from the interior of the black tower, the familiar form of Beelzebub appeared in the doorway. He'd lost his khaki shorts and ranger hat and was decked out in a black leather trench coat with a lot of decorative chrome studs and chains. The monster gestured to its underlings and stepped onto the hull, as more infernal sailors poured out, some of them with grappling hooks and lengths of black cable. These creatures fanned out along the length of the Black Scorpion and heaved their iron hooks. One cable sailed past only a yard or two from where we stood, continued the fifty feet across the deck and fastened into the granite lip on the far side of the deck. The cable went taut and several of the fly-men lashed it down to their sub.

A second grappling hook flew through the air and bounced off the tail section of our incubating rocket ship.

"Is our bun still in the oven?" I shouted as more and more cables whizzed and crisscrossed past where we huddled in the shadow of M-2500.

Jesus looked perplexed.

"The ship! Isn't it going be ready in time?" cried Sarah.

We watched in horror at the Captain of the Black Scorpion appeared on the threshold in the portal of his conning tower and surveyed with infinite satisfaction the handiwork of his fly-men. Yes, these were good times for the Lord of Evil.

Stepping over one of the chrome runners Sarah reached up under the midsection of our rocket ship and pounded on the red cherry hull.

"Are you about done in there, M-2500?"

There was no answer. We looked back at the Black Scorpion, as Satan raised an arm in the air pointing in our direction. The gangplank had reached our deck and settled into place with a clang.

"Fly my minions! Fly! Bring me the Rings of the Ophanim and the severed heads of the human beings."

Jesus looked down at me, "If we get out of this," he said, "We really have to do something done about that tattoo of yours."

I looked down at my insignia for an instant having forgotten that it had been burning like hot oil for the past ten minutes, but now there were new horrors as a dozen fly-men on the hull of the Black Scorpion leaned forward, trying their wings. The loathsome sound of buzzing filled the cold, afternoon air. Throughout these last terrible moments as the insect abominations took flight and the icy ocean finally overtopped our sanctuary and poured out across our ankles, Sarah continued to pound on the keel of the rocket.

"God," we heard her cry, "If you're out there, please do something," and she punctuated each syllable with the beat of her fist on the unbreakable red-cherry alloy, "Wake -- this -- ship -- up!"

The fly-men were out for blood and they would have had it as they descended upon us when suddenly I heard a sound that reminded me of the blue light bug zapper outside an ice cream stand on Chippewa one hot evening in South St. Louis in 2002.

Twitching faintly and trailing blue smoke a fly creature crashed onto the deck with a splash. Now another, "ZAP" and another creature careened past and slammed into the stone fingers of the Colossus with a sickening thud. Something from within our cherry-red, white hardtop super ship was generating an almost invisible blue aura of light enveloping everything within a twenty foot radius of the vessel. It faintly tingled on our skin and if one thought about it long enough it even began to tickle, but to the fly creatures it instantly flashed fried them from the inside out. One of the monsters had circled around the deck and approached from the north aiming a nasty looking spear at Jesus. It buzzed in at fifty miles an hour, sailed through the entire field of blue force before dropping its lance, overshooting the deck, and heading out for the Black Scorpion. The aura had so thoroughly cooked the minion that its internal fluids flash boiled over the gang blank and the creature exploded. Three pounds of hot green and yellow bug guts sailed through the air and splattered the Supreme Commander directly in his face.

Oh, he went on a rant after that: a big frustrated, ineffectual rage, punctuated by oaths and impossible orders.

"His henchmen are dropping like flies." I said to Jesus.

"Yes. Yes they are. Yes, that's rather funny!" he replied.

We turned back to Sarah who leaned against a chrome strut of the landing runners. She looked up into the overcast sky from the underside of the rocket ship. "Thank you, thank you, thank you," she repeated over and over.

"Sarah?" said Jesus.

"My prayer. My prayer was answered. He... it... Maybe it's a sign?"

"It's a sign if you want it to be."

"What about him?" said Sarah, looking at the submarine. The commander had kicked loose the now superfluous gang plank and disappeared into the conning tower with what remained of his crew. The bulkhead slammed shut with a metallic "clang" that resounded across waves.

"He'll dog us the rest of our lives," said Jesus.

"I don't know whether I like the sound of that."

"Trust me," said Jesus and next he turned to me. "You ready to go?" he asked.

"I don't know," I said honestly, "Where?"

Jesus smiled, reached up and knocked on the side of the rocket ship.

"You ready?" he called up at the cherry-red paint job.

In response, a pinhole of radiant white light appeared in the bottom of the hull. Like the aperture of a camera, seven panels appeared in the seamless underbelly of the craft and pin wheeled silently away to expose a four foot opening. In the next instant a spiral staircase of glimmering chrome corkscrewed down through the opening and stopped in the ocean water that was just pouring in over our knees.

"Watch that first step," Jesus said to Sarah as she climbed up into the waiting ship.

Jesus, turned to me, "Did you put out the lamps?"

"The lamps?" I looked back west in the direction of the stone fingers of the Colossus, suddenly overcome with the dreadful sensation that I had neglected to do something vitally important.

"The lamps? What lamps?"

Jesus smiled.

"Oh, for a minute you had me worried," I said.

"Have you given thanks?" he asked, once again catching me off guard.

We exchanged a long look and both laughed as I followed Jesus up the staircase. That Jesus, what a kidder.

* * *

We raced upstairs like kids in a carnival funhouse. As we passed up through the lower deck in the dimness we could see something that looked like a sleeping quarters in the stern and a full galley in the forward compartment. I was really tempted at that point to check to see if there was anything to eat in the pantry, but in the general excitement, I "followed the light" and the rhythmic sway of Sarah's exquisite rear-end up the steps to the flight deck.

The place was trim, sleek and what was known in the parlance of the 1950's and '60's as, "Futuristic." In other respects, the main deck reminded me of the motor home Jesus and I had boarded that first night in Nazareth, but way, way, way cooler, and of course, not in the service of someone possessed by Satan.

A diffuse blue green light emanated from behind a chrome valance that bordered the perimeter of the ceiling. There were cushioned seats and evenly spaced, tinted portholes on each side of the long narrow room.

"Good afternoon," sounded a deep, sultry voice from the forward section of the deck.

"Debbie," I cried, happily scooting past Sarah and striding up the slight incline toward the cockpit. Through the open bulkhead at the bow of the ship, I took two steps down into a glass windowed cabin behind two large flight chairs and half expected to see the sexy angel in her low-cut, cherry red gown. Instead I found two, empty, cherry-red leather seats, surrounded by an array of twinkling lights and complicated looking knobs, switches, gauges and LCD panels. The cabin seemed to pulsate with a life of its own. The configuration of the central crystal array reminded me of L-2500's face.

"Debbie?"

"I'm here."

"Debbie, is that you?"

"Yes."

"I can't see you."

"You're inside of me."

That was a weird thought, and I thought about it again, recalling the day I met M-2500, "I thought we agreed not to use that 'special' voice." I said.

"Naming the ship for a female of your species is a long-established tradition. Surely you're aware of the practice."

"Hi, Debbie," called Sarah, looking around the flight cabin, evidently, for the placement of concealed microphones and speakers.

"Hello, Sarah. We have about five minutes until the incoming ocean waves begin to compromise our current position on the pedestal. Good afternoon, Jesus."

"This sure beats our aluminum raft," said Jesus.

"So, Debbie, how does it feel having people walking around inside you?" I asked taking a seat in the pilot's chair.

"It tickles," replied the angel.

I felt a tapping on my shoulder as Jesus sat in the adjacent co-pilot's seat on my right. I looked back over my shoulder and up at Sarah. She pursed her lips, shook her head and motioned me out of the cabin with her thumb.

"What?" I protested.

"Do you even know what a rocket ship is?" she asked.

"Well, he doesn't know any more than I know."

"Look there," said Jesus, interrupting.

We followed his gaze from the center of the main console midway between the disputed flight seats up to a small control panel. The inner workings were conducted by chrome rods through two vertical slots ending in two identical levers. They were set, for the time being at least, in opposite positions along parallel groves that ran vertically beneath the crystal array that so closely resembled the countenance of our angel, M-2500. The lever on the right was at the very top of its track. The adjacent lever was set at the bottom of the second track. The levers were not all that remarkable in themselves, but looped midway around each of them, were the respective rings of the Ophanim.

"Hey Debbie," I said, reaching forward with my hand, "Are those what are left of your tentacles?"

"Don't touch those levers," shouted Sarah.

From his place in the seat beside us, Jesus' left arm shot out barring my path. I leaned back.

"Here," said Jesus climbing out of the ostensible co-pilot's seat. "I'll sit in back. You can take my place, but Steve, keep your hands off those levers. Do you understand? We have no idea what they're designed to do."

"Sorry, you guys," I said, getting up from the captain's chair, "You both go ahead and sit up front; you both know so much about rocket ships."

My feelings were a little hurt, but I was soon preoccupied with the thought of getting something to eat below in the galley. I made my way back into the main cabin and down the spiral stairway and climbed off into the galley. No sooner had my foot stepped off the stair than the forward section of lower deck was illuminated. I walked to a basin and a series of cupboards. I saw lots of stuff, but nothing to eat. I shook my head and pounded a metal countertop with my fist.

"Sorry, Steve," came a soothing voice. Once again I half expected to turn and see Debbie sitting at the round dining table behind me, and was disappointed that it was only M-2500's robot voice purring from some hidden speakers in the ceiling.

"The M-series is unable to synthesize chemical compounds and organic molecules. I'm afraid I have nothing for you to eat. I suspect our benefactors from the First Sphere intend for you to subside on something altogether different."

I was about to complain, when the craft lurched to the left. The lights flashed out and I was thrown down on the hard rubbery floor in the dark.

"Ye-ouch!" I cried. "What's happening up there?" There was no answer. "Are you playing around with those levers?" I shouted and smiled to myself. I was about to speak again when suddenly, a terrific shock wave coursed through the vessel and I flew in the dark and slammed up against metal cabinets. Pots and pans and utensils were falling from cupboard doors I'd left open and came crashing and banging down on the counter tops.

Outside, The Prince of Air and Darkness was back on his conning tower in the rain like a mad, heavy equipment operator at the controls of his Black Scorpion Flagship. He was currently bashing our rocket ship back and forth between his ship's enormous scorpion claws. The sound of our ship's metallic runners grating outside against the submerged granite slab sent nerve wracking vibrations up through the support struts into the metallic hull, to be followed by the boom and shock of a ten ton black metal claw bashing us. This went on for what seemed a full minute and then the sound of the grating metal fell away. I pulled myself to my hands and knees. The light flicked and came on and I tried to get to my feet but I felt dizzy, off balance. I felt the bruise on my head and got scared that I'd been seriously injured. Then I realized as the room dipped and rolled from side to side that we were adrift.

"Everyone okay, up there?" I barely got the words out when: BOOM. The force of an impact on the right side knocked me sprawling over the table and into the unyielding armrest of a metal chair. This time I had braced myself, rolled to my feet and dashed to the stairs. I was just coming up over the lip of the main deck when the thundering: BOOM sounded from the left, and I felt as though I cracked a rib against a metal joist. Debbie and her passengers suffered another volley before I managed my way back into the cockpit to see Jesus and Sarah powerless over the elaborate control console. They were shouting at Debbie and staring out the viewports to our north.

"It's Satan!" I cried, "He's toying with us!"

"Oh, is that what he doing?" shouted Sarah.

"Can you hear us!" cried Jesus desperately into the crystal array that flashed above the two motionless levers.

I swallowed hard as I listened to the robot angel's voice. She'd lost her feminine routine, but it didn't quite sound like good, old M-2500. The voice sounded scared.

"Forgive me," the voice began tremulously, "It is so — complicated here. It may be beyond my capacity!"

"Listen, M-2500," said Jesus, "All things are possible through he who created you."

"Yes... Yes... Of course..."

We prepared to brace ourselves for another salvo but felt only the eerily smooth rocking of the ship on the waves. The ship was slowly turning as a result of the last thunderclap from the left and the action of the wind blowing in from the west. The nose of the ship was turning to the east.

"Look!" said Sarah, pointing out the rain streaked view ports in front of the control console. We could see the wrists and palms and curved fingers of the Colossus -- like islands jutting out of the waves. Just the four finger tips of the eastern most hand were visible. Our craft continued to rock and slowly turn so that now we had spun 180 degrees from our original position and were facing the Black Scorpion.

"Wait a minute," Sarah continued.

"Quiet," I said.

"No! No. Its finger tips were facing down, gripping the platform." she continued.

"The platform? We don't need the platform. We're floating!" I shouted.

"But don't you understand? That means they've moved! The hands of the Colossus are moving!"

Jesus and I had more important things to think about.

"Yeah, well that guy out the window over there has other plans for us," I shouted and I was dead right.

"Now, the bastard is waving at us!" I exclaimed.

Sure enough, the Captain of the Black Scorpion Flagship waved at us from his perch on the conning tower. He pointed down at the two monstrous claws that floated on either side of his vessel. He smiled, raised his hands like a mime and opened and closed his thumbs and fingers.

"Ducks? Are they ducks?" I asked, breathlessly.

"They aren't ducks," said Jesus.

"Geese? Are they talking geese?"

"They're claws, Steve. Claws forged in the fires of Pandemonium. He wants us to see how he plans to destroy us."

Typical of an arch villain, and sure enough, the guy out there in the black and blue outfit with the purple cape threw back his head laughing in the rain and applied his "talking geese" to his own set of metal levers. At our close range the cranks and levers were clearly visible over the rim of the conning tower. He grabbed them and squeezed and instantly the gigantic claws responded, rising out of the waves on their enormous black metal stalks and opening to reveal rows of razor-sharp serrations. They snapped shut with a force that sent shock waves dancing across the water and vibrated in the metal beams of our ship. Once again that afternoon as we prepared to meet our deaths, something caught our attention on either side of our forward viewport. At first glance it looked as though the Black Scorpion Ship had drawn us into a channel between two rocky islands of columnar basalt. We looked quickly, one side to the other, even as the shadow of the enormous claws slowly yawned down upon us.

At the same time the islands of black rock sliced the waves like the dorsal fins of two impossibly large sharks.

"The hands of the Colossus," Sarah cried.

In the end, it was no contest. It was as though the ancient monument of the Cherub had discovered a member of our tribe at table in Nazareth with a delicious, but forbidden, Maine Lobster. The Colossus deftly snatched the claws, one in each hand, instantly crushing them beyond possibility of repair or threat to our vessel. Perhaps recalling the injunction against eating things that swim in the sea without scales, the two gigantic stone hands tore both claws off the floundering body of the submarine and with a flick of the wrists tossed the remains two hundred feet into the air in opposite directions where they spiraled down into the waves and sank from sight.

Inside Debbie's cockpit, we were stunned by what we had seen. I understood what Sarah had been trying to tell us and I apologized and shouted for joy. Sarah hugged me. Only Jesus stood and in the narrow space between the captain's chair and the control console and without expression on his face, he stared out through the rain streaked viewport.

As for the Captain of the Black Scorpion Flag Ship, well, his flagship no longer looked much like a scorpion. Really, it was no more than a smoldering metal tube taking on water through two enormous holes in its hull. It listed to port and we looked back in time to see her captain cling to the side of the conning tower with one arm and gesticulate wildly at us with the other. I went up to our window and pressed my face against the glass and laughed and waved until I felt Jesus hand on my shoulder, "Take no delight," he counseled.

"Oh come on, Jesus!" I protested, "You saw what he was going to do to us!"

"He really did have it coming," said Sarah.

"He dies a thousand deaths each day," said Jesus, "Look."

We turned back to the viewport. Outside, the being in the conning tower looked as though he were about to mount another attack from his bag of tricks, but he turned his face into the wind just in time to see an enormous black index finger breach the waves. Like a finger digging around in a nostril, the two ton digit slammed into the conning tower. Satan was pinned up against the bulwark and the wall of rock. We heard his bellows of rage even through the walls of our ship as the fingers of the other hand of the colossus closed over the ruptured hull of the Dark Lord's flagship and pulled it down with its master to the watery depths.

"Wow," I said

"Yeah, wow," repeated Sarah.

"I guess I do feel kind of bad for him," I said.

"Don't feel too bad," said Jesus.

"So, what do we do now?" asked Sarah. "Did you find anything to eat down in the galley?"

I shook my head.

"Debbie?" asked Jesus, looking up at the rafters, but nowhere in particular as we moved out of the cockpit and sat on comfortable divans in the main cabin amidships. "Debbie, are you there?"

"Yes…" the voice answered tentatively.

"Are we ready to take off?"

"No, I'm sorry to say."

"My people are going to need something to eat pretty soon, Debbie. Any estimate on how a long it will take you to be ready."

"A while, sir."

Actually, it turned out to be quite a while: two more days to be exact. For forty-eight hours we drifted to the east until the waters of the deluge covered over every mountain top on the face of the earth. Well, I don't know about EVERY mountain, but our mountain was covered over. We climbed up through the hatch on top of the ship and drifted right over it on the waves. We looked over the side of our ship and down through the water at the ice covered summit just below our keel. It's a good thing that we were drifting away; big, house-sized chunks of ice were popping up to the surface. No, that was a pretty impressive sight. It was pretty amazing too about Debbie. There wasn't a scratch on her. Up on her white hardtop we spent a long time that last day. We were mighty weak. We had pots and pans from the galley placed up on top to catch rainwater, so there was always plenty to drink. And then the clouds parted on the morning of the last day. Jesus had spent the night up top in the rain. Sarah and I climbed out of our bunks and climbed up on top and there was Jesus grinning from ear to ear and there it was, just like in the movies: a ray of sunlight streaming down out of the heavens and pretty soon it was coming down over our beautiful, cherry-red rocket ship and bathing our faces and we could see blue sky.

* * *

I suppose Noah and his crew up north had to wait a considerably lot longer for the sun to finally shine, but where we had drifted east of Eden there it was, and in some places a light golden rain was still coming down and a great big old rainbow filled the sky from one end to the other.

We smiled at each other and gave thanks and then we heard a voice coming up through the open hatch.

"I'm ready!"

15. Countdown

"Where should we go?" asked Debbie.

We looked at one another as we assembled back on the main deck.

"Food," I said looking around the compartment. Debbie's soft, sultry voice seemed to emanate from everywhere in the ship at once so it was difficult to know where to look when addressing her.

Sarah nodded her head, "Wherever we can find food."

"Three hundred miles to the North, aboard the wooden vessel?" replied Debbie.

"You mean Noah's ark?" I asked.

Jesus was climbing down the stairway from the observation deck where he had sealed the hatch. He shook his head.

"Raiding an ark's storehouse would provide only a temporary solution. They have rations enough only to support those on board. A visit from us would compromise their chances of survival."

"What if we just stopped in for a snack?" I asked.

"The unintended consequences of that decision would prove fatal to all aboard," he paused and looked sternly at Sarah, "And ultimately to the three of us."

"And what makes you such a genius all of a sudden?" she replied.

"My mind has been illuminated," said Jesus.

"That's just great!" I said, "We're real happy for you!"

"Thank you."

"I'm being sarcastic!" I shouted.

"Wait a minute," said Jesus, holding up a hand in truce. "Haven't we already covered this ground?"

"Hell, yes," I spat.

"We're starving, Jesus," said Sarah.

"What's changed since the last time we visited this subject?" said Jesus.

It turned out to be a rhetorical question, although I spent the next three minutes recounting the events of the past week and enumerating possibilities when Sarah interrupted.

"We have a rocket ship."

"Exactly!" said Jesus as he sat down and looked around in the air to address our ship.

"Debbie?" he asked.

"Yes?" came the disembodied voice.

"How fast can you travel?"

"As fast as you wish."

Sarah looked up at some vague point in the middle of the room, "Can you travel the speed of light?"

"Yes, but..."

"But what?"

"Well, it's difficult to put this into words that you and the others can understand..."

"Go ahead, Debbie," Sarah continued.

"My current configuration is meant to accommodate your 'mortal' sensibilities. I might have appeared as a wooden ox cart with a team of oxen, or an aluminum canoe, or three plastic lawn chairs on a patio."

"Yes..."

"The Ophanim suggested thrones."

"That would have been cool!" I said.

"They left it to me. I drew my inspiration from a science fiction comic book that you used to read at your grandfather's house on those summers in Cape Cod when you were a little girl."

For some reason Sarah got red in the face.

"The crude picture of that fanciful space ship pointing to the stars on the cover was my inspiration."

"Can you take me back there? Back to my grandparents'?"

"Hey, we're not going to go see that Broadway Show again, are we?"

"Hush, Steve," said Debbie.

"Well, is that what took you so long, trying to make yourself look like something out of a children's picture book?" I asked.

"My ability to travel through what you conceive as 'space' was never in question. Three point eight billion years ago when you first encountered me at the dawn of life on the planet's surface, I might have taken you to the outer planets of the Crab Nebulae in a heartbeat. It has never been purely a matter of space, but..."

"Eureka!" cried Jesus jumping up from the sofa. "The thrones! Beside the Cherubim and Seraphim in the First Sphere, the Thrones, the Ophanim! We may have their power at our finger tips!"

"A portion of it, yes."

Jesus looked straight down Debbie's keel line through the cockpit bulkhead to the control console and into Debbie glittering crystal array flashing brilliant white light. We gazed at the two control levers beneath.

"We can travel through time!" said Jesus.

"Are we going to Cape Cod?" I asked.

I followed Jesus and Sarah to the flight deck and down into the cockpit. Jesus climbed into the pilots' seat and Sarah sat to his right and buckled her seat belt.

"Cape Cod. The summer of 1993?" asked Jesus looking at Sarah as he buckled his seat belt.

She frowned, "No, I don't think I could go back there. What about you? Where do YOU want to go?"

"Sarah?"

"It's your rocket ship."

"Well..." Jesus looked down at his hands and then looked up with a boyish grin on his face, "Ever since you told me about Prince Siddhartha Gautama, I thought maybe, before I begin my ministry, I'd like the chance to meet him."

Sarah smiled and looked into the crystal array.

"Debbie?" she said.

"Sarah?"

"Lumbini, Nepal in the Himalayas."

I pulled down a folding auxiliary seat from the cabin wall behind them and fastened the harness, over my shoulder. "Some throne!" I said to myself.

"Set the date for 450 years before Christ," said Sarah in the cockpit reaching up and putting her hand on a silver lever and slowly pushing it forward up its vertical track.

"450 years before Christ?" said Jesus, "Why does the name sound so familiar? Who was that, Sarah?"

Sarah smiled as Debbie began the classic countdown from the pages of Grandpa Benton's favorite comic book.

"Five, four, three, two, one..."

"That would be you," Sarah replied.

16. Jesus in Space

The cherry-red space ship with the white hard top skimmed the surface of the ocean at two hundred fifty miles an hour and headed for a ray of sunlight breaking through the cloud bank on the horizon. We raced along the golden pathway and then slowly lifted off the surface of the earth. In the next minute Debbie climbed through the high cloud deck and the cabin was flooded with brilliant blue skylight. Debbie suggested that Sarah and Jesus open the compartments concealed in their armrests beside the cup holders, and help themselves to special designer sun glasses. Sarah tossed a pair back to me and I put them on just as Debbie reached the outer limits of the atmosphere. The sky turned blue black and I could see the faint glimmer of stars ahead in the sky.

Soon afterward when Sarah asked why we weren't experiencing any 'G's,' Debbie started in on a long explanation that seemed to fascinate Jesus and Sarah, but frankly got a little boring, with all sorts of references to famous and not so famous scientists from the future like

Galileo, Newton and Einstein, Hawking, and Auldmann, and a mess of others whose names I'd never heard.

I awoke with a start. We'd hit a big BUMP and in a passing instant of terror I opened my eyes and pulled off my sunglasses and looked ahead though the viewport but could see only grey mist. I was about to call out, when in the next instant the mist steamed away and we were looking ahead at an enormous planet encircled by rings hanging there before us plain as day.

"Saturn!" exclaimed Sarah.

"It is beautiful," said Jesus. "Hey, Steve, look at this!" he called back to me.

It was pretty awesome, I had to admit.

"Just giving you a little tour of the neighborhood before we head back," said Debbie, "And Steve, you might want to keep those sunglasses handy."

In the next instant we plunged toward a field of stars of such depth and variety that I shivered at the sight and as they wheeled away to the left another giant planet filled the view port, blue and serene.

"Uranus," said Sarah like a docent in a museum of astronomy. "It won't be discovered until the 1930's."

"Hanging out there all the while. Worlds I never knew existed," murmured Jesus as the space ship continued its arc.

"Time for those glasses," said Debbie and in the next instant she had completed her turn and was headed back toward the earth.

Of course it was the sun that caught our attention and left us breathless until we shot past Saturn and neared an enormous banded planet, itself surrounded by a dozen smaller worlds.

"That must be Jupiter," said Jesus. "And next…"

"The asteroid belt," said Sarah as Debbie slipped among thousands of whirling, tumbling boulders the size of small cities.

"The Creator wasn't satisfied with that one," said Debbie nonchalantly as another planet, red and laced with strange black markings wheeled into view on our right.

"Hey, there's Mars," I said.

"Really?" said Jesus.

"That's where Lucifer got his start before we moved operations to the earth," said Debbie.

"The angels had a base on Mars?"

"The Creator himself came by and toured the place four and a half billion years ago. He didn't like the climate and was really upset with XL-5000 over the shape of the moons. 'Moons are going be round,' I remember him saying. 'I'd rather have one round moon than two lop-sided moons any day.' We pulled up stakes and moved operations to the earth system. And here we are…"

We all of us had tears in our eyes as we peered through the viewport, none more than Sarah, I suppose, having seen pictures of it blue and green on TV the way she remembered it, hanging there so fragile against the enormity of the cosmos.

"Home," she said.

"For now," replied Jesus.

And that was pretty much it for my friends' first trip into space. After that we went on to have loads more adventures in the mountains of Asia and the Arabian Peninsula and then later, in a big, wild country called the United States of America. There were lots more battles with the Captain of the Black Scorpion and his minions to be sure. We even tangled with a demon emissary outside a great big church in a place called St. Louis that Sarah said reminded her of a cross between a shopping mall and an airport concourse where they played a new kind of music with electrical instruments called Christian Rock.

It was all new to Jesus and me, but not even what Sarah had read about in that book called The New Testament or what the Ophanim had revealed to M-2500 could have prepared us for our confrontation with Satan and the evil archangels on the Creator's home world at the center of the Ultimate Universe.

There would be plenty more temptations, trials and tribulations in store in the weeks ahead and through it all Jesus held up great. You can imagine what the first thing Sarah and I did when we landed in the Himalayas. Jesus didn't take a bite. I still don't really know how he managed, but he did, and when his time in the wilderness finally came to the end it was a pretty sad day.

We'd come through from another dimension with a super big BUMP and were gliding in from the West over the wine-dark Mediterranean. Jesus and I had been away exactly forty earth-days. We flew along the coast of Africa and Debbie switched on stealth mode so as not to scare the Egyptians. As we came up alongside the Dead Sea and followed the Jordan, out of the blue Jesus said he'd come far enough, and if we wouldn't mind, could we drop him off by the Sea of Galilee?

Man, was it ever a sad time for me and Sarah and Debbie, too. Sarah gave Jesus a big hug and he kissed her on the forehead, and said he'd always be with her, and of course she tried to be brave, but I think that made the tears come down her cheeks all the more. I know it did me. I was over on the dining room table in the galley and I just put out my hand to shake his in farewell and I kind of half stood and he reached down and gave me a big hug and for a second I felt better, like everything was going to be okay, but when I opened my eyes and looked ahead I could see where the hatch had swirled open in the bottom of the ship and the sight of that spiral staircase leading back down to our day to day life in the regular world – well, I'm not embarrassed to say, I really lost it.

Sarah came over and put her arm around me and we stood there in the dim blue light on the rubbery floor of the galley and watched as Jesus came back out of the living quarters dressed again in a white robe with a blue sash, like he'd worn the day we left. He stood, hanging onto the rail of the staircase, first with one hand, and then with the other, pulling on his sandals. For the strongest, smartest, most righteous, and merciful man that ever lived, he looked pretty lousy. I suppose forty days without food in a wilderness will do that to a guy. We waved goodbye to him. He nodded and smiled and turned to the stairway leading back to the earth.

After he got out he must have stumbled on the last rung, having not been used to going around in his sandals for so long, and he tumbled out of the ship and down into the dust. We started for the stairwell, but Debbie had already retracted the steps and sealed the hatch. We ran to the galley observation portals, where we waved our arms and tried to be of help, if only to encourage him, but, of course, we were invisible.

Jesus spit sand from his mouth and looked up. He shielded his hands against the glare of the afternoon sun, and pulled a tangled strand of hair from his lips. Slowly, carefully, he crawled to his feet and stood, holding the small of his back with one hand and shielding his eyes against the sun with the other. A hot wind was blowing from the west and Jesus squinted and strained his eyes. Through shimmering heat, he saw blue flecks on the horizon and recognized this was no mirage but the shoreline of Galilee. He saw the white sails of fishing vessels and the figures of three men going down to the sea with their nets. Jesus looked up into the sky, and then lowered his gaze, fixing his attention on the men.

He drew a deep breath and walked out of the wilderness to meet them.

Look for the further adventures of Jesus, M-2500, Sarah, and Steve in Parts Two and Three of the Jesus in Space Trilogy, coming soon to a book store near you.

Visit *Jesusinspace.com* today!

www.ingramcontent.com/pod-product-compliance
Lightning Source LLC
Chambersburg PA
CBHW020227260626
47156CB00002B/575